Dear Reader,

Thank you for selecting Under The Radar to read. Be sure to sign up for my newsletter for up to date information on new releases, exclusive content and sales. You can find the form here: https://bit.ly/MMorelandNewsletter

Before you sign up, add melanie@melaniemoreland.com to your contacts to make sure the email comes right to your inbox! **Always fun - never spam!**

My books are available in paperback and audiobook! You can see all my books available and upcoming preorders at my website.

The Perfect Recipe For **LOVE**
xoxo,
Melanie

UNDER THE RADAR by Melanie Moreland
Copyright © 2023 Moreland Books Inc.
Copyright #1202010
ISBN Print 978-1-990803-56-7
All rights reserved

MORELAND
BOOKS INC.

Edited by Lisa Hollett of Silently Correcting Your Grammar
Proofreading by Sisters Get Lit.erary
Cover design by Karen Hulseman, Feed Your Dreams Design
Cover Photography by Eric D Battershell
Cover Model Drew Truckle
Cover content is for illustrative purposes only and any person depicted on
the cover is a model.

Under *the* Radar

NEW YORK TIMES AND USA TODAY BESTSELLING AUTHOR

MELANIE MORELAND

Readers with concerns about content or subjects depicted can check out the content advisory on my website:
https://melaniemoreland.com/extras/fan-suggestions/content-advisory/

CHAPTER ONE

Chase

I sat down heavily on the sofa and ran a hand through my hair in frustration.

What a clusterfuck.

When I'd advertised for a roommate, I thought it would be easy to find someone.

Some of the people I interviewed today were downright scary. Two of them, I was certain, were only here to case the joint. I made a big point of talking about the state-of-the-art security system and the guns I kept in the house.

I had neither, but I hoped that would deter them.

One woman who showed up asked me for reduced rent. She'd "make it up in other ways," she informed me with a lewd wink. She even offered a sample.

I got rid of her as quickly as I could.

Another woman was searching for someone to look after her. When I explained the shared duties, she pulled on her hair and asked me if I could just "do all that stuff" and she'd stay out of the way. I could barely manage on my own, so I wasn't what she needed.

The obviously high dude who asked about using the basement to grow his necessary "medicine" was a no-go as well.

I was ready to give up.

There had only been one decent possibility, and he had called an hour after he was here to say he'd found another place.

I sighed, looking around. It was a great house. Easily shared, but if I didn't find a roommate, I would have to beg Charly to let me go back to the apartment since I couldn't afford to live here on my own.

I knew if I told her, she would laugh and remind me I had millions in the bank, but I refused to touch that money. It was used to help others because it had never done me any good when I'd needed it. I didn't want to use it now. She'd give me a lecture about letting the past go and that purchasing the house was a positive move. Financially responsible.

The doorbell sounded, and I frowned in confusion. I wasn't expecting anyone else. I opened the door a little faster than I should, startling the person on the other side.

Amber eyes, golden-red hair, and thousands of dots of cinnamon on a heart-shaped face that haunted my dreams met my astonished stare. It was a face I saw often when I shut my eyes.

I met Officer Gallagher on a day when I was dealing with some painful memories. Determined to rid myself of them, I sat alone at Zeke's, drinking far too many shots of tequila and chasing them with beer. When the agony of the memories became a dull roar, I hazily recalled stumbling outside to my truck, knowing I needed to sleep it off. The back bench had been used more than once for a quick nap, and I fumbled with the locks, which refused to work.

Like an angel, Hannah had appeared. Instead of busting my ass about how drunk I was, she talked to me, and I attempted to explain my problem. She was sweet and understanding, more concerned about my pain than the fact that I was drunk. I knew I said some inappropriate things to her, but she only smiled and kept me talking. I was in and out, drifting at times, and the next thing I knew, Brett and Kelly were there. I explained to Brett in what I thought was a quiet voice my instant fascination with the pretty police officer and her freckles. They were a particular weakness of mine. I called her Officer Cinnamon, although it came out sounding more like Occifer in my state. Brett was equal parts amused and annoyed, and he manhandled me into his car to take me home. I hated leaving the pretty police officer and apparently was quite vocal about it. I needed Occifer Cinnamon's contact information before I could go home and pass out.

I never got it.

The next day, Brett was quite happy to fill me in on every detail of how I embarrassed myself in front of Hannah. Yet the next time we met, she was as sweet and gracious as my foggy memories told me she was. I didn't pursue her, given the fact that she was a cop and I had a record.

But she was here. At my door.

Why?

I realized I had been staring at her, silent.

She smiled, her overwhelming prettiness becoming beautiful. I had to swallow before I could speak.

"Officer Cinn—I mean, Gallagher. Is there a problem?"

She shook her head. "You had an ad up in the general store looking for a roommate. Did you find one?"

I gaped at her.

"You wanna be my roommate?"

"Well, I need a place to live. You need a roommate. Solves two problems, I think." She frowned. "May I come in?"

"Oh, right. Yes, of course, come in."

She walked in, her scent swirling as she squeezed past me and headed to the living room. I followed in her wake, greedily inhaling. The urge to reach out and touch her was strong, but I resisted.

4

"So, you're looking for a new place?" I asked.

She smiled as she sat down. "Yes, I am." She winked. "So much so, I took down your ad. I'm the only one to apply."

"Ah, I had one in the paper." I leaned forward. "The applicants were scary."

"Good. Then I guess you've been waiting for me, right?"

She had no idea.

She crossed her legs. "Ask me anything, Chase."

My throat went dry.

Jesus. My wet dream was sitting across from me, her sexy calves on display. She wanted to live in this house. With me. I'd see her every day. Hear her talk and laugh. Maybe see her in a towel.

Or less.

I dropped my head. If I let her move in here with me, I would be in so much trouble. It was a really, really bad idea.

"When can you move in?" I blurted out.

She laughed. "Oh, you are a funny one."

I had to look away. I had been serious.

And my first instinct was right, except I was beyond trouble.

The fact was, I was totally fucked.

And I wasn't going to do anything to stop it.

She grinned at me. "May I see the place before I sign?"

I offered her a rueful smile. "Of course, ah, Officer—"

She cut me off. "Enough of that. It's Hannah. You can call me Hannah. Unless, of course, I have you handcuffed."

The mental image that came to my head wasn't helping my situation at the moment.

Hannah, wearing her police hat and belt and nothing else. Me, handcuffed to her bed while she decided what to do with me.

Jesus, this was a bad idea.

I stood. "Let me show you around."

We walked into the kitchen, and she smiled. "Oh, it's a good size!"

"You like to cook?" I asked.

"Oh yes. My mom taught me. What about you?"

"Well, Brett and I ordered in a lot, but I make a great breakfast and I can grill. Charly taught me how to cook pasta and grilled cheese," I replied honestly.

"Charly—she's Maxx's wife, right?"

I nodded. "My pseudo-sister slash mother too. She gives me advice—whether I want it or not."

Hannah laughed. "Sounds about right."

I opened the door in the hall. "This would be your room."

"*For now,*" I added silently.

She walked into the room, peeking in the closet, pleased to see she had her own bathroom. "Can I paint?" she asked.

I looked around, seeing the plain beige walls, scuffed and dull in some places. "Yeah, of course."

"Great. My mom will help."

"I was thinking of doing some painting too. We can help each other."

"Awesome."

I showed her the backyard, and she eyed the overgrown garden with pursed lips. "I'd want to clean that up. I love to garden in my downtime."

"Sure."

We returned to the living room, and I offered her a glass of water or coffee. She grinned and accepted the coffee, then followed me to the kitchen and sat at the table while I dropped a pod into the machine and hit the button. Luckily, I had cream and sugar. She mixed hers, and I noted the half teaspoon of sugar she added and the more than generous splash of cream so I could make it for her while she waited for me in bed.

Then I shook my head.

I sat across from her and added cream to my cup. We sipped for a moment before I spoke.

"Hannah, I want to apologize about the first time we met. My memory is rather foggy, but if I was disrespectful, I'm sorry. You were like an angel, and I thought you were very pretty. I know it's not an excuse, but I'd had a shit day. You were very kind, and I want to thank you for that. I rarely ever drink to excess, I promise you that."

She shook her head. "I understand bad days, Chase. I'm glad I was there. And you weren't disrespectful—you were adorable. I'm glad your friends came to help you." She wrinkled her nose. "I don't think anyone has ever considered me an angel. And you thought I was pretty?"

I only meant to nod. Instead, my mouth took over. "I still do. That's how I think of you. An angel in my dreams. And you're very pretty."

"Oh," she said and took a sip of coffee.

I ducked my head.

Angel in my dreams.

I had just made it awkward. I was an idiot.

But she smiled at me and acted as if everything was good. "What is the rent?"

"Two thousand plus utilities. At least for now. My lease is coming up, but Old Man Hyde has always been fair. If he raises the rent, it's nominal. I think because Brett and I do repairs and mow the grass, that sort of thing. So, you'd be half that."

She nodded. "And how would our relationship work?"

I almost choked on my coffee. "Re-relationship?"

She frowned. "Yes. For a while, I had a great roommate. We split all the chores, but if one of us was extra busy, we helped the other out. We often took turns cooking if we were both there, and we got along really well." She paused, taking a sip of her coffee. "When she got married a couple of months ago, I got a new one, and she's been a nightmare. She insisted that we each had to have our own shelves in the fridge and cupboards. She measured everything and often accused me of taking her food. When I would remind her I'd been gone all day on shift, she'd remember she ate it. She was a total space cadet. The day she informed me she knew I'd dipped into her shampoo, I lost it. She refused to move out, so I got my name off the lease and I moved out a month ago. Last I heard, her boyfriend moved in."

"I hope he's eating her."

Her eyes widened. *"What?"*

"Her stuff, I mean," I quickly added on. "And using her shampoo. Her razor too," I added for good measure.

Hannah laughed. "Oh. Yeah. Me too."

"I'm pretty easy. We can decide who does what, and I have no problem helping out. Brett and I did our own laundry and cleaned our bathrooms, but we divided the rest up. As for cooking, we can figure that out. Whatever works for us is good. I won't weigh my cereal. Just don't pick out all the marshmallows in the Lucky Charms." I winked at her.

She chuckled. "Deal."

"Where are you living now?"

"Crashing on a friend's sofa."

"Do you have a lot to move in?"

"My bedroom furniture, some boxes, and I do have a newer sofa I want to keep. And a couple of chairs. Some tables and pictures. They're all in my friend's storage locker."

"No worries. The living room is kinda sparse. I haven't really done much since Brett moved out with Kelly. Most of the stuff was his, although he left me a few pieces."

"So I can put that in the living room?"

"Knock yourself out."

"When can I move in?"

"Today works."

"Don't you want to check my references or do a background check on me? I could be trouble," she added with a wink.

"I think the police force is enough of a background check. And I trust you."

I didn't say anything about the trouble remark. I already knew she was going to be trouble. The very best kind.

She laughed and extended her hand. "You just got yourself a new roomie, Chase. I'll go get some paint swatches today."

I wrapped my hand around hers, pleased at how well they fit together. "Welcome."

"Awesome."

CHAPTER TWO

Chase

O n Sunday, I went to Stefano's for a barbecue. I loved being included in the group. These men and women had become my family. My own had wanted little to do with me, and once my father and brother died, I was alone. That was until I'd gotten up the balls to apologize to Charly for my past behavior and she had taken me under her wing.

Now I had all of them. Maxx and Charly. Stefano, Gabby, Brett, and Kelly. Theo and the smaller kids. Brett's dad, Mack, and Stefano's mom, Rosa, had recently been married, and they were often at the barbecues or get-togethers. Mary and her new beau joined us on a regular basis. All of them I now considered my family.

I grabbed a beer and headed to the barbecue pit where Stefano and Brett were basting a huge roast beef, the smell enticing. We clinked bottles in silent hellos and watched

Theo kicking a soccer ball with Mack and Thomas. Vivvy sat with her mom, occasionally investigating the game, toddling over to be closer, only to be led back by Theo, who always watched over her.

"How was the roommate search?"

I picked at the label on my bottle, trying to appear casual. "Some odd people out there. But I think I found a good one."

"Well, there might be a problem," Brett said with a frown.

"What?" I asked.

"Old Man Hyde called me last night. He was calling me back because I had left him a message about transferring the lease to your name only. But he said he thinks he's going to sell the place."

"Damn. Why?"

"He's moving closer to be with his daughter. He doesn't want the responsibility of being a landlord anymore, even though he says we were great tenants and he was sure you would carry that on."

I took a sip of my beer. I thought about how excited Hannah was the day before, mulling over colors, asking if maybe we could paint the living room too. She had walked around the garden again, full of ideas about what vegetables and flowers to plant. I could hardly wait for her to move in and get to know her more.

"…you should really think about it, Chase."

I looked up, startled. I had been so deep in my thoughts, I hadn't heard what Brett said.

"What?"

He laughed. "I said you should get over this issue with your money. Buy the house. It's a good, solid investment. You're not proving anything by keeping the money in the bank."

Stefano nodded, lifting the lid of the barbecue and basting the meat again. "You won't even touch the principal to buy the house. So technically, you're not using your dad's money. You're using the money you made with it. And Brett is right. You like the place. You can buy it, do some improvements, and make it yours—really yours."

I pursed my lips. They made sense. And if the place were mine, Hannah could do whatever she wanted and I wouldn't have to get permission. I could give her leave to do whatever made her happy.

"I think you're right," I said.

They both stopped what they were doing.

"Come again?" Brett said.

"You're right. I should buy it. It would be the smart move."

"But…?" he asked.

"No buts. I'll call Mr. Hyde later and sit down with him and figure out a price. We can avoid using a real estate agent, and I'll cover the legal fees. It can be quick."

They both looked shocked, and I clapped Brett's shoulder. "Good talk, guys. Thanks."

I grinned as I walked away. I knew that wasn't the last I would hear about this. But it was worth it to have rendered them speechless.

Even for a moment.

I joined Mack and Theo kicking around the ball. I lifted Thomas high, tickling him, and I pushed him on the swing for a while. I went to grab a cold water and noticed Charly talking to the boys. Maxx was with them, Vivvy cradled in his embrace, and they were all deep in conversation. I tried not to laugh as their heads turned my way and Charly spun on her heel, heading my direction. I sat down, knowing there was no place I could run, and waited for the invasion.

Three...Two...

"So, you've decided to buy the house now?" she asked, sitting beside me. "What changed your stubborn, pigheaded mind all of a sudden?"

"Hello to you too, Charly."

"Don't change the subject, Chase. Maxx has already been on my nerves today, and I am incapable of bull pucky."

I bit back my laughter. "Did he not approve of your outfit?"

"What the blazes is wrong with my outfit?"

"Nothing." I paused and took a drink. "But I'm not your husband."

She looked fine. Beautiful, in fact. She wore a pretty, loose tunic that fell to her knees. The problem was there was a way of gathering up the material at the sides, and she had done so. Her thighs were on display, which was hardly indecent, but to Maxx, it was like a target. He would zoom in on her exposed skin and rant for hours. It amused all of us, and Charly did it to rile him up.

"I have shorts on under this," she hissed. "Don't you start too."

I chuckled, thinking I had gotten her mind off the subject, but I was wrong.

"Now, the house," she continued.

"I decided you were right. I was being foolish not to buy a place, so I am going to buy the house from Mr. Hyde so I don't have to move. Simple."

She narrowed her eyes. "Really?" she drawled. "Just like that?"

"No, I've been thinking about it. You were right, Charly. I listened. You should be happy."

She pursed her lips. "I was right," she repeated.

"Yup. Your wisdom soaked in."

"Isn't that great."

I nodded. "Yup."

She leaned close, smiling. She tilted her head to the side. "Bull pucky," she murmured. "I'll find out, Chase Donner. I'll know the real story, and you'll be sorry you didn't tell me."

She got up and flounced away. I saw now why Maxx was freaking. There was no back to the tunic. It fell in folds to her butt, and her hair was up, so her back was on display. I was shocked he hadn't covered her with a blanket. Even if she was among friends. I had to laugh at the two of them.

I did wonder, however, how long it would take Charly to put two and two together and figure out the real reason I'd decided to buy the house.

To get Hannah.

Once she discovered it, she'd never let me live it down.

———

I sat with Mr. Hyde that night. He showed me the three estimates he had on the property, the tax bill, and a list of repairs he had done not long ago. I offered him a cash price, and we shook on the deal. We agreed to use the same lawyer and that the ownership transfer would happen as soon as the paperwork was complete. He could move closer to his daughter, and I would have the house. Simple.

He regarded me as he scratched his chin. "All cash? You got that sort of money, son?"

I nodded. "Yes, sir. It's not an issue."

"Your dad?" he asked.

Again, I nodded but didn't reply.

"You know, I knew your parents when they were younger. A couple of crazy kids in love. So proud of his boys. Of being a father. He wasn't always so bad," he offered quietly. "He was never himself after your mom passed. He couldn't let go of the grief, and he became bitter. Instead of finding his purpose being your father, he walked away."

"He totally checked out. He stopped being a father and ignored both of us. He didn't speak to me again when I got out of jail, even after I reached out. I wanted his attention, not his money."

"It happens. And your brother going wild happens too. But neither was because of you."

"I know."

"You should live. Really live. You could buy a bigger place than mine, I imagine."

"I like the house. The neighborhood and the yard. I can expand it if I wanted."

"I always thought so. A second story was planned when it was built, but I ran out of money. The foundation was built for it to carry the load. But after we had our daughter, we never had the need since she was our only child."

"Good to know."

"You don't want an inspection? Nothing?"

I laughed. "I've lived there long enough, and Brett and Stefano before me, to know if there was anything wrong with it. I want to buy it."

He held out his hand. "Then it's yours, Chase. I wish you much happiness in it."

I shook his hand. "Thank you, sir."

He reached over and pulled a cardboard tube from a shelf. "Here are the original plans. In case you ever decide to expand."

"Thank you."

I walked into the house later, wondering if it would feel different once Hannah was there. Right now, it was just me. Silence greeted me, and I was surrounded by it all the time.

Would she change that?

I sat on the sofa, looking around the room with fresh eyes, seeing what Hannah had seen.

Brett had taken his stuff, not that it had been much. We lived like regular bachelors. A couple of mismatched sofas, end tables, and a big TV was all we had when he lived here. We each had a bed and dresser, and we used the old kitchen table Mr. Hyde had left behind. We'd never painted after Stefano moved out or replaced the furniture he'd had, which had been much nicer. Now the place held my sofa, a table, and the TV. The same blinds in the windows. It was rather dull and dreary.

I'd let Hannah do whatever she wanted. As long as it wasn't pink and frilly—I'd lay down the ground rules when I told her.

I rubbed my lip, feeling the stirrings of excitement. Hannah had given me her cell number, so I sent her a fast text.

> **ME**
>
> Hey, it's Chase—we never really set a date. When are you planning on moving in?

She replied quickly.

> **HANNAH**
>
> I have some paint samples and was hoping I could drop by tomorrow. I'll find some hands to help me with my stuff on the weekend if that's okay?

I grinned.

ME

Great. Happy to help. I can provide a truck and some muscle. You don't have to wait until the weekend.

I knew Stefano and Maxx would help. Brett, too, if he was around. He was leaving for another trip with Kelly soon, so I wasn't sure. Dom was around now too, and we got along well. I was sure he'd pitch in if I asked.

HANNAH

You're amazing! Thank you. Dinner's on me on Sunday. I'll cook. And pizza and beer for your friends if they can help.

They'll love it. And it's a date

I replied, adding a winky face so she didn't think I was serious.

Even though I was.

CHAPTER THREE

Chase

First thing on Monday morning, I called my lawyer and gave him the details. He was pleased I was finally using some of the money and assured me he would contact Mr. Hyde and would get everything together. I headed to work, stopping to grab some donuts on the way to celebrate. It was still before eight when I arrived at the garage, and I had already accomplished a lot. I was grateful my lawyer kept such early hours. I really didn't want to be making personal calls at the garage, even though I could shut the office door.

I put the donuts in the kitchen and grabbed a coffee, heading for the desk. I opened the schedule and checked to make sure everything was good. It still felt odd to be in the office and not on the road. I started here as a gofer. Picking up parts, running errands. Everything asked of me. Anything to earn Charly's and Maxx's forgiveness. I worked and ran errands. Picked up lunch. Lived in the small back room without complaint, eating my meals alone. I read a lot, rarely ventured into town.

Forgiveness came first from Charly. Stefano and Brett were friendly but distant initially, then eventually they started joking around with me. Insisting I join them for a beer or pizza night at their place. I knew Maxx had forgiven me the first time he stopped by the stockroom, eyeing up the parts I was organizing so Charly didn't have to do it.

"You're doing a good job," he huffed as if it hurt him to admit it.

"Thanks."

"Charly made pot roast for dinner. And pie. We eat at six." He paused. "Come join us." He walked away before I could respond.

Sitting around their kitchen table that night, I saw what a family was really like. Stefano and Brett were there. So was Mary. They laughed and teased. Talked and really listened. At first, I was uncomfortable, unsure if I should be there, wondering if I should finish my dinner and leave. But Maxx leaned his elbows on the table. "So Chase, we're expanding the garage, and I'm planning a bigger apartment upstairs. You interested in staying on?"

"Um, yeah."

He nodded. "Good. There'll be a raise coming too. You did good, kid."

I gaped at him, and he grinned. "Now, eat. Charly's pie is not to be missed. After, we're going to go over the plans. You can sit in."

And the rest was history. Now Maxx and I were as close as

he was to Stefano or Brett. He was like a brother to me. They all were. I moved from runner to managing the office when Brett decided to travel with Kelly. I shared the responsibilities with Dom Salvatore, and when Brett was around, the three of us split everything. I took a course on upholstery. Taught myself how to customize interiors. I was learning new things every day and loving it all. And I enjoyed having a gofer to do all the tasks I used to handle, although on occasion, I still enjoyed a road trip to pick up parts. I planned on going to school to become a certified mechanic, but I was waiting for the right time.

Dom came in, carrying a cup of coffee and holding a donut. He lifted it in a mock salute. "Thanks, kid. I was running late this morning. I needed this."

"No problem. Everything okay, Dom?"

He leaned on the corner of his desk, nodding. He was tall and broad. Well-muscled with tattoos on his arms and chest. He had a thick swatch of scruff, and his hair was brushed high off his forehead. His voice was low and gruff, and he looked stern and unflappable. Confident. But he was a great guy. Dependable and knowledgeable. Friendly when dealing with customers. The opposite when handling a problem. Then he became no-nonsense and clipped, and he didn't mess around. We got along well, and I was learning a lot from him.

"Just had to wait for a new stove to be delivered. The one in the apartment crapped out." He chuckled. "The fridge last month. The stove last week. I imagine the dishwasher is next." He shrugged. "The landlord isn't happy but it's not my problem."

"I should replace the ones in my kitchen," I mused. "They're pretty old."

"Don't you rent?"

I grinned. "I bought the house last night. So soon, *I'll* be the owner."

"Congrats, kid. That's great. Real estate is a good investment. Any luck with a roomie?"

"Yeah. Found a good one."

He took a sip of coffee. "I'm enjoying the peace of my own place. I was living with two other guys in Toronto. You sort of have to, with the prices there. But they were getting on my nerves."

I bit back my grin. There was one nerve in particular I hoped Hannah would get on. A lot.

He stood and rolled his shoulders. "I have that engine rebuild today. You wanna be in on it?"

"For sure."

"Great. Everything okay with the schedule?"

"Yep. Going over receivables today and will send out reminders, then start on calls."

Luckily, we had very few receivables. More businesses than individuals. It was a matter of chasing down their accounting department and reminding them the work on their company vehicles needed to be paid before we did any more. Most of the time that worked. Our reputation was too good for them to risk taking their business elsewhere and getting shoddy service.

"Great," he said, looking past my shoulder. He whistled low in his throat. "Isn't she just a pretty little thing," he mumbled. "Always liked the redheads."

I turned and saw what or whom he was referring to. Hannah was walking in the garage, headed to the office. She'd been here once before and knew where it was located. I turned back to Dom, narrowing my eyes. "Way too young for you," I snapped.

He looked at me and my clenched fist then chuckled. He clapped me on my shoulder. "I hear you, Romeo. Off-limits. I got it." Then he winked. "And for the record, far too young for me. I like them my own age. Midforties and wiser. But she is still a pretty thing to look at."

"She's my new roommate."

His eyes widened, and he threw back his head and laughed. "Well, this should be fun," he said. "I think I'll get another donut." He nodded as he passed Hannah. "Miss. Have a good day." She smiled in return, her cheeks flushing a little. It was sorta cute.

She paused in the doorway. "Am I interrupting?"

God, she was pretty. Her hair was a mass of red-gold curls around her shoulders today, glinting in the light. She wore a simple T-shirt and jeans, but the denim hugged her curves and the shirt was slightly large and hung off one shoulder. The temptation to touch the skin it showed was strong.

I managed to resist. For now.

"No," I assured her, hoping Charly wasn't around. "What's up?"

"I have a big favor."

"Sure," I replied. "Whatever you need."

"I wanted to look at these paint swatches in the house. Any chance I could do that? I mean, would you trust me enough to loan me a key? I'll return it fast, I promise."

I chuckled and dug into my pocket. I had also stopped by the general store this morning and had Mack, Brett's dad, cut me an extra set of keys. I handed them to her. "Here. These are yours."

"But-but I haven't signed anything!"

I waved off her concern. "It's fine."

"No, really. I should sign something."

I pointed to the chair beside my desk. "Sit down, then."

I typed in the website I knew about and printed off the same form I signed with Brett. It was standard and simple. I scribbled in the rent amount and crossed off a few things and handed it to her. "Here. Read this and sign."

She looked at it, a cute furrow appearing between her brows. "Um, you said a thousand plus utilities. This says includes."

"Except phone. I only have my cell. If you want a landline, you pay for it. But yes, all in."

"Why?"

I blew out a deep breath. "I didn't say anything on Saturday since it wasn't official, but I bought the house, so I'm the new landlord. That is my rate. Now, sign."

"You bought the house?"

"Yep."

She was out of her chair fast and threw her arms around my neck. She pressed a kiss to my cheek. "Congratulations!"

Without thought, I wrapped my arms around her, hugging her close. She was small and warm, and she smelled incredible. Like flowers. As she bent over me, her hair fell around us, and I was lost in a curtain of red-gold tresses. I dared to fist the back of her hair, feeling the softness.

She eased back, and I released her, already feeling the regret.

"So," she teased. "Does this mean you can approve my paint colors?"

"I guess so."

She spread out some swatches. "This one for my room, I think. And I was thinking the living room would look great in this sort of taupe."

"I thought that was brown."

She chuckled. "It's sorta both."

"I like it." I sat back with a grin. "I'm kinda relieved it's not pink."

She shook her head. "I'm not much into pink on the walls."

"Good to know."

"Okay. I'll go see how these look in the rooms."

I tapped another strip of colors. "What is that one?"

"It's called Misty Moors. You like it?"

"I was wondering if I should paint my room, you know, while we're at it."

"It's a great color."

"Okay. Get whatever you need. Keep the bill, and I'll repay you." I held up my hand before she could argue. "I can write it off under house expenses."

She stood, then leaned down and pressed another kiss to my cheek. "Thanks, Chase."

"Sure," I mumbled.

A throat clearing from the door made me shut my eyes. I knew the sound of that rumble. I opened my eyes and met Charly's amused, all-seeing, all-knowing gaze. She grinned widely.

"Hello, Hannah."

"Hey, Charly. I was just leaving. Gotta run some errands." Hannah smiled at me. "I'll let you know about the paint, okay?"

"Okay."

She left, and I tried to act nonchalant.

"Hey, Charly. What's up?"

"Oh no," she replied. "You're not playing innocent with me. I walk in, and you're all cozy with Hannah and picking paint samples. And you bought a house? I think you and I need a chat, Chase."

She shut the door, and I knew no wasn't an option.

I turned to face my fate.

CHAPTER FOUR

Chase

C harly sat in the chair Hannah had vacated, crossing her legs and smiling her sweet smile. The innocuous one that gave you a false sense of security. Until she opened her mouth to speak.

"So, you've been busy."

I didn't say anything.

"On Friday, you left here, hoping to find a roommate, refusing to listen to reason about buying the house—any house, actually—and now Monday morning dawns, and not only have you got a new roomie, you purchased the house and are picking paint colors with said roomie. The girl of your no doubt torrid nocturnal fantasies, I might add." She lifted one eyebrow in question. "Have I got that about right?"

I cleared my throat, suddenly wishing an engine would catch fire or the oil cans on the wall would begin to explode and distract her, but all remained calm in the garage. And none of the bastards would dare come in here and rescue me. Not if it involved Charly. Even Maxx wouldn't attempt it.

"Things changed," I agreed.

She snorted. "Changed? Talk about doing a 180, Chase! What happened?"

I met her eyes and found the Charly I adored there. Caring, warm, and worried. She had always worried about me. She had been my staunchest defender, even when she could have turned me away for what I had done.

I sighed and yanked off my beanie, running a hand through my hair. "Honest to God, Charly. I have no idea. Some of the applicants were downright scary. One even tried propositioning me so she wouldn't have to do anything around the place. Another guy wanted to grow drugs in the basement. I was about to give up, and Hannah showed up. She was like a miracle. Normal, fun. Has a full-time job. And..." I waved my fingers. "It was *Hannah*. She wanted to live with me."

Charly grinned, nodding for me to continue.

"She loved the house, asked about painting her room, and planting some stuff in the garden. I could see her there—with me. Then Brett told me Old Man Hyde wanted to sell the house. And I thought about what you had said. What Maxx and Stefano, even Brett, have been telling me. I had to stop thinking of the money from my dad as bad. That I should use it for good things. And making Hannah happy is a good thing."

Charly leaned forward. "You realize you bought a house, and all she might be looking for is a roommate, right?"

"I know. But there's something between us. I can feel it. Maybe it's nothing. Maybe living together will make it ease off. But maybe..." I trailed off.

"Maybe not," she finished.

I nodded. "Regardless, you have all been right. The money just keeps growing. At least I've invested some of it in something worthwhile." I swallowed. "My dad—the one I remember from when I was a kid—would have liked that."

She took my hand and squeezed it. "He would have, Chase. He'd be proud. I think somewhere deep inside him, he was still that guy. He just lost himself. Use the money and do lots of good things. Support the local food bank. Do things that make you smile." She paused. "Like buying a house so the girl of your dreams moves in with you."

I chuckled. "Like buying a house so I can live with Hannah, yes."

"I don't want to see you get hurt if all she is looking for is a place to live and a friend, Chase."

"I'm a big boy, Charly. I can look after myself. I'm not going to rush this or do anything stupid. I'll see what happens." I winked at her. "But I have a better chance if she's living with me than not. I'll see her every day. I'll charm her."

Charly snorted again. "Then make sure to pick up after yourself and keep your room clean. And for God's sake, get a cleaning lady so your bathroom isn't disgusting."

I began to laugh. "Good advice."

She stood and pressed a kiss to my head. "Good luck, Chase. I'm afraid it's going to be complicated, but for your sake, I hope it works."

I smiled as she left, sauntering over to Maxx and saying something to him. He laughed and cupped her head, kissing her, then swatted her butt. I had a feeling he was telling her to mind her own business, not that she would listen to him. He watched her leave, his expression saying it all. He adored his wife and everything about her. Stefano looked at Gabby the same way. So did Brett. His eyes spoke volumes when he glanced at Kelly.

I wanted that. I wanted what my friends had found. Their home. Their place. Their entire world revolved around a woman they loved fiercely.

I didn't know yet if Hannah was that woman for me, but I certainly wanted to find out.

On the way home, I stopped by the lawyer's office and signed some papers. Everything was going to happen quickly since it was a cash sale, no real estate agents were involved, and I already lived there. Mr. Hyde would get his money immediately, and the ownership would transfer to me. I picked up a pizza at the local shop and headed to the house.

I was pleased to see Hannah's car parked in the driveway. I took the pizza and headed inside, smelling the paint fumes as I opened the door. Loud music was playing, and I put the pizza in the kitchen then followed the thumping beat.

I found Hannah in her room, the floors covered, the trim taped off, and a fresh coat of paint on the walls. I leaned on the doorframe, watching her for a moment, silently enjoying the show. She wore a loose T-shirt and leggings, both paint-splashed and obviously well used. The shirt fell from one shoulder, exposing the creamy skin. Her hair was up in a ponytail, swinging as she moved. She was singing as she painted, her roller covering the last of the dull beige that had been there before. She had a pretty voice, which made me smile. I smiled even wider as she shimmied her hips in time to the beat. It was eighties music, which she obviously liked since she knew every word. She was sexy and cute all at the same time.

I lifted my hand and rapped on the wall. She spun around, and I began to laugh. She had a streak of paint on one cheek. She grabbed her phone and stopped the music, and I waved. "Hard at work already." I touched my cheek. "You're wearing some of it."

She chuckled. "I had a little fight with the lid, and it got me."

"Looks good. Ah, gray? Green?"

"Sort of a blend. Mossy Gray, it's called."

"I like it."

"Me too."

"Can you take a break and have some pizza?"

"Oh God, I love pizza."

"Then come and join me."

"I'll just finish this wall, and I'm done for the day."

"Okay."

She joined me in the kitchen a few moments later, her face washed. I noticed her feet were bare, the toenails painted a deep red. She sat down and picked up a slice of pizza.

"There are hot peppers on it," I advised. "I should have only gotten them on half, but I forgot. Feel free to pick them off."

"That's fine. I love hot peppers." She took a bite. "Oh, this is awesome."

I was pretty sure I fell in love right there. She ate her pizza with gusto, sipping a beer with me. There was no pretense about her. She even burped once—a delicate sound, unlike when Brett or I would belch. She covered her mouth, coloring a little. "Excuse me."

I chuckled. "Pretty lame."

"I'm easing you in. I don't want you to kick me out before I've even moved in."

"Not gonna happen."

She smiled, and I reveled in the warmth of it.

"You got a lot done today."

She nodded around a mouthful. "My friend Sara came with me to get the paint, and she helped me tape everything and fill in the holes. So once that was done, it was fast. My mom is going to come and help paint the living room if that's okay?"

"Sure. Does she live here?"

"No, in Toronto. She'll come out on Saturday. I'll have my room and the bathroom done by then."

"Great. I can help too. We'll get it done."

"I love all the wood trim in the house. It's so nice."

"Yeah, it is." I took another slice, folding it in half and eating it like a sandwich.

"Have you lived here long?"

"A while. Brett and Stefano were roommates here first. When Stefano got married, I moved in with Brett. Now he's with Kelly, and it was going to be just me. I thought having another person around would be nice."

"And you bought the place."

"Yes."

She sighed, looking around. "I'm glad. It's a great little house. So much potential."

I had never thought to change anything in the house, but I was surprised to find I wanted to hear her ideas. "You mean besides paint?"

"Paint will help. Spruce it up, you know? But you could refinish the floors, update the kitchen and bathrooms, all sorts of little DIY projects to make it really nice."

"Good thing you're here," I joked. "I have no idea about sprucing or DIY projects."

"I love to putter."

"Putter away, Hannah. Just keep me up-to-date and in the loop."

She laughed and stood, taking the empty pizza box to the counter. "I'll do that. Let me know when to stop."

She paused in the doorway. "I'm going to go and put everything away and head to my friend's place and crash on the sofa. I'll be back tomorrow."

I carried my plate to the counter and leaned against it. "We could move your stuff in tomorrow, you know. Put it in the living room. You can crash here on the sofa until the walls are dry and we move your bed in. Give me the address, and the guys and I will take care of it."

"Really?"

"Sure."

She rushed toward me, flinging her arms around my neck. "That would be awesome!"

I hugged her back, liking how she felt in my embrace. She was shorter than me, but not as tiny as Charly. She was warm and soft pressed against me. She stepped back, still in my arms, gazing up at me. The air grew warm as we stared. "You're incredible," she murmured. "I'm not sure how I got so lucky."

I smiled, my eyes drawn to her mouth. Her lips looked soft. Sweet. I wanted to taste them. To feel them move underneath mine. She shocked me when she rose up on her toes and kissed me. It was a fast, light kiss. But I felt it all the way down to the soles of my feet.

"Thank you," she murmured, then turned and eased from my embrace. "You're—" She shook her head, touching her lips. "Thank you," she repeated, then hurried down the hall.

I touched my bottom lip with my tongue, still feeling her mouth there. I tried not to read too much into the gesture. She was grateful. It was a spontaneous kiss between friends. Roomies.

Except, I had never kissed Brett. Nor had I wanted to.

I wanted to kiss Hannah again.

And much more.

Fuck, Charly was right.

This was going to be complicated.

And yet, I wouldn't want anyone else here with me.

In the morning, I asked the guys about helping me move Hannah's possessions, and they agreed without hesitation. Maxx indicated the two larger trucks. "We'll take both and get it done in one load. You just want it piled in the living room?"

"Yeah. We can move her bedroom stuff in once the walls dry. Then she wants to paint the living room."

Maxx shared a look with Stefano, who chuckled. "She works fast. Charly didn't paint for at least a month," he stated dryly.

I laughed at his ribbing. "Whatever. Gotta make sure my investment is looked after."

He rolled his eyes. "Whatever, kid. We'll go around two. I'm booked until then."

Dom looked up from a motorcycle he was working on. "I'll come with. The boys can watch the shop. I can help on the weekend too if needed."

"That would be great."

Stefano grinned. "Brett wants me to update him on the house happenings while he is gone."

"You got him to the airport okay?" Maxx asked.

He rubbed his chin. "Ass-crack of dawn, yeah. He was pretty excited. Kelly was a little more laid-back, but she's traveled more than he has. It was good to see him happy, even if we're gonna miss him around here."

"I'm stoked for him. He deserves to be happy. Travel."

"I agree."

"Okay, let's get at this so we can help Chase this afternoon."

I clapped my hands. "Let's go then, boys. I got a lady to impress."

That made them all laugh.

Later, we loaded up the contents of the storage locker for Hannah. It was neat and organized, something I had already discovered about her. With four of us, it was fast work, and it all fit in the trucks easily. At the house, we carried everything in, Hannah excited and looking prettier than ever. She'd greeted us at the door, her eyes shining.

"I have coffee!" she exclaimed. "And I made cookies!"

The guys all smiled in appreciation and accepted the mugs of coffee happily. The cookies were still warm and filled with chocolate chips. My favorite. The guys were pleasant and polite, all grinning when she insisted she would make them lunch one day and send it to the garage to say thanks. None of them turned it down—not when it was food. They teased me a little about the house, saying it was a good thing Hannah was already increasing the value of my sudden purchase with her improvements. I ignored them.

I stood when we finished our treat and indicated the piles in the living room. "I'll help you sort that when I get home," I said, pausing at the front door. She had been effusive with her thanks to everyone, and they were all grinning with the bags of cookies she'd shoved into their hands.

"Great."

I was shocked when she kissed my cheek again. "Thanks again, Chase."

She called out to me as I got to the truck. "Have a good afternoon! I'll see you later when you get home."

It hit me. She'd be there tonight. Tomorrow. All the time.

Hannah. In my house. With me.

I was still smiling as I swung myself into the passenger side. Dom side-eyed me with a wide grin as he backed out of the driveway. "Roomies, huh?" He chuckled.

"Yes."

"I say that girl is far more than that in a month," he muttered. "Maybe less." He reached into the bag and took another cookie. "Hell, if she can cook like this, marry her up, boy. Fast."

I looked out the window.

I had no desire to bet against that.

CHAPTER FIVE

Hannah

The sounds of the trucks faded away, and I shut the door and headed to the living room. All my boxes were there. All my things. I sighed in happiness as I sat down on my sofa, ignoring the crinkling sound of the plastic that covered it. It would look nice against the far wall once the room was painted. It went okay with the one Chase had. Even the chairs matched well enough. I studied the room, mapping out the layout of everything in my head. It would be cozy when I was done.

I still couldn't believe I was going to live here. With Chase.

When I had seen the handwritten advertisement in the general store, I had looked at the address, the location striking a memory. It was the cute mechanic. The one with the sad eyes. I had helped him one night in his drunken state.

He had been so adorable, insisting he wasn't trying to drive. Then he peered at me, getting far too close for it to be comfortable. Yet, with him, I was fine.

"You got hit with a cinnamon truck," he slurred a little. "Little dots ever-ry-where!" He drew out the last word into three syllables. Then he winked. "Are they everywhere, Occifer Cinnamon?"

"Gallagher," I corrected, trying not to laugh at his inappropriateness. "It's Officer Gallagher."

"To everyone else." He waved his hand. "To me, you're Occifer Cinnanum. Cinnamon." He hiccuped. "Oops." Then he patted his chest. "Mine."

I bit back my smile. He was utterly endearing.

"Can I call someone for you?" I asked. I didn't want to throw him in the drunk tank.

"You could take me home. I wouldn't tell anyone. We could cuddle. I bet you'd be a good cuddler."

"A friend, maybe?" I prompted, shocked at the fact that I was actually tempted. He looked as if he needed a good cuddle.

"Oh, okay. Brett," he said, sounding disappointed.

Once his friends came to get him, I felt sad he was gone, which was ridiculous. He probably wouldn't even recall meeting me.

The next time I saw him was at the garage where he worked. Something had sparked between us, and I had hoped he would ask me out, drop by the station, or even call me, but aside from his changing my oil and being extremely sweet, I had heard nothing.

I had hesitated, then untacked the ad from the board. Mr. Conner had chuckled.

"My boy's old place. Chase is looking for a new roommate. You need a place? He's a good kid."

"Yes."

"You'd be safe there."

His words struck something in me, and I smiled. "Thanks. I'll just, ah, take this."

He had laughed again. "You do that. Once he gets an eyeful of you, he won't want another applicant."

I had hoped he was right.

Seeing Chase again had made my heart beat faster. He was still sweet and sort of shy, yet at times, he became funny and sexy. He looked at me in a way that made my stomach jump and my chest warm. But he was polite and courteous and wasn't upset when I told him I took down his sign. He seemed shocked at my desire to live there, then immediately agreed to it. Showed me the place. Told me I could paint.

When I saw him on Monday and he told me he had bought the house, I assumed it was a coincidence that it happened when I wanted to move in. Yet the way his friends had teased him, I wondered.

But that was ridiculous. There was no way he would have bought the place on a whim because I was going to move in.

Right?

I shook my head to clear it and went back to my room. The walls were done, and I had most of the tape off the trim. I was going to prime the bathroom and paint it next. Each bedroom had its own en suite, and there was a small guest bathroom in the hall with a sink and a toilet. It needed painting too, but I would concentrate on my room and the living room first. Chase mentioned his room, and I had picked up the paint for it as a surprise. I was excited to live here.

I had tried to tell myself it was because I was going to be away from my nightmare of a roommate and off the sofa at Sara's, but the truth was far more complex than that, and it all involved the sad-eyed man I was going to be living with.

Thoughtfully, I recalled more from the first time I saw him, drunk and trying to put his house keys into a lock that didn't exist. He had looked up at me, his light-blue eyes widening.

"Whoa," he mumbled. "You are sooo pretty."

I tried to keep a straight face.

"Sir, have you been drinking?"

"Yes. I am so wasted," he admitted honestly. "I need a nap. I sleep in the back seat a lot when I'm tired." He sighed. "I'm tired now, Occifer Cinnamon. But I can't get in my truck."

His nickname made me smile, even though I tried to fight it.

"Why have you been drinking so much?" I asked.

He shook his head. "Bad stuff. I have no one to talk to."

"I can't let you drive."

He stared at me, aghast. "I can't drive, Occifer. I am drunk!"

"Right. Maybe I could call someone?"

"Brett," he slurred. "He'd come get me. He's my friend."

"Can you tell me his number?"

I had called Brett, who showed up with Kelly. He was upset that Chase was so drunk and assured me it wasn't usual for him.

"From what I gathered from his mumblings, your friend is upset about a fight with his brother," I said.

He sighed. "A bit more complex than that, I'm afraid."

Chase had been so funny, adorable, and sad. He said I was like an angel. He kept calling me Occifer Cinnamon and telling me how much he liked my freckles. My nose. My hair. Then he'd look upset and say he wished he'd done things differently. He wished his family still loved him. When I would try to comfort him, he'd ask if he could sing me a song about how beautiful I was.

I found it impossible to forget him, and days later, I saw him at the garage.

He was in a tight T-shirt that showed off the ink on his arms. His shoulders were broad and his waist narrow. He was tall, and his light-

brown hair was tucked up under a beanie. His eyes were as beautiful as I remembered. And just as sad. His light-blue irises reminded me of a summer's day early in the morning just as the sky was getting brighter. I wanted to make them shine in happiness. He'd taken my hand, allegedly to help me over some uneven ground, but I felt the tremor in his arm and saw the way he looked at me. I had hoped for more, but it hadn't happened.

Then I saw his ad.

And now I was living with him.

And I really hoped to get to know him more. To get a chance to erase that sadness.

Why it was so important, I didn't want to dive into. At least not yet.

Maybe one day soon.

Chase walked in, carrying a bag. He frowned when he saw me lifting a box.

"What are you doing?" he asked, hurrying over and taking the box from my arms. "I said I'd do that tonight."

I laughed, taking back the box. "Chase, I packed them and put them in the storage unit all on my own. I'm used to doing it by myself."

He shook his head and set down the bag he was carrying. "But you don't have to anymore. I'm here." He tugged the box out of my hands.

I gave up. "Fine. It goes in the kitchen."

He nudged the bag on the floor. "So does that. I brought Chinese."

"Oh my God, you are spoiling me. Stop it."

He shrugged, grinning as I picked up the bag. I followed him to the kitchen.

"Get your room done?"

"Yes. Maybe you can help me move my bed tomorrow when I get back from work?"

"What is your shift?"

I grabbed plates from the cupboard as Chase set out the food. "Three days on, four off. Then four on, three off. Six to four. I was lucky and got the day shift."

He nodded. "Nights must be hard."

"They were in Toronto," I said, hoping my voice didn't shake as a memory swept through me.

He placed his hand over mine. "Sorry, Hannah. I didn't mean to upset you."

I looked down, realizing my hand was trembling. My whole body was. Simply mentioning Toronto upset me. I sighed. I had thought it would stop once I left the city—obviously, I was wrong.

Chase leaned across the table and slid a finger under my chin, and I met his gaze. He looked upset, his eyes worried. "Are you okay, Cinnamon?"

I clutched his wrist, drawing in a shaky breath. "Yeah, I'm okay."

"I'm sorry. I obviously brought up something painful."

I blinked at the wetness in my eyes. Before I could say anything, he stood, pulling me up with him and wrapping me in his arms.

"I'm here, Hannah. Everything is okay."

I let him hold me. I drew strength from his solid form, his tight embrace. He smelled good. Clean and masculine, the hint of fresh-cut grass lingering. I stepped back and blinked, desperate to change the subject. "Did you shower before coming home?"

He chuckled and sat. "I had to. I was helping install a newly reupholstered interior on a car Maxx is restoring. I was covered in sweat and grease." He smiled at me, his voice low and tender. "Okay to eat?"

"Yes."

"Good."

"You work in the office and the garage?" I asked.

He nodded around a mouthful of egg roll, swallowing before he spoke. "I enjoy designing custom interiors. I've been taking courses, and Maxx lets me play."

"Do you have any pictures?"

With a grin, he showed me his phone, and I scrolled through the images. "Chase, these are gorgeous."

He looked bashful, color flooding the tips of his ears. "Thanks. I like it."

"I love it. You're so talented."

"Thank you."

Silence fell, but it wasn't uncomfortable. We ate and put away the food. "Dinner tomorrow is on me."

"You will have worked all day."

"You too," I pointed out. "If I was on my own, I would cook, so it's no big deal, Chase. Anything you hate?"

He made a face. "Liver and brussels sprouts. Salmon."

"I can relate to both." I nodded in sympathy. "Not a fan."

He shuddered. "I agree."

"If it's nice, we could barbecue. I saw you had a grill."

"Oh yeah. I'm good at grilling."

"Then I'll pick up something easy. Next week, we can figure out a plan going forward."

"Sounds good."

After dinner, Chase moved some boxes, his muscles flexing, showing off his tattoos.

"I like your ink," I said without thinking.

He grinned. "Yeah? Thanks."

"Is it, ah, all over...I mean, just on your arms?"

He pulled up his sleeve. "Both go to my shoulder. Stefano drew them for me. He's really talented. He does a lot of the custom work at the garage. I told him what I was thinking, and he came up with these."

"They are incredible."

"Incredibly sexy," I added in my head. I reached for a box, and he stopped me, chastising me sweetly over dragging my bed into my room when I got home from work. "Stop with the heavy lifting," he ordered. "I'll do it. You take a little one."

I tried not to laugh at him. I was used to doing things on my own. I had to admit it was nice to have someone worrying about me, though.

I carried a couple of lighter boxes to my room, deciding to leave the furniture until the next day. The walls would be dry enough then; I could position it all the way I wanted.

I returned to the kitchen, where Chase added the last box to the pile. I poured us each a glass of water, and we sipped the cold liquid.

I rolled my shoulders, feeling the ache from the painting and moving the bed.

"Why don't you have a bath?" Chase asked.

"My room only has a shower."

"Mine has a soaker tub. You can use it. Relax for a bit and go to bed early."

I smiled. "That would be awesome."

He grinned. "I even cleaned it last week to show off the house. It was pretty dusty."

"Not a tub guy?"

"No."

"Okay, I'll use it."

I stopped as I went past him and pressed a kiss to his cheek. I felt like I did that a lot. He seemed okay with it, so I kept doing it. "Thanks, Chase. For everything."

He caught me around the waist. "Anytime. And, Hannah?"

"Yeah?" I asked, trying not to cuddle right into him. He relaxed me more than any bath could.

"If you want to talk, I'm here. Okay?"

I sighed and lifted my head. We looked at each other, the room disappearing. There was only him and me. His blue eyes, so understanding and warm, met my golden-brown ones. They locked and held. He bent and pressed a kiss to my mouth. It was so light and fleeting, I thought I imagined it. Except the way my body lit up, I knew it had happened.

"Anytime," he repeated. "I'm here."

"Okay," I whispered.

"Enjoy your bath," he said, stepping back.

I nodded as I walked down the hall.

I touched my mouth.

I had a feeling life was about to get interesting.

And I wasn't sure how I felt about that.

CHAPTER SIX

Chase

I went outside, puttering in the garage to give Hannah some privacy while she had her bath and got ready for bed. She had already dragged her double mattress into the room and planned on sleeping on it, even though it was still on the floor. Tomorrow, I would surprise her and put the bed together so she would be more comfortable.

I poked around the worktable and looked in the drawers. Old Man Hyde told me whatever was left in the garage or house I could keep or throw out. There were some cool old tools and equipment. I found a box and loaded it up. Charly was always looking for stuff to hang in the garage. She'd love the items I found. I walked the yard, looking at it with new eyes. The fence needed replacing, and the yard needed to be cleaned up. It would be a good project to work on with summer approaching. The deck was small, and I wondered about expanding it. I enjoyed sitting outside, and it would make sense. I stood back, eyeing the roof. It might need replacing too. And the windows were original.

I shook my head as I chuckled. Buyer beware. But the house was solid, the basement dry, and I could easily afford to fix it up. I got it at a decent price, and I was trying to let go of my ideas of not touching my father's money. Instead, I was trying to think of it as my *dad's*. The man I remembered from my childhood. The one who would be pleased I bought a house and planned to look after it. When I was little, I remembered how he and Mom always worked on our house together, keeping it neat and tidy. Once Mom passed and after he had made a lot of money from a business venture, we moved in to a bigger place and he had people who looked after it. That house never felt like home. I looked around again. I wanted this place to feel like a home. I had a feeling, with Hannah here, that was going to happen.

I paused as I walked into the kitchen, listening. The house was quiet aside from some soft music I could hear. I headed down the hall, seeing Hannah's door wasn't shut tightly. I peeked in. A lamp was burning in the corner, and she was curled up on her mattress, a blanket thrown over her. Her hair was spread out around her head, shimmering in the dim light. She was on her side, her knees drawn up to her chest and her hands clasped under her chin like a child.

Except she was far too sexy to be a child. I stared at her, unable to look away. She was incredibly lovely. No makeup, her hair a tangle of curls, and sleeping, yet she called to me on a level I had never experienced before. The draw to her was strong.

I shook my head and stepped back, pulling the door closed behind me. I was acting like a stalker. Watching her sleep. I headed to the kitchen and got a beer and a pad of paper. I sat at the table, making a list of the things I wanted to do for improvements. I noted the items I thought I could handle with help from Maxx and Stefano and those I would need to bring in contractors on. Luckily, we serviced a lot of company vehicles, so I would be able to use one I trusted.

I glanced at the clock, seeing it was past eleven. I decided to go to bed, and I stood, stretching.

I was walking down the hall when I heard it.

A whimper and a soft sob coming from Hannah's room. Startled, I opened her door, looking in on her. She was curled into a tighter ball than before, clutching her pillow and mumbling, obviously in the throes of a bad dream.

"Please, no," she whimpered.

I crossed the room, kneeling beside her. I wasn't sure what to do.

Should I wake her up? Shake her? Leave her?

Of all the options, the last one appealed to me the least.

Tentatively, I placed my hand on her head, stroking her hair.

"Hannah," I murmured. "It's okay. Everything is okay."

Her whimpering stopped.

"I'm right here, baby," I said quietly. "You're safe."

She let out a little puff of air, her body relaxing. I kept stroking her head and murmuring words to her. She shuddered and went still, her breathing evening out.

I kept stroking her hair until I was sure she was deep into sleep again. I carefully stood and backed out of the room, keeping her door open.

In my room, I yanked off my shirt and jeans, then brushed my teeth. I dragged on some sleep pants and lay on my bed, keeping my door open as well. I wanted to be able to hear her if she had another nightmare.

I wasn't sure what brought it on.

Maybe she was overtired? Or being in a new place? Thinking about going back to work? I recalled how tense she got when I mentioned Toronto. Maybe she'd had a bad experience there and talking about it brought back an unwelcome memory. I would have to tread carefully.

In the meantime, if she needed me, I was there for her.

I was at the table when she walked in the next morning. I smiled at her and tipped my pretend hat. "Morning, Officer."

She laughed and shook her head. "Why are you up so early?"

"I'm often at the garage early. Gives me a chance to get things organized before everyone shows up." I eyed her carefully as she poured a cup of coffee into a travel mug. "How'd you sleep?"

She frowned. "Okay. Why?"

I decided not to mention the nightmare right now. I shrugged. "I was wondering how comfortable you were on the floor. We'll move your stuff tonight."

"I was fine," she assured me, twisting the lid on the mug tight. She offered me a smile.

"See you tonight."

"No breakfast?"

She shook her head and grinned. "Cop. Donuts."

I laughed as I carried my mug to the sink. "Well, have a good day, dear."

She stopped beside me and smiled. "You too, Chase." Then she kissed my cheek.

I watched her depart, leaving the warmth of her lips on my skin. I wanted to drag her into my arms and kiss her thoroughly. Send her to work with a real smile.

I hoped that one day, that would happen.

Dom chuckled. "You listening, kid?"

I shook my head. "Yeah, sorry. I missed that."

He sat back, crossing his arms. His muscles bulged, and he looked scary. But he smiled. "What's on your mind?"

"Oh, nothing important. I was walking around the house last night, looking at some jobs that needed to be done."

Maxx came over, pouring a cup of coffee and taking a sip. "Houses and cars. Expenses never end."

"So I'm discovering. I need to replace the fence and the roof." I scratched my chin. "And I want to enlarge the deck out back. I like sitting there, but with the grill, there is really only room for one chair." I had to laugh. "Never thought about those things when I just rented the place."

Stefano came around the corner, hearing what I had just said. "Ownership. Whole other ball game. And you helped with my deck. I'll help with yours. Fence too. Roofs, I know nothing about."

Maxx nodded in agreement. "Decks and fences, we do. But roofs, nope."

Dom grinned. "I do. I spent three summers working at a roofing place. Put myself through mechanic school working in the hot sun installing shingles. I can help there. I can teach you guys. You get the dumpster bin and supplies, and we can do it in a weekend as long as there isn't a lot of rot under the current shingles."

"That would be awesome."

"I'm looking for a place right now." He grinned. "I don't want to rent if I can buy. So when I'm ready, you can return the favor."

Maxx chuckled. "That's how we do it around here."

"I'll drop over tonight and have a look if you want," Dom offered.

"Awesome. Maybe you could help me carry Hannah's dresser and bed frame into her room? She slept with her mattress laid out on the floor last night."

"Not a problem." He stood. "Now, back to this invoice."

That night, Hannah came out of the kitchen as I walked in, Dom following. She smiled at us.

"Hello again," she greeted us, recognizing Dom from the garage.

I introduced them, and Dom shook her hand. He was polite and friendly.

"We're going to move your bed, and Dom is going to check out the roof."

"Well, you should eat first. I made my mom's famous casserole, so there's lots. It'll be ready in about ten minutes."

Dom grinned. "Never say no to a casserole. Especially a famous one." He glanced into the living room. "We can get some of this done fast."

We carried the bed frame in and set it up, adding the box spring and mattress once Hannah pointed where she wanted it. Then she informed us it was time to eat. We sat down, and I inhaled deeply, the scent of the food making my mouth water. "That looks awesome," I commented with a wide grin. "I don't think I've ever come home to a meal before. Brett or I would pick up something or throw a burger on the grill. But a real meal?" I shook my head. "And on matching plates?"

She laughed and patted my arm. "I unpacked a couple of boxes."

"This is great." Unable to resist, I kissed her cheek. "Thanks, Hannah."

She laughed, and Dom looked between us with a grin on his face. We ate dinner, chatting about Lomand and Littleburn. Dom said he planned on looking in both places for a house. He asked Hannah about working here. "Must be different from the big city."

She swallowed and nodded, pausing before she spoke. "Very much. Fewer people, less crime, far too quiet for some officers, but it suits me."

"Were you in Toronto a long time?"

She paused before speaking. "About two years. I realized the big city wasn't for me. Luckily, I saw this posting." She picked up her glass, and I noticed the slight tremor in her hand.

Dom abruptly changed the subject, and I wondered if he saw the tremor as well. After we ate, she insisted on cleaning up, and we went outside, climbing up onto the roof. Dom walked around, inspecting it, and was pleased. "I think the plywood is still strong. It feels sturdy—no bouncing. We'll scrape off the old shingles, and as long as it's good, we'll have the new ones up in a weekend. Faster if I get a couple of my buddies to help out." He paused. "Maybe a couple of weeks from now?"

"Yeah, great. I'll have finished the sale by then, so everything will be in order."

"Great. You can order the dumpster bin and pick your shingles. Make sure to go with thirty-year shingles. You don't really get thirty out of them, but they are far better quality."

"Great. I'll do that this weekend."

We looked at the fence, and he even gave me a couple of ideas on the deck outside. "Two levels would be nice. Put your grill up close to the door and a nice seating area below. Great entertaining spot."

"Good idea. I hadn't thought about that."

He grinned. "I love home improvement."

Inside, we moved the dresser and night tables and carried the last of the boxes marked "Bedroom" in for Hannah. She smiled as she looked around the living room. "I'll start painting in here this weekend."

Dom smiled. "I'll help. With the hall leading to the kitchen, that's a lot of painting area. Many hands and all."

She smiled at him, laying her hand on his arm. "That would be awesome! My mom is going to help too. She's going to be in charge of taping, bottom trim, and food." Her eyes danced. "She's pretty little and hates heights, so she sticks to ground level."

Dom laughed. "Works for me. I don't need the top trimmed. I'm great at cutting in. We'll make a good team." He paused. "Your dad coming along too?"

Hannah's smile fell. "No, he died when I was younger. It's just my mom and me."

"Sorry, kiddo."

"Thanks." She smiled again, although it looked forced. "I'll go call Mom and tell her it's on." She rose up on her toes and kissed his cheek. "Thanks, Dom."

I felt an odd feeling as I watched her kiss him. It was fast and friendly, yet somehow I didn't like it. Hannah left the room, and Dom looked at me with a wide smile and he chuckled. "Relax, kid. She was just being sweet. She's young enough to be my daughter, and even if she weren't, it's obvious you two are getting close."

I blinked. "Is it?"

He threw back his head in laughter. "With the touches and the smiles at dinner? How she was worried about you being on the roof? The way she's making this place homey? Kid, you got yourself way more than a roommate." He grasped my shoulder and shook it. "Open your eyes. She likes you the same way you like her. Take it slow and treat her well. I think you got a good one there."

He left with a wave, and I wandered down the hall. Hannah was unpacking a box, and I grinned at how different the room already looked with her furniture in place and a throw rug on the floor beside her bed. When it had been my room, I'd had a bed, a dresser, and a side table. That was it. I rubbed my chin. That was how my room still looked. I had just moved what I had into the bigger bedroom, not really caring. But seeing Hannah's space made me want to fix up mine too.

I rapped on the doorframe, and she looked up.

"Hey."

"The room looks really nice." I complimented her.

She looked around, pleased. "It does. Once I hang a few pictures and some curtains, it'll be great."

"And your mom is coming this weekend?"

"If that's okay."

"Of course. I'll be at the garage until noon or so, then I'll come home and help. Dom will too."

"Great. Mom and I will tape and get the room ready. With four of us, the room will go fast."

I grinned. "It wouldn't surprise me if Maxx or Stefano showed up either. Or Charly and Gabby."

She looked delighted. "They are all so awesome. You're so lucky to have them, Chase."

"You have them too, now."

She hugged my arm. "Then I'm lucky too."

———

She had another nightmare. I heard her from my room, and I hurried next to her bed, finding her in the same curled-up position as the night before. Tonight, I saw tears on her face, but her whimpers and distress eased when I stroked her head and murmured quiet words to her that seemed to soothe her.

"I'm here, Hannah. Right here, baby. You're safe."

I worried about her all the next day, but she seemed fine when I got home. I grilled some burgers, and she tossed a salad. It was easy and comfortable. After dinner, she made me look at the paint swatches she had taped to the wall in the living room, asking my opinion.

"Um, they all look…fine?" I offered.

She tapped one. "Too green, I think." Another tap. "And this one is more purple. I wanted a nice coffee-mocha. My sofa is taupe, yours is chocolate leather. We want it to complement both."

I narrowed my eyes and studied them. I touched the end one. "I like this."

She hummed in agreement. "Yes. The perfect blend. You have a good eye."

I chuckled. "Working with the upholstery side of restorations has helped. Customers are very particular about the colors."

"Okay, we'll look at that one and this one in the light tomorrow and decide. I'll pick up the paint after my last shift." She stood close, the heat of her soaking into my skin. "I get a weekend off. That doesn't happen much." She looped her arm around my waist, leaning her head on my shoulder. "I love this house, Chase. I'm so happy to be here." She paused. "With you."

I pressed a kiss to her head. "I like having you here."

She looked up, her eyes wide and shining. "Yeah?"

I turned, facing her fully. I pulled her closer. "Yeah."

I wanted to kiss her with everything in me. Know what it felt like to have her lips move with mine. Taste her. I'd been fantasizing about that since I'd first met her.

I began to lower my head when my phone rang. It startled us both, and we pulled apart. We stared, realizing what had been about to happen. Her breathing was fast. My pulse raced. My phone rang again, and I pulled it from my pocket, answering it.

"Charly," I almost growled into the phone.

"Chase. I hear there is painting this weekend."

I stepped back, running a hand through my hair, trying not to sound upset. "Yes, we're painting."

"I'm coming. So is Gabby. The boys have the kids. They both suck at painting. I excel. We can do the living room and your room. Get it all done."

"Um." I was about to protest when I saw the happiness on Hannah's face. She picked up a pile of samples, pulling out the one I had mentioned I liked and waving it. I had to smile.

"Sure, Charly. Many hands and all that."

"Awesome. We'll talk tomorrow!"

I hung up and shrugged. "I guess it's turning into a party."

"Great!"

For a moment, neither of us said anything. She smiled sadly and lifted a shoulder as if silently acknowledging the lost moment. "I'm going to head to bed."

I nodded. "Night, Hannah."

"Night, Chase."

CHAPTER SEVEN

Chase

I stayed in my room in the morning, listening to Hannah move around and get ready for work. She was quiet, the sounds muffled. I smelled the scent of coffee and heard the front door click locked behind her. She'd had another nightmare in the night, and I'd gone in and soothed her again. I wanted to ask her about them, except she didn't seem to recall having them in the morning or the fact that I'd gone into her room to comfort her. I wasn't sure how she was going to feel about that. Our almost-kiss troubled me. I wanted to kiss her, and I was certain if I had last night, she would have kissed me back. How far things would have gone, I had no idea, but in the dull light of the morning without lust or her scent in my nose, I wondered if it was a good idea to pursue a different relationship with her. We were close in age, her twenty-eight compared to my thirty. But she was a cop, and I had a record. How would she feel about that? I knew I had to tell her, but I was worried. I would hate to lose her as a friend and roommate. It hadn't been a long time yet, but still, I felt different when I walked in the door. If she left, I would go back to being alone, and the thought didn't sit well. If we were just friends and I was her landlord, I didn't have to divulge my past.

Except, my omission felt like a lie. And given how closely my past was linked with Charly and Maxx, she would find out.

I scrubbed my face in vexation. I had no idea what to do.

But I knew one person who would tell me.

And her name was Charly.

Charly poured us a coffee and looked at me across the table. "What's up?"

"I almost kissed Hannah last night."

"Kissed, like you did me this morning?"

I shook my head slowly. "No."

Her eyebrows lifted. "Well, that was fast." She sat back, sipping her coffee, looking around the kitchen. "When I first got here, Maxx and I struck sparks off each other. He made me mad, and I liked to push his buttons."

"You still do," I pointed out dryly.

She grinned. "But now I know what to expect. He's going to get all growly and pissy and throw me down somewhere and get all his frustrations out."

"TMI, Charly."

"There is a point here," she replied.

"Can we get to it? I'm getting uncomfortable."

She laughed. "Whatever. Mom and Dad do have sex, Chase. A lot of it."

I wanted to cover my ears, but I nodded. "Well aware. Everyone is."

She chuckled. "It took us a while to admit our feelings. Especially Maxx. I knew I loved him early on. You've had feelings for *Occifer Cinnamon* for a long time." She paused. "I think she has some for you. But you both have pasts. Your record." She paused and took another sip of her coffee. "Whatever she is running from."

I hunched closer. "She has nightmares, Charly. She cries in her sleep."

"Do you wake her up? Or does she wake up on her own?"

"Neither. The first night, I went in to check on her. I stroked her head and talked to her a little, and she stopped. I-I've been doing it every night."

Charly studied me. "You need to show her she can trust you."

"How?"

"Show her that you trust her. Tell her about your past."

"She could just look it up in the system. She might already know."

"I don't think Hannah would do that. But if she knows, then you have your answer. She does trust you. If she doesn't, she has to know—it's only fair." She studied me. "I can tell you are feeling guilty about withholding it from her."

I huffed out a deep breath. "You're right. I am. I want to be honest, but I'm scared."

"If this was just a roommate scenario, I'd say to leave it, but it's obviously not. You have feelings for her, Chase. You have to be honest."

"I know. I'm worried she'll reject me."

"Then at least you'd know. Don't push this relationship forward without being honest, Chase. You saw what happened with Kelly and Brett. With Gabby trying to do everything on her own. Take it slow, and tell her when the time is right." She leaned forward, clasping my hand. "I don't want to see you get hurt."

"Thanks, Charly."

She nodded. "You were right to come to me. I am wise about this stuff."

"Maxx would call you nosy."

"Maxx is a man of few words. Same thing."

I laughed as I stood and drained my coffee. "I'll head into the garage now."

"Okay." She waited until I was at the door before she called, "Chase?"

I turned. "Yeah?"

"I like her, and I think the two of you would be an awesome couple."

I grinned. "Me too."

"I think she'd be lucky to have you."

I laid my hand on my heart. Coming from Charly, that meant more than I could express. She was my sister, pseudo-mother, and friend, all rolled into a smart-mouthed redhead I adored.

"Thanks."

She winked, but I saw the glimmer of tears in her eyes. She pretended to be tough, but we all knew she had a heart of gold under the swagger.

She waved her hand. "Be off with you. Make me money."

"Okay, boss."

The garage was swamped, and the rest of the week flew by.

Hannah was there when I got home, and we spent a little time together at night. Conversation was easy between us. She would share bits of her day. I would tell her about amusing incidents in the garage. We sat at the kitchen table, leaning on our elbows, chatting. The living room and hall were now shrouded in plastic, the furniture and floors covered, the holes filled in and primed. Waiting for the weekend. Hannah had the paint mixed, and all the supplies were ready. Friday night, we ordered a pizza, and I laughed when I opened the fridge to grab us a beer.

"Enough food in there?" I asked. "When do you plan on using all of that?"

"Tomorrow. Stuff for sandwiches, burgers, and sausage to barbecue. Condiments and fruit. Mom will make some macaroni salad, and I got cupcakes."

I began to laugh. "Okay, Cinnamon."

"Your nickname makes no sense. I'm not a redhead like Charly."

I tapped the bridge of my nose. "It's the sexy little dots of cinnamon on your skin. Not your hair."

She wrinkled her nose. "You find my freckles sexy? They're annoying."

"Nope. Totally sexy."

Color fused her face. "You're just being sweet."

"Never. Telling the truth. I find them fascinating."

She picked up her plate and carried it to the sink. "Then you need to find a better hobby."

But she was smiling as she left the room.

And there were no nightmares that night.

The next day, I worked in the garage, grateful when we were done ahead of schedule and I could go home. The place was bustling when I got there. Gabby and Charly were working in the living room, waving as I went by. I was shocked when I went to my room, finding my furniture already in the middle of it and my walls ready to be painted. I turned and found Hannah leaning on the door, grinning. "We got it ready."

"I don't want you to hurt yourself moving furniture."

She laughed. "I'm stronger than I look, Chase. I'm fine." She winked, teasing me. "Don't worry, I didn't riffle through your drawers and find the hidden porn stash. I tried, but you must hide it well."

I gaped, and her eyes widened. "I was kidding, Chase. I'm sorry…"

I started to laugh. She joined me. "You brat."

I had to sling my arm over her shoulder and pull her in for a hug. "I use the internet now for porn, Cinnamon. I don't buy magazines."

Now it was her turn to gape. Then we both laughed, enjoying a moment of levity together.

"Seriously, thank you. I'm shocked how much you have done already."

"Get into your painting clothes and grab some food. Everyone will eat, and then we'll split off to divide and conquer."

I pressed a kiss to her cheek. "Awesome."

I was tugging my T-shirt down as I walked into the kitchen and met the hazel eyes of a pretty woman who was busy setting out food. I stuck out my hand. "Hi, I'm Chase. You must be a friend of Hannah's. Thanks for doing this."

She began to laugh, tossing her braid over her shoulder. She was short and curvy. Her hair was red, but not like Charly's brilliant hue. It wasn't as light as Hannah's either. More of a rusty auburn color. She was older but not much. Her smile was wide and familiar. So were the freckles on her nose and cheeks. "Friends, yes," she murmured. "But a bit closer. I'm Cherry Gallagher."

"Hi, Cherry," I responded. Then I paused. "Wait. Gallagher?"

Hannah walked in. "Oh, good. You met my mom."

I gaped at her. "Your *mom?*" I looked between them, seeing the similarity now. "That is your *mom?*"

They laughed, sounding quite a bit alike in their amusement. "Yes, that is my mom."

Cherry smiled, the resemblance striking. "I had Hannah young."

"No shit," I mumbled.

Dom walked in, carrying a case of beer and another one of pop. He stopped, frozen for a moment, his gaze focused on Cherry, then he shook his head and set down the cans. "I, ah, brought refreshments."

I looked at Cherry, who stared at Dom. His frank appraisal of her was almost embarrassing. Her return of the same gaze was surprising. Then he held out his hand. "Dom," he said in his deep baritone. "Dom Salvatore."

"Hi," Cherry murmured. "Cherry Gallagher. I'm Hannah's—"

He cut her off. "Older sister."

"…mother," she finished.

He blew out a whistle. "Impossible."

"I assure you, I am."

"They don't make mothers like you where I come from."

She blushed, and I looked between them, feeling as if I should leave them alone. I glanced at Hannah, who was watching, as fascinated as I was.

Cherry tossed her hair. "Then you've lived a sheltered life."

He grinned, the movement changing his countenance. His eyes crinkled, and he looked younger. Almost relaxed. "I guess I need to expand my horizons." He crossed his arms. "Maybe you could help me with that—" he paused, rubbing his bottom lip and staring at her "—Cherry Gallagher."

She lifted her eyebrows. "I wouldn't hold my breath, Mr. Salvatore."

He grinned again, playful. "We'll see about that."

He was still grinning as she swept past him. "I'll go tell the girls to come get something to eat."

He spun on his heel and followed her. "I'll make sure she finds them."

I looked at Hannah, who was wide-eyed and shocked. "What was that?"

"I'm not sure. But I think it's going to be interesting."

Hannah began to laugh. "I hope he's prepared. She is stubborn, independent, and knows her mind."

"Hmm, I wondered where you got that from."

She laughed and slapped my arm. "Stop it. Help me with the food so we can get back to painting."

I assisted her as best I could since I had no clue about what she was doing. She knew where everything went. What dishes belonged where. What utensil was needed. I just handed her things. It seemed safer.

"You might want to separate those two," I muttered as her mom came back in, Dom following. "Or get a hose."

Hannah giggled, nudging me with her elbow. "Stop it," she repeated. "He's your friend. Tell him to back off."

"I am not telling that man anything. She's your mother." I shook my head. "How the hell that is possible, I don't know, but that's what she says."

"She had me when she was eighteen. I'm twenty-eight. She is forty-six."

"Doesn't look it."

"I know."

"Dom is forty-eight. Perfect age for each other."

"She lives in Toronto and isn't looking for a man."

"I wasn't looking for you either," I said, without thinking.

Hannah's hands stilled, and our eyes met. "I mean, I thought I'd get a roomie with balls. You know. A dick. Like mine. *Fuck*. I mean, a guy. But I got you. You are so much better than balls."

"Or a dick?" she asked, her lips twitching.

"Definitely better than a dick. You smell way better."

"Sniff dicks often, do you?"

I began to laugh. She joined in, and without thinking, I pulled her into my arms and hugged her. I dropped a kiss to her head and stepped back, grabbing the plate of meat she handed me. I met Charly's all-seeing gaze and her knowing wink as she came into the room. I tried to ignore it.

"Smooth," she muttered as I went by. "The whole dick conversation. You sure know how to woo a woman."

"I try."

She shook her head. "You should try harder, Chase."

I looked at the way Hannah was still laughing as she poured a bag of chips into a bowl. I liked making her smile that way. She was fucking beautiful.

"No, I'm good."

Charly's smile was soft as she looked between Hannah and me.

"Yeah, you are."

CHAPTER EIGHT

Chase

The Gallagher women were drill sergeants in another life. There was no doubt about it. Lunch was served —trays of crusty sandwiches, dips, veggies. Cheese and crackers. Cut-up fruit. Cupcakes. Then they organized us all into pairs—each getting a different area to paint. I tried not to grin when Dom announced he and Cherry would do the hall. "I'll do the high parts. Cherry here can look after the bottom. Once we're finished, we'll move into the living room since it's the biggest area, and we can help with that," he said with a satisfied nod.

I had a feeling he wanted to take on the hall since the chances of brushing up against Cherry were high in the narrow space. I noticed the way he situated himself close to wherever she was. He did it casually, moving to get another sandwich, walking over to pour another coffee or get a soda for someone. He'd end up beside Cherry, talking to her or simply watching her, the look on his face intense. Hannah and I exchanged more than one amused glance, and Charly was practically vibrating in her seat. She loved matchmaking and pushing couples together.

She was enthusiastic with her response. "Good plan, Dom. I bet you'll make a great team. Gabby and I will start the living room. We've painted together before." She smiled innocently at me. "You and Hannah can tackle your room, okay, Chase?"

"Sure," I agreed easily, ignoring her subtle little wink.

"We have the brushes, rollers, and paint trays in each area all ready to go," Cherry said. "And the right paint. Lots of rags plus the stepladders."

"So organized," Dom muttered. "I do love me a woman who is organized."

Cherry snorted. "You have to be. Try being a single mother who has to get her kid ready for school and be at work on time every day. You learn fast."

The look he sent her was filled with admiration, and yet somehow, it still smoldered. She met his gaze without backing down, then turned and said something to Hannah, who grinned and tried to hide it behind her sandwich.

The front door opened, and Maxx and Stefano walked in, their voices booming. "We're here!"

Charly frowned. "You are supposed to be watching the kids."

Maxx grinned, dropping his head and kissing her soundly. "Mary, Nonna, and Papa have all the kids. Not only that, Rosa is making a huge lasagna, and they expect everyone at their place for dinner tonight. You get us for the afternoon."

I grinned at the shocked look on Cherry's and Hannah's faces. I wasn't surprised. This family always pulled together. When Rosa and Mack got married, they had moved to a place next to Mary's, and the three of them hung out a lot. Mary was an adopted grandmother to all the kids, who loved spending time with them. Rosa, Stefano's mom, was Italian, loved to cook, and adored having her family around, which now included all of us.

"How lovely," Cherry said. "Are you sure?"

Stefano flashed her a grin and introduced himself. Both he and Maxx were as surprised as I was to find out she was Hannah's mom and not a friend. He was fast to reassure her. "Mama would love to meet all of you. Including you again, Dom. Mack was keeping the kids busy in the garden, and she and Mary were bustling in the kitchen. They'd be disappointed if you didn't join us."

"Awesome. I remember your mama's cooking fondly," Dom said with a grin.

"Great." Stefano clapped his hands, taking the plate of food Gabby offered him. He bent and kissed her cheek. "Thanks, *Tesoro.*"

The house was suddenly overfull, the sounds of laughter and teasing nonstop. I leaned against the wall, enjoying it. My friends gathered together, helping one another. Nothing new, except this time, I was on the receiving end of that help. It was a great feeling. I gazed at Hannah across the kitchen as she laughed at something Charly said. She looked so right with my friends. She fit in well, and everyone liked her. God knew, I liked her.

I caught her eye, and we shared a smile. It occurred to me I had never experienced that before. Usually in our group gatherings, I was the odd man out. They never made me feel that way, but it was the truth. Everyone else was coupled up. Even Mary had a beau these days. An older gentleman who had bought a house down the road from her. Now she, Larry, Mack, and Rosa hung out as a foursome. And until this second, I was always solo.

Internally, I shook my head at my thoughts. Hannah was my roommate. We weren't a couple. She'd been here a week.

But we'd bonded so quickly. I already forgot what the house was like before she walked in the door. I looked forward to the end of the day, knowing she'd be around. Getting to have dinner with her or hear her laugh.

But it was too soon, and there were so many reasons for us simply to remain roommates. Good friends were hard to come by, and I truly liked her as a person.

And yet the thoughts persisted.

And I didn't stop them.

I didn't want to.

I wasn't sure painting was supposed to be this much fun. I stood on the ladder, edging the walls, and Hannah did the bottom then followed behind, rolling. I kept stealing glances of her bent over, trailing the paintbrush along the top of the baseboard. The movement caused her shirt to lift, and I caught glimpses of the bare skin of her back. A few times, her stomach as she stretched to get the roller to reach. At one point, she stood below me, pointing out a piece I had missed. Her T-shirt gaped at the neck, and I caught a peek of her lacy bra and the breasts it so carefully guarded. I wanted to free them, play with them. Taste them. Just the thought made my mouth water.

"Chase?" she prompted. "Earth to Chase."

I shook my head. "Sorry. I was, ah, thinking."

She put her hand on her hip. "About?"

"Work. A car," I lied. "Some upholstery I want to get my hands on."

"Uh-huh," she grunted, knowing I was lying. I was sure she'd caught me staring at her rack. But damn, it was fine. Really, I had no choice.

She put down the roller. "I need a drink." She pointed to the wall. "Fix that."

Laughing, I corrected the line and climbed down from the ladder, picking up the roller and finishing the wall. I headed to the kitchen to grab a drink, pausing when I overheard Hannah and her mom in her room talking quietly.

"Are you sure, Hannah?"

"Yes, Mom. He is just a friend. Nothing else."

"He wants more. I saw it."

"Well, he isn't getting more. I am not ruining a good partnership for that. I like him, but I'm not interested. He's—he's like a brother to me. We're friends. Nothing more."

"Is there someone else?"

Hannah paused. "Yes."

I felt a wall of disappointment swamp me. I hurried to the kitchen, not wanting to hear any more.

I had misread the signals. Hannah thought of me as a friend. She was affectionate and sweet. When I thought about it, she hugged and gave out cheek-kisses like they were nothing. I was the one who saw more than there was. Felt more.

Unable to stay, I grabbed a bottle of water and headed outside to the deck. I looked around, thinking of how I had jumped ahead. Seen us as a couple. Entertaining. I blinked away the moisture in my eyes.

What an idiot.

The door opened, and Hannah stepped out onto the deck. "Hey—you okay?"

"Absolutely. Just getting some fresh air. Rid my lungs of the paint."

She stepped closer, and I turned, walking down the steps. I couldn't take it if she touched me right now. I knew it wasn't her fault. This was on me. But I was hurt and disappointed. I felt stupid. Buying a house to make a stranger happy. Making plans for a future that was never going to happen. All because she was pretty and soft and she smelled good. Because I thought she saw me. That she liked me the same way I liked her.

"Chase?"

I looked up at her. "Yeah?"

"Are you sure you're okay? You look a little funny."

"I'm good. I'll be there in just a minute, and we can finish the first coat."

She frowned, not looking convinced. "Okay."

She headed inside, and I breathed a sigh of relief. I drew in some much-needed air and stared at the blue sky.

I had two choices.

Act like a dick and confront her. Make her uncomfortable and hope she moved out so I didn't have to look at her every day and remember what an idiot I had been.

Or not say a word. Enjoy her for the person she was. Kind, sweet, and wonderful. Keep her as a friend, exactly the way I had hoped to feel when I'd advertised for a roommate. Eventually, this feeling would go away. It had to. I didn't want her to move out. I didn't want to lose her.

Even if she didn't feel the way I did.

We could be friends.

Roommates.

Buddies.

Right?

It killed me to go back inside and keep painting as if nothing had happened. As if overhearing a few words hadn't devastated me. I managed to smile and return Hannah's teasing as we painted, although I knew it wasn't as heartfelt as it had been before. I made sure to stay far enough away that there was no touching, no cheek-kisses or arm-hugs.

The living room and hall were totally done. Two coats. My room would be ready for a second coat in the morning. I planned to get up early and get it done before Hannah woke up. I wasn't sure I could be in that room with her again. The close proximity was too much.

We went to Mack and Rosa's place, the one-story house large and welcoming. The gardens were being prepped, and they had a big area of play sets for the grandkids. We sat around in the warm summer evening, eating lasagna and the multitude of other dishes she'd prepared. Rosa Borelli-Conner had no clue how to make only one dish for a meal. I ate like I was starving, even though the food on my plate tasted like sawdust. I played with the kids, laughed with Maxx and Stefano. Let Rosa fuss over me a little.

I stayed as far away from Hannah as I could without making it obvious. I sat beside Dom, and we discussed the roof and the deck. Charly was enthusiastic about the tools and other items I had taken her, planning on adding to the garage décor. I made sure Hannah and Cherry were okay, insisting on getting them second helpings and bringing them the delicious dessert at the end of the meal. I hid everything deep inside. I was good at that. I had done it for years with my brother and my father.

Charly nodded her approval, and I smiled at her, sitting beside Rosa.

"Thank you for doing all of this for us, Rosa."

She smiled and patted my cheek. "You good boy. I like you. I am glad you buy a house. You need roots."

I chuckled. "Yes, Mama Rosa."

"I like new girl." She turned, lowering her voice. "But she make you sad, Chase?"

"Um, no, she's great."

She shook her head. "No, I see your heart is sad when you look at her. How much you like her?"

"Just as a friend. It's the same way she sees me."

She pursed her lips. "Be patient. Sometimes we have to be patient. It is hard, but worth it."

I didn't have the strength to try to explain it to her. "Sure, Rosa. I can do that."

She patted my cheek again. "Good boy. You deserve to be happy. Like my Stefano."

I had to look away.

I doubted that was in the cards for me.

Later, back at the house, Hannah turned to me with a smile.

"I can't believe how much we got done today," she said, looking around the living room. "We'll move the furniture against the walls in a couple of days," she explained. "But it's usable, and you can watch TV."

"Awesome." I forced a smile to my face.

"Chase, are you sure you're all right?" she asked. "You look as if something upset you."

"No," I lied. "I'm good. Just a long day and I'm tired. But you're right. We accomplished a lot, and thanks to Rosa and all the food you bought, we don't have to worry about groceries or cooking for a while. Lots of leftovers."

"That's true." She looked at her phone, following me into the kitchen. "Mom got home."

"That's good." I grabbed a soda, offering one to her. She took it and nodded. "I always worry about her driving."

I sat at the table. "Isn't that her job? To worry about you, I mean?" I asked, curious. They had an interesting dynamic. More friends than mother/daughter.

She pushed the hair away from her face as she sat down. She opened her drink and took a swallow. "Oh, she does worry. Believe me. Having me young and my dad dying, it was always just us. I think she sort of grew up with me. I mean, she was—is—a great mom, but we've always been close since it was only the two of us."

"She never remarried?"

"No. Between raising me, running her salon, she was busy. I remember her going on a few dates, but no one special."

"She owns a salon?"

"She did. The building was sold, so she closed it. Now she works at another place. She says she likes working for someone, not being the boss all the time with all the worry."

"How old were you when your dad died?"

"Seven." She swallowed. "He was a great dad. I remember his hugs and snuggles. His booming laugh. The way he would dance with my mom in the kitchen. I got his eyes and her freckles."

"They're beautiful," I said before I could stop myself.

She blushed. "Thanks." She looked over my shoulder. "He was a cop. He was on a regular traffic stop, and the driver was carrying drugs. He panicked and shot my dad."

"Shit. How awful." I frowned. "How did your mom feel when you decided to become one?"

"She wasn't happy, but she wasn't surprised either. I always wanted to be a cop."

"What made you leave Toronto?" I asked. "I mean, with your mom and your life there, moving here to a small city must have been a shock."

It was as if the shutters came down. Her face paled, and her shoulders stiffened. "More room for advancement," she replied.

She was lying. Everything about her suddenly screamed panic. Wariness. And for me to back off.

I stood. "Well, I wish you luck with that. I'm off to bed."

She blew out a long breath. "Night, Chase."

I left, pausing at the door. I glanced over my shoulder. She remained at the table, staring at her soda. I wanted to go back to her, to drag her into my arms and ask her what really happened. To get her to tell me if her reasons for leaving Toronto had something to do with her nightmares, but I didn't have that right. If she wanted to tell me, she could have.

But we were only roommates. Buddies.

I had to remember that.

She had another nightmare in the night, and I did the same as usual. Slipped in and comforted her then left her alone. At first, I was determined to ignore her, but her cries were stringent. Louder. I couldn't shut out her pain. She grasped my hand as I stroked her hair, and for a moment, I thought she'd woken up, but she remained asleep, holding my hand, her breathing evening out again. I hated leaving her. But I had to.

I was restless and gave up at dawn, getting off the bed in the middle of the room and beginning to paint. I finished my room, opened the windows to let in fresh air, then grabbed a shower and left when I heard her shower come on. I needed the space.

I pushed aside the thoughts of wondering how I was supposed to remain aloof and friendly.

Cursing the day I had put up the ad. Impulsively bought the house.

I should have just moved back into the apartment over the garage and saved myself the heartache.

I was an idiot.

To make matters worse, I already knew I was going to keep being an idiot.

And there was nothing I could do to stop it.

CHAPTER NINE

Hannah

I was surprised to see that Chase had gone out when I got up the next morning. I was even more surprised when I saw his door open and that he had already done the second coat on the walls. The paint stuff was all cleaned up, the brushes soaking, the roller covered in case it was needed.

I frowned as I made a coffee then sat at the table. I wondered if he was out for the day or just on an errand. I wasn't sure why it bothered me that he hadn't said anything or left a note. It wasn't as if we were a couple. We were roommates—except I thought perhaps we were already closer than that.

Maybe I had misread the signals? Chase was affectionate with Charly, Gabby, and the kids. He offered and accepted hugs and kisses all the time. Maybe he simply added me to that category. But I was sure I had seen the flare of interest, more than once. Felt his lips linger longer than just a fast, friendly kiss.

Had I misinterpreted that?

I shook my head as I took a sip of coffee. I was tired today. I'd had bad dreams last night. Fractured images of bad memories. It happened often when I talked about Toronto or my dad. I frowned as another memory surfaced. An indistinct, blurry one. A quiet voice murmuring my name, assuring me I was safe. A gentle touch that soothed and eased my fears. It had to be another dream, yet it felt real. But how could that be?

I pushed my hair off my face and finished my coffee. I had no idea what Chase's plans were today, but I knew what mine were. And I was determined to get them done.

I stood and carried my cup to the sink. I looked out on the yard, already envisioning what it would look like in a few weeks with some hard work. I'd heard Chase talking to Dom about the deck he wanted to build and the plans to do so. It would look amazing and be a fun place to hang out. A great one to relax on.

A wonderful place to spend downtime with Chase.

If he wanted me to.

That was the question that plagued me.

Because I wanted him to want that as much as I did.

But if all I could have was a great roommate and a friend, I would take that too.

Because when it came to Chase, I would take whatever he offered.

———

He came home around four, looking tired. He walked in and stopped, looking around in amazement.

"Wow, Hannah, the place looks so great."

I smiled at him from the sofa. I had arranged the furniture and added a rug I had already. It went well with his sofa. I added the chairs and tables, plus put together the TV stand and managed to get his TV on top. The room looked inviting, and once I hung some pictures and blinds, it would be a cozy place. I kept it minimal, not wanting to overpower him with toss cushions and knickknacks. He looked at the keys in his hand, then the table in the hall. "Is the bowl for these or decoration?" he asked.

I laughed. "Whatever you want it to be. It's your bowl."

He picked it up, studying it. "Really?"

"It was in the cupboard."

His face cleared. "Right. Charly gave it to me for Christmas. I thought it was for salad."

"No. Decoration."

"Makes more sense," he mused, turning the beautiful wooden bowl in his hands. "With the hole in it and everything. I thought maybe she got it on sale, and I didn't want to ask."

I began to laugh, and he grinned at me, looking more like Chase than he did last night.

"Working today?"

"Yeah. I had some stuff at work I wanted to do. Retooling some leather and I needed the quiet."

"You were gone early," I said lightly. "I wasn't sure."

He sat down and pulled off his beanie. His hair stuck up everywhere, and I had to bite back my grin. "I guess I should have left a note or something. I'm not used to roommate etiquette. Brett and I would just come and go. If we wanted information, we'd call."

"I didn't want to bother."

He frowned, running his hand over his head. "I need a shower." He stood, heading to the door, pausing. He turned and met my gaze. "You could never be a bother, Hannah. Ever."

Then he disappeared.

It was like that for the next week. Moments of politeness. Long periods of him being absent. I had no idea if that was normal. He'd kept close the first week, but maybe that was the anomaly and his being gone was the usual. If he was there, we'd eat dinner together. He told me amusing stories about the garage. Tuesday, he had a new bed delivered for his room, and he'd asked advice on where to put it. It was a king-sized mattress with a nice, heavy headboard that curved, made of black metal with brushed nickel accents. I suggested the spot, and he instructed the delivery men to situate it there.

They left, and he rubbed his chin. "I should have bought a new dresser," he surmised. "That one is kinda old."

"But it's solid wood. Holds a lot," I pointed out. "We could strip it and paint it black and add knobs to match the headboard. Same with your side table. It would look awesome with the blue-gray walls."

He swallowed. "If you have time."

"Of course I do. We can go get the stuff on the weekend if you want." I looked around. "Do you want help making the bed?"

He paused, then chuckled. "I guess my sheets won't fit."

I had to laugh. "You had a double, and now you bought a king? No, they won't."

He shrugged. "I'll just make do for a couple of days. No biggie. I'll get some."

"There's a big warehouse sale this weekend in Toronto. I'm going to pick up a few things with my mom. Tell me what you like, and I'll find you a set. It's cheaper there and has a bigger selection." I offered, hoping he'd say he would come with me.

"You can pick it. I trust you."

"You have plans this weekend?" I asked lightly, feeling an odd frisson of hurt in my chest.

"Picking out shingles and wood for the deck with Dom and Stefano," he replied.

"Oh, cool." My chest felt better with his words.

"Dom and I are going to go to a place he likes later. It's about an hour away."

My heart sank. He wouldn't be around at all. "Well, have fun."

"I plan to. You got any big plans other than shopping?"

"No, just going to see my mom."

"You can have friends over, you know. It's your place now, too," he informed me.

"Thanks. Maybe soon." I hadn't really made many friends; I was usually too busy working or spending time with my mom.

"Sure." He turned, pausing in the doorway. "I'd prefer no overnight guests, but if that happens, try to keep the noise down."

His words surprised me. Made me angry for some reason. "I'd ask the same," I snapped. "I'd prefer no naked women in the kitchen, if you don't mind."

I passed him in the doorway. "And keep them off my sofa too."

I slammed my door behind me, unsure why I was so mad. I had a feeling Chase thought he was being nice. Traitorous tears filled my eyes, and I wiped at them impatiently. The thought of Chase having another woman here made me crazy. But it was his house. He owned it, and the bottom line was, he could make the rules. But the thought of him bringing another woman here really upset me.

I sat on my bed, wondering why I'd thought this was a good idea. Moving in with Chase—a man I was secretly crushing on. He was handsome and sweet. Of course he'd have women all over him. I should have known that. But I had hoped he liked me too. In fact, I thought he did until this past weekend.

What if he came home from the bar with another woman?

I laid a hand on my chest at the sudden pain the idea of that happening caused. The way my days off were lining up, I had the weekend off again. But the thought of sitting here, waiting for Chase to show up with a guest, made me feel ill.

Imagining his mouth on someone else's made me want to punch something. I decided I needed to stay busy and away from the house. If I didn't see it, I could handle it.

Right?

"What are you up to this weekend, girl?" Annette in dispatch asked me the next afternoon.

"Going in to Toronto for a few hours tomorrow to do a little shopping."

"We're going to Zeke's for some drinks and dancing Saturday night. Why don't you join us?"

"Oh, ah—"

"Girls only," she added. "Dan isn't invited. None of the guys are."

I shot her a grateful look. A fellow officer, Dan, was a great guy. Steady, loyal, and yes, good-looking. We worked well together when we were partnered up. Not long ago, he had confessed that he liked me and asked me out. I was shocked. I let him down gently, telling him I didn't date fellow officers and that I was seeing someone. He took it well enough, but it seemed lately that he was around more and demanding my attention. I didn't want to hurt him, but I had no desire for a relationship with him. He felt like a brother to me. We had always gotten on well, but my feelings were strictly platonic. I hoped he would get the message and move on. I was beginning to be a little uncomfortable around him.

"I'll see what time I get back," I promised Annette.

"Great. I'll save you a seat."

I left the station and got in my car, unsure what to do. I had barely seen Chase since our interaction on Tuesday night. He came home late on Wednesday, and last night, he'd walked in carrying a pizza. He'd been polite, asking if I wanted a slice, but I told him I had already eaten when I got home. I sat in the living room while he ate in the kitchen. I quietly went to my room, shutting the door, and I heard the TV come on a while later. I wasn't sure how to clear the air between us. What had felt easy and great was now laced with anxiety and awkwardness.

I took a hot shower and sat on my bed, sighing as I brushed my hair. Maybe I had made a mistake and should look for another place. I had seen a small studio apartment in Littleburn when I was looking. Emphasis on the word small. But it would be okay, although the idea of moving again made me feel tired. Plus, the expense.

As I was mulling it over, there was a knock on my door. I looked down. I was in my nightgown—a ridiculous white cotton one I loved with long sleeves and lace. But I was covered and decent, so I called out for Chase to come in.

He opened the door and leaned on the frame, gazing at me for a moment.

"Hi."

"Hi," I responded.

He scratched at his chin, a habit I had noticed he had whenever he was nervous.

"So, I think we had our first fight," he said at the same time as I blurted out, "I'm sorry."

We both laughed, the sound slightly brittle.

"I shouldn't have slammed the door. I didn't really mean to…" I trailed off as he shook his head.

"I don't bring women home, Hannah. Ever. I wouldn't do that."

"It's your house," I reminded him.

"You live here as well. I respect you too much to do that."

I strove for levity. "So, you'll go back to theirs, then."

He shook his head. "I don't do that. I don't sleep around."

"Me either."

For a moment, silence surrounded us. He nodded. "Glad we cleared the air."

"Me too."

He paused, looking as if he wanted to say something.

"How's the new bed?" I asked.

"Big."

I laughed. "Comfy?"

"Yeah, pretty good." He looked around. "You're all settled, I see." He indicated the pictures on the walls and the curtains I had hung. "Looks, ah, pretty."

"It is. I'm glad I don't have to—" I cut myself off. "It's nice."

"Don't have to what?" he asked.

"Nothing."

He frowned.

"Move things around. I got them all in the right places," I ad-libbed. "No paint touch-ups."

"You can't leave," he murmured. "You were thinking of it, weren't you?"

"No," I insisted.

"You were," he breathed out. "You were thinking you should leave." He shook his head, his voice panicked. "Don't leave. Please. You can't, Hannah. I like having you here. I was in a bad mood, I said a couple of things. I'm sorry."

I held up my hand. "I'm not leaving, Chase. I like it here. I'm sorry too."

He stared. "Promise?"

I nodded. "Promise."

He sighed. "Okay. Sleep well." He left, shutting the door behind him.

I was glad he'd come to see me, but I still felt unsettled. As if we hadn't entirely cleared the air. But short of admitting my feelings for him, there wasn't much else I could say.

I lay down and pulled the blanket up to my chin.

I hoped I'd sleep tonight.

CHASE

I heard her cry out once in the night, but there were no other noises from her room, and I stayed put, lying on the big bed I had bought on impulse. I'd wanted a new mattress but only planned on buying a queen-size until I saw the bed in the showroom when I walked in. I liked it, and my room was big enough to hold a king-sized mattress. Brett and Stefano each had one, so there was no question there. I liked the metal headboard and the way it bent and curved. It was heavy and masculine-looking. I'd never owned anything that nice, and suddenly I wanted it.

I hadn't thought of sheets or pillows. Hannah said she'd get me some this weekend, and I hoped she would since she wasn't mad at me anymore.

Or was she? We hadn't exactly kissed and made up.

I felt awful about the angry words we exchanged. The sudden coolness between us. It was as if a wall had been erected, and I had no idea how to scale it. Even going to her earlier hadn't fixed whatever had broken between us. It felt as if we were both holding back. I wondered who it was she was seeing. If I would ever meet him. How I was going to feel when and if I did. How I would handle it if he started hanging here with her.

But the thought of her leaving upset me even more. If friendship was all I could have with her, I would take it. I just had to move on.

After a long, sleepless night, I wondered how much time would have to pass for me to do so. I headed into the garage and shut my door, working on paperwork to force myself to concentrate. Around eleven, I got a text from Hannah, telling me she wouldn't be home that night. I frowned, my thoughts immediately going to the one place they shouldn't. I made a big deal about not bringing women home. Did that mean she was spending the night with whoever she was seeing at his place? I scrubbed my hand over my face, feeling my scruff under my fingers. I had no idea how to respond. If I should respond. I decided to play it light.

> ME
>
> See you tomorrow, then.

Her reply almost sent me over the edge.

HANNAH

I'll be late. Don't wait up!

My beanie ended up on the floor, and I dug my hands into my hair, yanking on it. She was definitely spending the weekend with the guy she was seeing.

I already knew the answer to how I would react if I met him. I could barely handle the thought of it, never mind seeing him in person. I hated him. With the fiery passion of hell. I was going to introduce him to my fist. Repeatedly.

"Chase."

I looked up, meeting Charly's concerned gaze.

"If you yank on your hair any harder, you'll pull it out."

I bent over and picked up my beanie, tugging it back on my head. "Great. Bald *and* alone."

She shut the door and sat beside me. "Tell me what's going on."

It all came pouring out. The closeness I felt with Hannah. The conversation I overheard between her and her mother. How devastated I felt. The way I tried to stay neutral, even friendly, but staying away at the same time. Our angry words. My awkward apology last night. The certainty that what I thought was the start of something great might have been the biggest mistake for both of us and how I worried she was going to leave. Then I showed Charly the text.

"She's seeing *him*. I know it."

Charly was quiet for a moment, reading the text, thinking about what I said. I could practically hear her mind working as she sat there, her legs crossed, one foot swinging in agitation as she mulled over everything I'd spewed out.

"First off, I think there is more to this than you know. Than I know. Hannah isn't that sort of person. If she'd been seeing someone, she would have told you. He would have been around when she was moving in. She would be moving in with him, not you."

"But I heard—"

She interrupted me. "You heard part of a conversation. Maybe not all of it." She held up her hand. "But if she is seeing someone, then you have three choices."

"Which are?"

She held up her finger. "One. Be exactly what you are supposed to be. Her roommate. Not her jealous, want-to-be lover. Not her dad or her brother. Live your life. Be friends. Suck it up if she brings him around. If she does that, it means she trusts you. Act like the Chase I know."

I really didn't like that option. "The Chase you know wants to kick someone's ass."

Charly chuckled.

"What is my second option?"

"Act like a jealous asshole. Make her life miserable so she does move out. You may miss the opportunity of having a great friend and confidante. You may be the one she turns to if whoever she is seeing breaks it off. You may find, after living together for a while, she isn't the person you thought she was and be happy you didn't overreact. You might meet someone to have as yours."

"I doubt it," I mumbled. "The third?" I asked, hopeful it was something great, although I doubted it.

"Or..." She leaned forward, her expression serious. "You could man up, tell her how you feel, what you heard, and ask if you have a chance."

"Yeah, not happening."

Charly shook her head. "It amazes me how every man alive only thinks with his big head when the little one is in trouble. Option one is the simplest. Option two would put *her* out of reach of *your* misery at least and let you wallow in the house. You know. *The. One. You. Bought. For. Her.*" She paused dramatically. "Option three would give you the answer you want right now, and you could lick your wounds and maybe keep her as a friend. Or find you have it all wrong and she feels the same way. But you would know exactly where you stand. But you know, go ahead and second-guess everything while you fist yourself into a Hannah-induced coma nightly." She stood, flouncing to the door. "I'll buy you some extra lotion."

She slammed out of the office, and I dropped my head to my desk.

Why was this happening? The women in my life were all mad at me and slamming doors.

I thought of Charly's words. *The one you bought for her.* Yeah, great idea.

So far, home ownership sucked.

CHAPTER TEN

Hannah

I decided some distance between Chase and me was a good idea, so I came in to Toronto early to spend time with my mom. I sent him a message, letting him know I wouldn't be home and I would be later tomorrow so not to worry. I wasn't sure if he would even notice I wasn't around, but in case, it seemed the right thing to do.

So Friday evening, I sat across from Mom at our favorite pho restaurant. There was none anywhere close to Lomand or Littleburn, and I craved it all the time. We split a soup and some of their delicious spring rolls, chatting over the savory broth and dumplings. I showed her some pictures I took of the living room and my room.

"Looks great, jellybean," she said, making me smile as she called me the nickname she had used my whole life. Apparently even in her womb, I couldn't stay still long and her stomach resembled jelly. As I grew up, I was into everything and liked to move around, and my dad called me his jumping bean. They sort of melded, and jellybean was the name I lived with.

She swiped again with a frown. "What is this?"

"Oh." I wiped my mouth. "Chase bought a new bed. He never thought to buy sheets, so I'm going to pick him up a set."

"He's a nice boy."

I smirked. "He is hardly a boy, Mom. He is a couple years older than me."

She waved her hand. "Everyone is a boy or girl to me these days, Hannah. I'm far too old."

I laughed. "Please. Did you see the shock on everyone's faces when I introduced you as my mom? They all thought you were a sister or a friend." I dipped my spring roll in the spicy mixture of soy and sriracha. "And Dom was certainly transfixed."

She rolled her eyes. "Bossy, that one. Far too forward."

I bit back my grin.

"And we're not here to talk about him." She picked up her teacup, sipping it. "What is going on with you and Chase?"

"He's my landlord. And roomie. We're friends—I think."

She shook her head. "Hannah, baby. I'm your mom. I could

see the sparks between you from across the room. You light up like a Christmas tree when he's around. And he zeroes in on you the second he walks into the room."

I sighed as I finished my spring rolls and wiped my fingers. "I thought there was something, but since we painted, he's been...I don't know...off. We even argued. He apologized, but he is upset about something. I feel like I've hurt him somehow, and I don't know how to fix it." I tugged on my braid. "He's polite and accommodating, but distant."

"Do you think the whole painting his house was too much? All the people invading his space?"

"I don't know. Except he adores Charly and Gabby. He's very close with the guys, and they help one another a lot. The only new faces were us. I think maybe he's rethinking having a female roommate." I barked out a laugh. "Me, specifically."

"Has he said that?"

"No. In fact, last night, he looked upset when he wondered if I was questioning the whole thing. He told me he liked me there. He practically begged me not to move out."

Mom finished her soup, then pushed away her bowl. "Maybe he has stronger feelings for you and isn't sure how to express them. You two looked pretty cozy on the weekend."

"Well, now we're two icebergs crossing in the ocean. Close but not touching."

"What is he doing this weekend?"

"Spending the afternoon tomorrow supply shopping, then he and Dom are going to some bar Dom likes an hour away."

Mom snorted. "No doubt a great stomping ground for pickups. Not too close to home that you have to worry about a relationship developing."

Her words didn't help, and I grimaced. She patted my hand. "Sorry, jellybean. I was thinking more of Dom than Chase. He has that love 'em and leave 'em vibe. The whole bad-boy thing. Except he's a little past that." She shook her head. "I'm just not sure he knows it."

"You liked him."

She tossed her hair defiantly. "No, I didn't."

"He is pretty sexy with that intense look and the tattoos and all. Lots of swagger."

"Takes more to turn my head than some swagger, daughter of mine." She paused. "Although his, ah, swagger, is pretty nice. Especially from the back view."

We both started to laugh.

"You told me on Saturday there was someone else," she said once the giggles died down. "Is it Chase?" She met my eyes. "Be honest."

"Yes. I like him, Mom. He's sweet and sexy. Kind and

strong. And he has this vulnerability about him that he tries to hide."

"Do you know anything about him?"

I paused, then nodded. "He was in jail when he was younger. He was a troublemaker and led astray by his brother, but he learned his lesson. I read his file the day after I met him."

"Are you sure he is different now?"

"His crime was against Charly, and she has more than forgiven him. She treats him like a son or her little brother. He lost everything when he stepped up to come clean. I think if she can trust him, so can I."

"Does he know that you know?"

"No. I want to tell him, but there hasn't been a right time."

"Does he know about, ah, you?"

"No. He thinks I moved for the job, not *because* of the job. I don't have to tell him unless we move forward."

"Do you want to? Move forward, I mean?"

I hesitated before I answered. "He makes me feel safe, Mom. And cared for. He listens, and he makes me smile. If we can figure it out, I think I do."

"Then it sounds like you need a conversation with the boy. An open, honest, direct one."

"You're right."

"Don't wait, jellybean. Life has a habit of making those decisions for us, and we run out of time," she said sadly.

I covered her hand with mine, knowing she was thinking of my dad. "I know."

She blinked at the moisture in her eyes. "Enough heavy. How about some deep-fried bananas and ice cream then we can go home and watch a movie? Tomorrow morning, we'll hit the warehouse sales."

"Perfect."

———————

I peered around Zeke's, spotting the girls from headquarters. They were from dispatch, paramedics, front desk, and another female cop like me. Seven of them, sitting at a big table, laughing, drinking, and dancing. I joined them, getting hugs and greetings.

"How was shopping?" Annette asked. "I'm so glad you came!"

"It was great. Huge warehouse sale. My car was full, and I stopped at home to unload it. I got towels and sheets and all sorts of stuff. My mom and I barely got it all in. She went crazy too."

"Awesome."

I looked around. "Wow, the place is busy tonight."

"It is. There were a couple of bigger groups, but they already left." Annette pushed a glass of wine my way. "Drink up!"

I sipped at the glass of white wine. I had walked to the bar, leaving my car at home. Another girl came to the table, carrying a tray. "Tequila shots for all!" she crowed.

I grimaced. Tequila and I were not good friends. Annette laughed at my facial expression. "Just one," she said.

I picked it up, lifting my glass in a toast. "Just one."

CHASE

"You wanna stop and have a drink?" Dom asked. "Zeke's is hopping."

"Sounds good."

It had been a busy day. We worked in the garage, and I helped on a restoration, totally geeking out over the interior with its burgundy-and-ivory leather diamond stitched seats. Recreating it was going to be a blast. Then we headed toward Toronto, going to a larger home reno store. I chose and ordered the shingles, and Dom and I spent some time with a sales guy before ordering the supplies for the deck. I went with composite decking—more expensive to start, but

I would get years of wear from it. Then we went to a little place Dom knew and ate the best ribs and wings I'd ever tasted. The smoker out back was massive, and since Dom knew the owner, Harvey, he gave me a tour of the whole place. It was incredible, and we sat with him and his family, eating and enjoying ourselves, watching the customers come and go until they were sold out. Harvey smiled as he locked the door. *"Went fast today."* *He stretched.* *"Now I have to start tomorrow's supplies."*

"So you're only open until you sell out," I mused. *"Is that hard to plan?"*

"No. We have regulars, and we post the rules. You want a huge order, I gotta know in advance. Otherwise, we base it loosely on open at eleven, closed by eight. Sometimes it's seven, sometimes it's eight. Never later."

"I like it when it's six," his wife said with a laugh. *"Those are my favorites. Home by nine and soaking in the hot tub."*

"Thanks for taking me, Dom. It was great. We'll order a bunch of stuff for everyone, and I'll pick it up one weekend."

"Sounds good."

We headed into the building, the music loud, the dance floor full. We pushed through the crowd to the bar, and Dom got us each a beer. We clinked bottles, and I took a deep swallow then turned toward the dance floor, leaning against the bar. There was a group of women dancing together, obviously having a good time. They separated a little, and I caught sight of a flash of red-gold hair I would know anywhere. I shifted a little and watched as Hannah danced with her friends, her arms high in the air and her hips moving to the beat. There was a slight shift of relief inside my chest. She was here with a group of women. Not on a date.

I leaned back against the bar, blowing out a long huff of air. Dom looked at me, then followed my gaze, smirking as he saw what I was staring at.

"Your girl's having a good time," he observed.

"Not my girl," I replied, taking a long draw on my beer.

He chuckled. "Then you need to do something about that, son."

"I don't know how," I replied honestly. "I don't want to jeopardize the friendship we have. Or lose her as a roommate."

"But you like her more than a roomie."

I turned, facing the bar. "Yeah, I do. I like her a lot. But I come with some baggage."

"We all do."

I glanced at him. "You been in touch with her mother?"

He grinned, shaking his head. "Nope. That one is stubborn. I need to take it slow with her."

"So is her daughter."

He finished his beer. "Not a surprise."

"You want another?" I asked.

"Nope. I am heading home. I'm looking at a couple of places tomorrow. One close to you, actually. On Boulder."

"Oh, the two-story place?"

He rubbed his chin. "I like older places. More character. It looks decent from the pictures. I saw a brand-new build one town over last week. Hated it. Felt like a box. I would rather fix up a place a little and make it my own, you know?"

"I hear you."

"You want a ride home?"

"Nah, I'll walk. I might hang around a little."

His eyes danced. "Maybe dance with a pretty officer?"

"We'll see."

He clapped me on the shoulder. "I'll see you Monday, kid."

He left, and I ordered another beer, chatting to a few people I knew. I leaned against the bar again, my gaze immediately finding the group Hannah was with. Some of the women had sat down, but Hannah wasn't with them. I scoured the bar, not seeing her, until a glimpse of her hair caught my eye again. My heart sank at what I saw. Hannah was dancing with a man who wasn't me. His arms were around her possessively, while her hands rested on his shoulders as they moved to the music. Well, not really moved so much as swayed in one spot, his back to me, which was why I didn't see her at first. Slowly, they moved, him backing her up, going closer to the corner. I hated seeing another man's hands on her. I took another long pull on my bottle, grimacing when I realized I had drained it. Turning, I slammed it on the bar, making Fletch, the bartender, frown at me.

"Okay there, Chase? You want another?"

I wanted an entire case. I wanted to get drunk and forget what I saw. Ignore the feeling of pain that flickered in my chest and the sensation of loss. But I was being ridiculous.

"Nope. Just a tonic for now, thanks."

He poured me a glass, and I turned back to the dance floor. The music had turned up to a faster song again, and the crew Hannah was with were all back on the dance floor. She wasn't with them. I looked around, spotting the guy's blond hair. He had one arm braced on the wall, Hannah in front of him. He was bent, talking to her, looking serious. Something about his stance and the odd look on Hannah's face made me set down my drink and push my way through the dancers and toward the pair. I moved quicker when I saw how he had his other hand wrapped around her arm, preventing her from moving. She was shaking her head, and with a lull in the music, I overheard her. "No, Dan. I said I wasn't interested. I-I have a boyfriend."

She looked to the right, spotting me. "There he is! Chase, baby! I'm right here!"

She broke away, racing to me and flinging her arms around my neck. "Please play along," she murmured into my ear.

And then, her mouth was on mine.

I yanked her tight to my chest and kissed her back. I had no idea what was going on, but she wanted me to play along?

Then we were playing by my rules.

I kissed her with everything in me. All the frustration, want, and need I had been feeling. I licked into her mouth, tasting the flavor of the tequila lingering on her tongue and the sweetness I instinctually knew was her.

She whimpered softly, meeting my onslaught with the same level of passion. It was only someone yelling, "Get a room!" that broke us apart.

I looked down at her. Her eyes were glossy, slightly unfocused. I grinned. "Sorry I was late."

"You're forgiven."

"Who the hell is this?" Blond Guy demanded.

"Oh, ah, this is Chase," Hannah said, turning to face him, staying in the circle of my arms and resting her hand on top of mine. "Chase, this is Dan. We work together."

I met his glare, not liking how he looked at her. I felt the tension in her body again. "Hey," I greeted him coolly. "Dan. Right. Hannah talks about you on occasion."

"Is that right?" he replied, almost gloating.

I nodded and pressed a kiss to her head. "Well, we live together, so work comes up in our conversations."

His face flushed. "You live together?"

I could barely hold back my glee at his indignation. "Yeah, we do."

He narrowed his eyes, focusing on Hannah. "You never said that."

"I said no. That should be enough. I don't broadcast my personal life. I told you there was someone else."

Her words hit me. That was what her mother asked her. *"Is there someone else?"*

Hannah had said yes.

Had they been talking about this guy? Not me?

Hope flickered.

He stormed away, and Hannah sagged in my arms.

"Well, that will make next week interesting," she muttered then turned to me, still in the circle of my arms.

"Thanks."

I looked down at her, seeing the weariness on her face. The blurriness of her gaze. I felt how she swayed a little in my embrace. "Hannah Gallagher, are you drunk?"

She shook her head, then stopped. "Maybe a little. I had tequila. Only one. Maybe two." She pursed her lips. "Might have been three. That's never a good idea." She waved her hand. "Then Dan showed up. Only supposed to be girls," she muttered.

I laughed, feeling relief. Joy. Hope again.

"You ready to go home?"

"Yes."

"You want to go home now?"

She nodded, leaning her head on my chest. "I walked."

"Me too. We'll get a cab."

"M'kay."

I stood as she said goodbye to her friends, trying not to laugh. They'd all been indulging in tequila shots, and the over-the-top affection was rampant. Hugs and kisses. "See you Mondays" were exchanged. Lots of "I love you, girl." I tried to recall if I was that way when drunk. It rarely happened, and usually, it was to forget something painful. I was pretty sure I didn't tell Brett or Stefano I loved them.

They'd never let me hear the end of it if I had.

I couldn't help my smugness at the comments from her friends.

"Oh, this *is him."*

"Hannah, you dark horse. You never said he was so handsome."

"Oh my God, no wonder. I'd take him over Dan too."

My favorite, though, was, *"Oh, this is your man?"*

I wanted to be her man.

Outside, waiting for the cab, I chuckled as she leaned into me.

"Talking about me, were you?"

"No."

"I see. They just all were making up stories?" I teased.

"I may have said one or two things. Just that you were nice."

I helped her into the back of the cab, bending down and pressing my mouth to hers again.

"I am more than nice, Cinnamon. And we're gonna talk about that."

I shut the door before she could respond and climbed in on the other side. I knew the driver from the garage, and we chatted on the five-minute drive. He laughed and waved me off when I asked him the fare. "You do lots of extras for me. It's on the house—I didn't even bother with the meter."

I pressed some money into his hand. "Buy the kids a pizza," I insisted. I knew he worked two jobs to make ends meet.

"Thanks, Chase."

I helped a half-asleep Hannah from the back, and we walked up the sidewalk to the door. "You're such a good guy," she mumbled. "No wonder I want you."

I almost face-planted right there, but I managed to stay upright and get her into the house. I took her to her room, knowing our conversation needed to wait.

"Get ready for bed. I'll get you some water and Tylenol. You're going to need them."

In my room, I stripped and pulled on some sweats and a T-shirt, then went to the kitchen and got the water. I brought the pills from my medicine cabinet. Standing in her doorway, it was all I could do not to laugh. She was on the bed, her shirt pulled halfway over her head, obviously caught somewhere. I could tell she'd been tussling with it, then gave up. I walked in and set down the water and pills and, with a gentle tug, got her shirt off.

I tried not to notice how her breasts filled the lacy cups of her camisole. How soft and inviting they looked. Her nipples hardened at the change in temperature, and I bit back my groan. I wanted to fall to my knees and suck one into my mouth. Taste it. Taste her all over.

But we had to talk first, and she was in no condition to do so.

I looked around for her nightgown. It was lacy and pretty, and it drove me to distraction the one time I saw it. But I couldn't find it, so I pulled off my shirt and tugged it over her, covering her torso before I gave in to temptation. I pushed her back on the bed and divested her of the skirt she'd been wearing. I put it on the chair behind me, turning around, the breath catching in my throat. Laid out on her bed, wearing my shirt and a pair of pretty pink lacy underwear, she was a vision. Already hard, my cock kicked inside my pants, wanting out. Wanting her. It took everything in me to get her in the right place and under the covers. I went into her bathroom, running warm water over a facecloth and returning to the bed. I wiped the cloth over her cheeks and forehead, recalling how she told me once she never went to bed without washing her face first. I had no idea which of the many products on her shelf she used, so this would have to do.

"Hmm, that feels nice."

I tossed the facecloth into the hamper, then returned to the bed.

I tapped her lips. "Open, Hannah."

She smiled, running her hand along my thigh. "You got something for me, big man?"

My cock almost burst through my sweats, and I held back my moan.

"Yeah, Cinnamon. Something you really need."

She frowned as I pressed the pills to her tongue, urging her to drink the cold water. She swallowed and frowned. I wiped at the droplets by her lips, unable to stop my groan as she licked my fingers.

"Tease," she muttered.

I shook my head. "You are one to talk, baby. I'm going to have to use a splint on my wrist tomorrow."

She giggled and frowned at the same time as she turned on her side, curling up. "You're funny."

Funny wasn't what I was feeling right now. Fucking turned on, frustrated, hopeful, disappointed, and confused was a far better description.

I ran a hand over her hair. "Sleep well, Hannah. We'll talk in the morning. Or the afternoon, more likely," I added with a smile.

She made a funny little noise, burrowing under the covers. I swore to God she mumbled, "I love you," but I couldn't be sure, and if she had, I was certain it held the same meaning as the lovefest in the bar. Nothing. It was the liquor talking.

I paused before I turned off the light, looking down at her.

I really wished it were true, though.

CHAPTER ELEVEN

Chase

Hannah had only been asleep about an hour when she cried out. I sat up, throwing off my covers and heading to her room. Her cry was different some nights, and I knew those were the times she needed comforting. She was clutching her blanket, tears on her cheeks, her limbs jerking, and jumbled words falling from her mouth.

"Please, no."

I hunched beside the bed, running my hand over her head, whispering in a soothing voice.

"It's okay, Hannah. I'm here. It's just us. Hush."

Slowly, the tears stopped, her body relaxing. I kept stroking her hair for a few moments, then stood, making sure her blankets were tucked around her. But as I stepped back, her hand reached out, clasping mine.

"Chase?"

I shut my eyes, unsure how she was going to react to my being in her room. "Yeah, Hannah. It's me. You were having a bad dream."

She was quiet for a minute. "You've been here before."

I drew in a deep breath. "Yes. You calm down when I'm close."

"I thought I was dreaming that part."

"No, I've come in before," I said honestly.

"Thank you."

I passed my hand over her head again. "Go back to sleep. You're safe, okay?"

Her voice was quiet in the room. "Stay. Please?"

"Until you fall asleep?" I clarified.

"Please."

"Okay."

I rounded the bed, lying behind her, staying on top of the blankets. I wasn't sure what to do, what she wanted me to do, but she nestled close, her back pressed to my chest. I wrapped my arm around her, holding her tight to me. "I'm right here, and you're safe. Go to sleep," I whispered.

"I'm always safe with you," she mumbled. "It's my favorite place to be."

She fell silent, and soon, her breathing was deep and even. I wasn't sure if I should stay, but as soon as I shifted away from her, she moved too, keeping our bodies aligned. Her head was under my chin, the aroma of her shampoo filling my senses. It felt so good to be with her. She was warm and soft. Peaceful. I inhaled deeply, bringing her scent into my lungs. I pressed a kiss to her head, wishing that every night could be like this. That I could hold her, protect her from whatever frightened her in her sleep. Let her presence soothe me as well.

I sighed, knowing I would have to leave soon. I wasn't sure how she would feel about waking up with me in her bed. If she would even recall this happening.

But for now, I would hold her and enjoy it.

I thought about what she had said earlier. The guy I had stopped and what it could mean.

Was there a chance for us?

Tomorrow, I decided.

Tomorrow, I would be brave enough to have the conversation we needed to have.

One way or another, I would know.

In the meantime, I could hold her. Just for a little while.

That would be enough—for now.

I woke up, warmth surrounding me. My pillow smelled better than usual. Sweeter. I opened my eyes, blinking at my surroundings. I tried to move, but there was something holding me down.

Or someone.

I woke up fully when I realized I was still in Hannah's bed. Sunlight drifted through the window, telling me it was morning. I had fallen asleep beside her. And somehow in the night, she had turned and was currently nestled into my chest, her head tucked under my chin, her breath soft on my skin. The blanket had disappeared, her arm was draped over me, and we touched everywhere. Our chests were pushed together. Our legs entwined. One of my hands fisted her hair, the other held her tight to me.

And my cock was pressed between us, hard, aching, and needy.

I shut my eyes, trying not to panic. Trying to figure out how to ease away from her without waking Hannah up. I had to get away before she woke up. I was worried the screaming and yelling would start.

I decided slow and meticulous was the best way to go. I would let her go, slide out of her hold, and tiptoe from the room.

Except, when I opened my eyes again, I met her lovely irises. Her gaze was wide, curious, but not angry. Cautious. Questioning.

"Hi," she murmured.

"Hi," I croaked in return.

"Not a situation I expected to wake up to this morning," she quipped.

"Me either."

She bit her lip, trying not to smile. "I think maybe you have more than one situation happening right now."

"Ah, yeah, sorry. Can't help it."

She nodded, not moving, not pulling away the way I expected her to.

"How's the head?" I asked.

"Surprisingly good. I only had a few shots, but tequila gets me every time."

"I hear you. I avoid it."

"I think I will from now on." She frowned. "You rescued me in the bar. From Dan." Her eyes widened. "Oh my God, I threw myself at you and kissed you."

I chuckled. "It, ah, wasn't a hardship, Hannah. I kissed you back."

"Why?"

I decided to be honest. Here in her room, surrounded by the quiet of the morning, I knew I had to be.

"Because I've wanted to kiss you for a while."

"Oh."

"And I hated seeing him touch you."

She blinked. "You're touching me right now."

"Do you want me to go?"

"No." She paused, nibbling at her bottom lip. She only did that when she was really nervous. "You came in here to comfort me. I had a nightmare."

"Yes."

"Was it the first time?"

Again, I was honest. "No. You've had several."

"And you come to me every time?"

"Yes. You calm down when I talk to you." I swallowed. "When I stroke your head. I stay until you're asleep again."

"I thought I dreamed that part as well."

"You mentioned that last night. But it was real. I'm sorry I invaded your privacy—"

She stopped me with a frown. "I'm sorry I disturbed your sleep. You should have told me and bought some earplugs."

"I would rather lose sleep every night and comfort you than put in earplugs and not hear you. And I could never ignore your pain, Cinnamon. It would bother me too much."

"Chase," she whispered.

"Hannah."

"I like you."

"Yeah?"

"More than I should."

"Why would you think that?"

"Because I don't think you like me the same way."

"I don't."

Her face fell, and I cupped her cheek, leaning close. "I like you more."

Her eyes widened. "Oh."

I flexed my hips, letting her feel me. "I like you so fucking much."

"*Oh*," she breathed out.

"We have to talk."

She gripped my waist, holding me close. "Yes, we do."

"But all I want to do is kiss you again."

"Wait."

She rolled over, out of my arms, grabbing something on her nightstand. I chuckled as she pressed a TicTac to my lips, popping two into her own mouth and chewing furiously. A little morning breath wasn't going to stop me from kissing her, but I appreciated her worry.

She snuggled against me, gripping my T-shirt. "Ready."

"Eager, are we?"

"Chase, I don't remember much from last night, but I remember your mouth. I want it again."

That was all I needed. I brushed her hair back from her face, cupping her cheek, I stroked the soft skin, smiling at the feel of it under my fingers. Her breathing picked up as I lowered my head, barely touching her lips. "This changes everything," I whispered.

"I know," she responded, pursing her mouth and following my movement as I eased back a little.

"Slow, Cinnamon. I've been wanting this so much, I want to enjoy it. Savor you."

She growled. A real, actual growl and she fisted my shirt. "Savor it later, Chase."

And she crashed her mouth to mine.

I decided TicTacs were a gift from God. Her mouth was minty, and whatever reservations she had fled as soon as our lips touched. I kissed her hard, fisting her hair in my hands, needing her as close as possible. The only thing between us was the thin cotton of her shirt. I explored every inch of her mouth, letting her do the same to mine. I groaned as she nipped my top lip, then licked it to ease the sting. She pushed at the material of my shirt, her hands finding my skin, gliding up and down over my back and making me shudder. My cock leaked for her, and I gasped as she moved her hand from my back to cup me through my sweats. "Is this all for me?"

"Every inch."

At the same time, she plunged her hand under my waistband, I dipped my fingers under the edge of her lacy underwear. The slickness of her made me groan. Her hand wrapped around my dick made me harder.

"We have to talk," I said, trying desperately not to thrust into her hand as she stroked me. "You have to listen—"

She cut me off. "We will. But I want this, Chase. I need it. *Please.*"

I covered her mouth again and gave her what she asked for. I teased her clit with my thumb, stroking it and giving the hard button the attention it was demanding. I slid two fingers inside her, pumping them in a steady rhythm, keeping the pressure on the nub that made her pant and open her legs wider. She stroked me steadily, the feel of her palm soft and firm all at the same time. She ran her thumb over the crown, gathering the wetness and using it to glide her fingers over me. I grunted in pleasure. She moaned in satisfaction. I went faster, racing toward my release. Desperate for hers. She stiffened and cried out, and I buried my face into her neck, coming hard with her.

We stilled, our movements slowing. I withdrew my hand, gathering her close. She nestled into my chest, her breathing choppy and fast, matching mine. I pressed a kiss to her head. Then again. And again. I couldn't stop. She laughed, nuzzling my chest. "You're so affectionate. I like that."

She glanced up, and I kissed the end of her nose, then traced the bridge of it and along the top of her cheeks. "These dots, Hannah. They drive me to distraction. They are so fucking sexy. *You* are so fucking sexy."

She blinked, smiling shyly at me. "No one has ever told me I was sexy."

"How is that even possible?" I asked, ghosting kisses over her sweet freckles.

"My last boyfriend said I was cute. Not sexy. When we broke up, he told me, if he was being honest, I was a little funny-looking. He had overlooked it long enough."

I pulled back, meeting her eyes. "Give me his address. I'll overlook the fact that he's standing in front of my truck and knock him down a few times until he's funny-looking."

She smiled, cupping my cheek, stroking the skin in gentle passes. I leaned into her caresses.

"You are too sweet," she murmured. "No one has ever offered to drive over an ex either. But no need. I don't want you to go back to jail."

I stiffened, and her eyes flew open wide when she realized what she'd said.

"You know?" I asked. "You know about my past?"

"Yes."

"And you're still letting me touch you? Wanting to have a relationship with me?"

"Yes."

"How?"

"The day after I found you in the parking lot. You were so sad about your family, and I looked up the details of your dad's and brother's deaths. One article mentioned you'd been in prison."

"And you looked at my files."

"Briefly. I know the charges, but I don't know why or how you came to be the man you are now." She pressed her hand into my cheek harder, making me look at her. "And that's what I care about, Chase. The man you are now. Not your past or whatever mistakes landed you in jail. You are obviously a changed man."

"I am. And I want to tell you. I've been feeling so guilty about not being completely honest with you, but I was afraid…" I trailed off and swallowed. "I didn't want you to look at me differently. The way so many people do."

"I'm not judging you. I know you're different now. I like the Chase I know."

"But I have to tell you. I want to tell you."

"I'll listen," she assured me.

I studied her, seeing only acceptance in her gaze. I drew in a deep breath. "Will you tell me what makes you cry out at night, Hannah? What you have nightmares about?"

She averted her gaze, then nodded. "I thought I was past them, but for some reason, they are happening again."

"I want to know. I'll listen." I repeated her words.

"Okay."

"Shower first, I think," I said, trying to make her smile.

"Yes."

I kissed her, my mouth lingering on hers. "Okay."

CHAPTER TWELVE

Chase

I was at the table when she walked into the kitchen, her hair wet, the color dimmed but still visible. She poured a cup of coffee and sat across from me, taking a sip. Our eyes met, and her gaze skittered away, the color on her cheeks high.

"Something wrong?" I asked, teasing.

"No."

"You're kinda far away, Hannah."

"This is where I always sit."

I hooked my foot around the rung of her chair, pulling it sideways and closer to me. She gasped, grabbing the edge of the table. I tugged on the chair until she was beside me. "I like you closer."

She rolled her eyes. "Are you planning on being possessive?"

"Oh, I'm very possessive of you," I replied, taking a sip of my coffee. "I've felt that way since the moment I met you."

"You've hidden it well."

"I wasn't sure how you felt. How you feel now," I admitted. "But after last night and this morning, I've decided to be honest about it."

She looked oddly vulnerable. "How do you feel?" she whispered.

I leaned over, cupping the back of her head. I tugged her close and kissed her, licking into her mouth. She tasted of coffee, the mint of her toothpaste, and Hannah. She whimpered, gripping my T-shirt and kissing me back. I kissed her until I was breathless, until my head was swimming, and then I dragged my mouth across her cheek to her ear. "I am fucking crazy about you, Hannah Gallagher."

I eased back, watching as she slowly opened her eyes. I smiled and ran my finger across her swollen lips, still wet from my tongue. "Clear enough?"

She blinked and smiled. It was wide and honest. Her eyes shone with happiness.

"You may have to keep reminding me," she replied.

"Anytime." I pressed another kiss to her mouth. "But we need to talk."

"Okay."

I stood. "How about we sit in the living room? This feels like a living room conversation. Not a kitchen one."

"What constitutes a kitchen conversation?"

I shrugged. "Weekend plans, dinner ideas, deciding to say screw it and going back to bed to make love all day, that sort of thing."

"Oh." Her cheeks flushed again. "I see."

I laughed, tugging her out of her chair and running my fingers over her cheek. "I like this. I haven't seen you blush before."

"I haven't heard you talk like this before," she replied.

I kissed her again. "Get used to it."

I brought us fresh coffee, and we settled on the sofa, turning to face each other. Our knees touched, and I was glad. I needed to be close to her for this conversation.

"What do you know?" I asked, feeling strangely calm.

"Not much," she admitted. "You and your brother were in jail. Your charges were minor compared to his. You were released early for good behavior. Your brother died in jail. I know the charges but not the story." She took a breath. "And I know your dad died not long after you got out of prison."

I nodded, feeling the sense of loss drift over me again. "My mom died when I was younger, and my dad sort of lost interest in us. Wes was older. He acted out, and since I hero-worshiped him, I followed him. As we grew up, his actions changed. He changed. What used to be done in fun or to get Dad's attention was more focused. Devious. Intentional." I ran a hand over my head, feeling the anxiety creeping in. "I didn't know the extent of what he was doing. All the illegal things he was getting himself into, but I suspected at times and I joined him on occasion. Our father bailed us out. He had little else to do with us, but he gave us the money to keep being horrible people."

Hannah reached over and pulled at my hand. "I like your hair on your head," she said with a small smile. "Hold on to me, Chase. I'm right here."

I lifted her hand to my mouth and kissed her knuckles. I hoped she would still be there when I finished.

"We were known as the Donner brothers—trouble. Wes ruled his little kingdom. As I got older, I pulled away a little. I met a girl from another town. She was sweet and kind. I wanted to be a better person for her. Wes kept dragging me back, and out of some weird loyalty, I let him."

"He was your brother. You loved him."

"I did. But he became even angrier at the world. He wasn't the brother I knew anymore. He set his sights on Charly. He hated Maxx simply for the fact that he was Maxx and didn't take Wes's BS. Maxx would stand up to Wes all the time and protect whoever Wes was bothering."

"Especially Charly," Hannah surmised.

"Yes."

"The day he hurt Charly, I was with him. I was driving. He thought it was great. I was sick. He had physically hurt someone. A woman. A defenseless woman whose only crime was not putting up with his over-the-top ego." I shook my head. "I had no idea how badly she was hurt. Wes refused to let me stop the truck. We had a huge fight. Later, I went to the police and confessed. Told them everything I knew. Even things I only guessed."

"You turned your brother in," she said, sounding surprised.

"Yes. I knew if he hurt Charly, he would hurt other people —maybe even worse. I couldn't sit back and let that happen."

She squeezed my hand. "Because you're a good person, Chase."

"Long story short—we went to jail. Wes for a much longer sentence. I got out early, but I took advantage of every program I could while I was there. I wanted to come out better than when I went in. When I was released, I went to

Charly and Maxx to ask for forgiveness after I had gotten more counseling. Charly gave it instantly. I had to win Maxx over. But they became my family."

I huffed out a long sigh. "You have my permission to look through all my files, Hannah. Dig deep into the darkness of my past. Ask me any questions you want."

She shook her head. "I don't want to do that. You can tell me whatever you want to share, and that is good enough." She paused. "And your father?"

"He died. He died never speaking to me again. Wes refused to talk to me after the one time I went to see him once I got out. He said he hated me and called me a bunch of names. Told me he never wanted to see me again. Not long after that, he picked a fight with the wrong person in jail, and he lost."

She shifted closer. "I'm sorry, Chase."

I nodded. "Me too. My father stayed away and didn't return my calls, letters, or try to get in touch. I lost them both. I had no one until Charly decided she needed to look after me. Forced Maxx into letting me be a gofer and live in the little back room at the garage." I laughed. "I was so freaking happy there. A little place to call my own. I could shut the door and be safe. Charly checked on me all the time. Fed me. Talked to me. Listened when I had a bad day." I met Hannah's eyes. "I love that woman. She saved me."

"I'm glad you have her."

"I wasn't a good guy back then, but I've changed, Hannah. What I want from life has changed. My heroes are my friends. Maxx, Stefano, and Brett. I see what a good dad should be with Mack. With how my friends are with their kids. How I feel around them. How I feel about you."

"The girl you loved…?"

"Got married and has her own family. Ellen is happy, and I'm pleased for her. We run into each other on occasion. Her husband is a great guy." I was quiet. "She helped me change, Hannah, but she wasn't the love of my life. She was just a piece of it." I looked up. "You are already more important to me. I can't describe it, I simply know it. I want to try to build something with you." I paused. "If you want."

HANNAH

I looked at Chase. I saw the broken pieces he tried to hide from the world. How he covered up his feelings with a smile and a joke to disarm people. But the lingering sadness I had glimpsed in his eyes was there.

And he had just laid out his heart for me, waiting to see if I would accept it.

"I have feelings for you too," I admitted. "Strong ones."

His shoulders lost a little of their tension, but he still looked worried. "I sense a but."

"No. I want to explore this with you. And as weird as that sounds after this morning, slowly."

He smiled. "We can do that. I'll take you however I can get you, Hannah. You set the rules. Having you here in the house with me is already more than I ever expected to get."

"Have you had many relationships since you got out of jail?"

"None." He paused, meeting my eyes. "Ellen was the first and only girl I have ever been with, Hannah."

His words shocked me. I gripped his hand, terrified suddenly.

"Were you…"

He shook his head. "I was fine in jail. Scared every day I was in there, but I was okay. I avoided fights, groups, and people my age. My cellmate was older, and I hung with him and his cronies if I needed to. I avoided all the pitfalls. I just wanted out of there. I kept my eyes down and my nose clean."

"I see."

"Wes slept around like it was his career. My father had women come and go. I never wanted to be like that. Ellen meant something to me. You mean so much more. You mean everything. I'll wait until you're ready." A smile tugged on his mouth. "Despite, as you pointed out, what happened this morning."

"Wow." I shifted in my seat, pulling my legs up to my chest. Chase looked upset.

"Too much?" he asked.

"No. But a few things I didn't expect. I hate you've been so alone. Handling all this on your own."

"I have the crew," he said. "I didn't tell them the whole truth until after that night you, ah, found me. Charly became even more motherly. The guys listened and offered their support in a more, um, subtle way. But yeah, I rarely talk about it." He waited a moment, seemingly thinking. "And you should know. I'm rich. Well, I have a big bank account I don't use, but the money is mine."

"I don't understand."

"My dad left me everything. Millions. I refused to touch it after he died. Maxx tried to talk to me about it. Give me advice. So did Charly. I set up a trust fund, and money goes to charity every month to do some good. The foundation built the food bank in Lomand, and I make sure money goes to them monthly to keep food on the shelves."

"I didn't know that was you."

"I don't want anyone to know. I don't want them to know I rebuilt the school, or added to the fire station, or that the nice break room you have in the police station came from me. It's my way of making amends for what Wes did. Some of the things I was part of."

I shook my head. "That is amazing."

He shrugged. "The first thing I used the money for personally was to buy this house." He met my eyes. "So you would come live with me."

"Chase," I gasped, astounded. "Why?"

"I realized my friends were right. Not using the money was stupid. Paying rent when I could buy a place wasn't smart. Buying this house helped Mr. Hyde. I gave him more than he would have gotten if he'd used an agent. It was my way to say thanks. The added bonus was you would be with me." He smiled. "My dream girl."

I shook my head. "Nightmare girl is more like it."

He inched closer, laying his hands on top of mine. "Why do you have nightmares, Cinnamon? What happened to you?" He lowered his voice. "Trust me enough to tell me. Please."

All I could do was look at him, my throat too thick to talk. He shifted and moved closer, pulling me in between his legs, surrounding me. "I'm right here, Hannah. Nothing can hurt you."

"My mom wasn't happy about my being a cop because of what happened to my dad."

He nodded in understanding.

"But she supported me. I passed and got a job with the OPP. Ontario Provincial Police. I had an older man as a partner. Ross. We got on well, and he taught me a lot. He knew my dad. Not well, but enough. I think he saw it as a chance to look after a fellow officer's daughter and give her the benefit of his experience."

"Sounds like a good guy."

I had to swallow before I could talk again. Chase reached beside him to the thermos of water he carried everywhere and pressed it to my lips. "Drink, baby."

I swallowed the cold water, grateful for it. When I was done, he laced our fingers together and squeezed my legs. "Right here," he affirmed.

"We got a domestic dispute call. The wife answered the door and let us in. She said her husband had beaten her and then fell asleep. She was too afraid to try to leave. He appeared and said she was lying, that he'd pushed her around a little but she'd provoked him. That she did it all the time."

Chase stroked the tops of my hands. They were beginning to tremble.

"One moment, they were arguing. The next, he backhanded her. Ross and I went for our guns, but he was faster. He had one in his waistband under his shirt we didn't see. He shot Ross in the neck and me in the chest."

"Jesus."

"It hit just above the vest. Ross went down, me beside him. The wife was shrieking—these god-awful noises. I'll never forget the terror they made me feel. I sat up, trying to get my radio, the husband was yelling and waving his gun. I was trying not to lose consciousness. Ross was bleeding out. The husband kicked me, knocking me down. He was going crazy and screaming he was going to kill us all."

Chase reached over and pulled me to him, wrapping his arms around me and sitting back, holding me to his chest. He was breathing hard, a slight tremble to his arms. *"Jesus, Hannah. Jesus Christ."*

I kept talking, unable to stop now I had started. "I kept blacking out. I remember telling the husband to let me call in to dispatch—to try to save Ross. Not to kill his wife." A sob escaped my throat. "To please let me live. All I kept thinking about was my mom getting that visit. My superiors telling her I was dead."

"What happened?"

"The neighbor heard what was happening and she called 9-1-1. They sent reinforcements." I shuddered. "He was ready to die rather than go to jail. Take all of us with him. But the other officers distracted him somehow, and they got a clean shot. He was dead before he hit the floor. I recall crawling to Ross and holding his hand, saying we were going to be okay." I had to shut my eyes as the tears flowed down my cheeks. "I was too late, and he died in front of me." More tears followed. "I passed out from blood loss, and when I woke up, I was in the hospital and my mom was there. I'd had surgery to remove the bullet."

His arms tightened. He held me so close I could barely breathe, but I didn't want him to loosen his hold. I felt safe and protected. Loved. I rested my head on his shoulder, letting his closeness soothe me. Keeping one arm banded around me, he ran his hand up and down my back, the motion gentle and warm. He murmured hushing noises, whispered my name, and pressed kisses to my head.

"I'm sorry, Hannah. I hate knowing you went through that. That it is still affecting you."

I sighed and drew back. He kept his arms around me, gazing at me with worry.

"Have you had counseling?"

"Yes. Lots of it. And it helped. But when I'm stressed, it resurfaces."

"Being here stresses you?" he asked, horrified.

"No. Talking about Toronto does. Remembering it. And yes, I've been upset because I thought I misread the signals, so it happens."

"You haven't," he assured me.

"And you've been coming to me at night and comforting me?"

"Yes."

I pressed a kiss to his lips. "Thank you."

"How does your mom feel about all this? You still being a cop?"

"She struggles with it. I tried to go back. I was assigned a new partner. But I couldn't handle it, and the nightmares were endless. The first time I had to knock on a door about a problem, I froze. My mom was a nervous wreck all the time. They put me on desk duty, but I hated it. This posting came up, and I spoke with my superiors about it. Fewer people, less crime. Still with the dangers, but I could be a cop. I agreed to doing some desk work and some patrol. The first few weeks, I was terrified, but I slowly got back into it. More counseling helped. The people here helped. I found desk duty gave me a breather. And I like it here. Mom relaxed. I mean, she wants me to be anything but a cop, although she has accepted it. For now anyway." I smiled at him. "Then I met you."

He returned my smile, chucking my chin. "Irresistible, right?" he teased.

"Totally," I responded.

He hugged me suddenly, holding me tight. "Thank God

you're okay, Hannah. You were meant to be here with me. I know it."

I snuggled closer.

I didn't know if he was right, but I was glad to be there with him.

For the first time in a long while, I felt as if I belonged.

Right there—with Chase.

CHAPTER THIRTEEN

Chase

I held Hannah close for a while, neither of us trying to move. I thought we both needed it. She was warm and soft in my arms, and her trembling stopped. I hated hearing her story, knowing how terrified she must have been. How horrific that she saw her partner die, that she almost died. The thought of that made me hold her tighter.

She didn't object. If anything, she snuggled deeper into my chest.

"Are you always this affectionate?" she murmured. "I like it."

I laughed quietly. "Until Charly and everyone, no. She is a big hugger. All the girls are. I think I liked being affectionate with Ellen, but not as much as I enjoy touching you."

She lifted her head, meeting my gaze. "So you haven't been with anyone since her?"

"No. Sex means more to me than a release. It has to be with someone I care about. I dated a few women, but I never found someone I wanted to be intimate with." I shrugged self-consciously. "I suppose that sounds rather lame."

"No. I don't think it's lame. It's a lovely way to think. I haven't been with anyone for a while either. Since before the incident."

"Were there any lasting effects physically from your injuries, Hannah?"

She frowned, her hand drifting up to her chest, rubbing a spot on her sternum. "It aches sometimes. And I have a scar, but nothing major."

I covered her hand with mine. "It is major, baby. It shows you survived something." I paused. "Will you show me?"

She pulled aside the neck of her shirt and revealed her scar. A small, twisted round knot that rested not far above her heart. "The doctors said it was a miracle the bullet didn't do more damage. If the trajectory had been slightly different, I would have had permanent repercussions." She swallowed. "Or I would have died."

I traced the scar in wonder. "Thank God, baby," I breathed out. "Thank God." I lifted my gaze to hers. "You were meant to be here. For me."

Her smile was tender and sweet. "You and my mom. I think you both need me."

I pulled her back into my arms.

"Yes."

We needed normal. Whatever our normal was anyway. I pressed a kiss to her head. "Did you buy me sheets, Cinnamon?"

She pulled back, wiping under her eyes and offering me a smile. "Yes, I did. Did you know you had one tea towel and one dishcloth in the whole kitchen?"

I smirked. "Do you need more than one?"

She rolled her eyes, my question doing exactly what I wanted it to do. She pushed off me. "When they both are disgusting, yes. I bought new ones. And towels. Plus some other kitchen stuff. Good thing I found out you were rich. I spent a lot."

I laughed at her drollness. "Show me."

We spent the rest of the day doing things around the house together. We washed sheets, towels, and other items she'd purchased. Made up my new bed with the linens she'd bought me. The comforter was deep blue, gray, and black, the sheets coordinating with it. She put shams on the new pillows, which I eyed skeptically as she fluffed them and added them against the headboard.

"You expect me to keep it looking like that?" I asked. "I mean, it's nice and everything, but not sure I'm into the, ah, fluffing and all."

She shook her head and chuckled. "I am quite certain this is the only time I'll see it this way. Let me enjoy it."

I hid my grin as I tackled her onto the mattress, looming over her. "I like how it looks now," I said. "With you on it."

She giggled, pushing at my chest. "You are messing up all my work."

I lowered myself on top of her, our chests pressing together. My weight sank us lower into the fluffy bedding and the mattress underneath. "What can I do to make it up?" I asked.

Her eyes darkened. "Kiss me," she whispered.

I didn't have to be asked twice. I dropped my head, our mouths meeting. Her lips were soft and pliable. Full. They opened for me with a flick of my tongue, and I sank my tongue deep into her sweet mouth. She wrapped her arms around my neck, kissing me back. Her sweetness filled my senses, drenching me in her scent. Her taste. The feel of her fingers in my hair. The way her body felt underneath mine.

Then her phone rang out, the sound of it loud in the room. We broke apart, breathless and startled. I was amazed how quickly I lost myself with her. How easy it was to do so. I rolled off and handed her the phone from the table, helping her off the mattress as she answered the call.

"Hey, Mom."

She leaned against the dresser, watching me, amused, as I straightened the bedding. Ineffectually, I might add. She made it look so easy. In fact, she hip checked me out of the way, and in a few quick movements had the bed righted, the corners neat, and the pillows tidied. All while speaking to her mom.

"No, he likes the stuff. Honest," she said into the phone. "And I love mine."

Her bedding was much more girly than mine. There was even lace on the top sheet. She informed me I was a heathen not liking top sheets. But I found them constrictive and too much. All I needed was the comforter, and I didn't want to tell her that was a first for me. Usually, it was just a blanket. I looked at the room with the bedding in place. It looked like a real bedroom. In a home. I felt an intense satisfaction when I realized this place was home now. Hannah was here. With me. *Really* with me.

Soon, I hoped this would be our room. So, whatever she did that made her happy, she could do. I might draw the line at the lacy sheets, though. I had to put my foot down on that one.

I mean, a man had to do what a man had to do.

Unless it was a deal-breaker.

Then, I supposed, I could live with it as long as it meant she was in my bed.

I tried not to laugh at the voice in my head calling me pussy-whipped.

It was right.

I was.

The rest of the day was spent in what felt like an odd sense of normalcy. It reminded me of being at Maxx and Charly's place on a Sunday. Everyone was laid-back, there was a game on TV, and Charly puttered around, sitting on occasion, snuggled into Maxx's side, then heading to the kitchen or going outside with one of the kids. Folding laundry, laughing, and teasing. It felt like what I imagined a real home was like. And today, I was experiencing that here. Laundry, cooking dinner, watching TV with Hannah. Talking about the week ahead. Planning a barbecue once the deck was done. Cooking side by side in the kitchen, listening to her enthusiastic ideas when I mentioned upgrading the kitchen. Her little sketches on Post-it notes made me smile. Later, we sat on the sofa watching a movie. Her head began to droop, and soon it settled on my shoulder with her curled into my side. I finished watching the movie, my arm draped over her knees, holding her close.

When it was over, I carefully stood, hating to wake her. I scooped her up and carried her down the hall, regretfully taking her to her room and setting her on the bed. She woke up, bleary and confused. "Bedtime, Hannah," I whispered.

"Okay."

I pressed a kiss to her head. "I'll see you in the morning. Sleep well, baby."

I hated leaving her, but I changed and brushed my teeth, sliding into my new bed with the soft sheets she had bought me. I left my door open, worried about the fact that with everything we talked about, Hannah might have nightmares, and I wanted to hear her. I lay there for about half an hour, sleep eluding me. I was staring at the ceiling when I heard the creak of the floors in the hall. Hannah hurried across my room, sliding into bed and tucking herself against me. I slipped my arm around her, holding her close. "What's the matter?"

"I don't want to be alone tonight," she whispered. "Everything is too close. When I shut my eyes..." She trailed off.

"Okay," I agreed easily. "I got you."

She snuggled into my side, her head on my chest. "I like it here. I feel safe."

"You are. Go to sleep. I'll keep the ghosts away, okay?"

"We'll protect each other."

I passed my hand over her head. "Okay, baby. Sounds good."

Nothing could bring me down on Monday. Not the customer who bitched about his bill. Not the fact that some parts we needed were on back order. Not even the news that the shingles I wanted were only available in a dark gray, not the light gray I wanted. I didn't care.

"I don't spend much time staring at my roof," I said to the salesman on the phone.

"I can offer you a five percent rebate."

"Sure. Order them."

I hung up, and Charly cleared her throat from the doorway before sauntering in and sitting down. I kept my eyes on the pile of paperwork in front of me. "Yeah, Charly? What's up?"

"That's what I am wondering," she said, tapping the pile of paperwork. "I'm over here, Chase."

I sat back, meeting her gaze. "I have no idea what you're talking about."

She leaned close. "Horsefeathers. When I saw you last, you were moping around, all worked up about Hannah seeing someone. Regretting buying your house."

"Your point?"

"Today, you're Mr. Sunshine. Solving problems, dealing with assholes with a smile. Accepting a five percent discount. You should have held out for ten."

I burst out laughing. "I don't care about the color of the roof, Charly. Whether it's light gray or dark gray. And I don't need the money, so why make the guy's life miserable? He probably dreaded making the call, and five percent is fine. As for the assholes and problems, it's part of my job. I'm only doing what you pay me for."

She crossed her arms and legs, one foot swinging in agitation. "How's Hannah?"

"Not dating anyone else."

Her eyes widened, her irritation with me forgotten. She grabbed my arm. "You talked to her?"

I bent over and kissed her cheek. "Yes, Mama Charly. I took your advice, and I talked to her. She and I spent all day yesterday talking. Sharing our stories. She knew about me being in jail. I gave her all the facts. She told me why she has nightmares." I huffed out a long breath. "That was hard to hear."

She rubbed my shoulder. "But you listened?"

"Yes. And I admitted my feelings to her. She told me she felt the same way. So, we're working on that."

Charly smiled, big and bright. "Oh, Chase. That's awesome."

"We're going slowly. Neither of us wants to mess it up. It's too important."

"But you cleared the air."

"Yes. The guy she was talking about to her mom is someone at the station. The someone else she mentioned was me."

"I knew I liked her."

I chuckled. "She is pretty awesome."

"I'm so glad, Chase."

"Thanks for the advice, Charly. It didn't happen as organically as you suggested, but I did tell her the truth."

"I am pretty smart."

I kissed her cheek. "Yeah, you are. Maxx is a lucky man."

"He is," she agreed drolly. She stood, smoothing down her loose shirt. I noticed her outfit was normal. Jeans, sneakers, and an oversized shirt tied at the waist. Probably Maxx's.

I had to chuckle. "Giving him a break today, are you? No tank tops, shorts, or overalls?"

She grinned. "He's getting older. I need to throw him a bone on occasion."

She paused at the door. "Why don't you bring Hannah for supper one night?"

"Maybe next week. She is on the longer rotation right now."

"Okay." She grinned. "I might call her. Have coffee on her break or something."

"I'm sure she'd like that."

She left in a much better frame of mind than the last time we talked. There was no door-slamming this time. I saw her stop to talk to Maxx, who smiled at her, bending low to kiss her. I looked away with a grin, enjoying the fact that I didn't feel that pull of jealousy seeing their affection. This morning, I had woken with Hannah in my bed, still nestled against me. I had kissed her before heading to the shower, and we sat at the table sharing coffee before I left. Neither of us had moved in the night, and she looked well rested and refreshed. I felt that way.

She had shyly handed me a container as I went to leave. "I made you lunch."

"You did?" I asked, delighted.

"We had lots of leftovers from the chicken we grilled. I made you sandwiches."

I pulled her into my arms and kissed her hard. "Thanks."

"Have a good day at work, dear," she teased.

"Are you home tonight?" I asked.

"Yes. I'm going to finish unpacking and hang the curtains in my bathroom."

"Don't fall."

She laughed. "I won't."

"Then I'll see you later." I kissed her again. "Tonight." Kiss. "Here." Kiss. "At home."

She laughed and pushed on my chest. "If you don't leave, you'll be late."

She called to me from the door as I got to my vehicle. "I'll be waiting."

Those words made me smile all the way to the garage.

Thinking of them now made me smile again.

My phone beeped, and I picked it up, my smile getting bigger when I saw a text from Hannah.

HANNAH

Can you get some sour cream on the way home?

I stared at the simple words. So ordinary, yet to me, they meant something different. Home. Hannah. Her texting me to pick something up, like we were a couple.

Because we were.

ME

Sure

I replied.

Anything else?

She sent back a smiley face.

HANNAH

Nope. Just you.

ME

Okay. See you at home.

HANNAH

I'll be here.

Those words kept the smile on my lips the rest of the day.

CHAPTER FOURTEEN

Chase

I stopped at the general store, heading in to grab the sour cream. I was surprised to find Mack behind the counter, a newspaper open on the surface, his crossword puzzle partially done.

"Mack?" I asked. "You were retired when I last checked."

He chuckled. "I cover when needed. Lyle's wife went into labor unexpectedly. He called me, and I came to cover for a few days." He shook his head, looking around. "Feels odd to be back, to be honest. The place got some upgrades. I spent most of the day trying to figure out where everything was."

I laughed. "It needed the upgrade. And it looks good."

He smiled. "Yeah, it does."

"Heard from Brett?"

"He called. They're in Bora Bora. He is sending some pictures later. He sounds happy."

"Good."

I left with a wave, tossing the container into the front seat. I stopped as I looked across the street, an idea hitting me. I looked both ways, but as I suspected, the road was empty. I jogged across the street and headed into the little florist shop. I looked around, confused. I had never bought flowers before, and there were blooms everywhere. Flowers, plants, arrangements. Big ones, little ones, droopy ones. A woman approached me and smiled.

"May I help?"

I nodded, relieved. "I want to give my girlfriend some flowers."

"The occasion?"

"Occasion?"

"Anniversary, birthday, forgive-me flowers?" she questioned.

"Holy shit," I muttered. "I'm not in trouble yet. At least, not that I know of." I scratched my head. "Um, none of those. I can still give her flowers, right?"

"Flowers to brighten someone's day are the best kind of flowers to give."

"Perfect. But I don't know what kind. She likes pretty things."

I followed the woman around as she picked some stems, explaining to me what they meant. I had never known that flower choices could have meaning. I liked the bouquet she put together. The alstroemeria were pretty, and I like the symbolism of friendship and loyalty. The hydrangea symbolized gratitude for being understood, and they added a nice pop of color I knew Hannah would like. The florist added a bunch of other blooms, then paused and slid a single red rose into the center.

"For true love," she explained.

"Perfect."

She wrapped them, and I thanked her, walking back across the street and adding them to the front seat. As I rounded the truck, a police officer was standing there on the sidewalk. The sight of him waiting, his hands crossed in front of him, made me feel oddly nervous, although I had done nothing. He wore his hat and sunglasses, and I didn't recognize him.

"Officer," I greeted him.

"In a hurry?"

"Sorry?"

He pointed to the left. "You know there is a crosswalk thirty feet down the road. That is where you, as a pedestrian, are expected to legally cross the road. Not just race across randomly, causing a distraction. Against the stoplight as well. That's jaywalking and illegal."

I was sure he was fucking with me.

"A distraction?" I repeated. "To whom?"

"The drivers."

I glanced left and right. "Which drivers am I distracting? I'm the only car around. And I didn't see the light from where I crossed."

"Because you were crossing in an unlawful area."

Unlawful area.

Was this guy totally shitting me?

He spoke again. "If an owner leaves his store for a moment, does that give you the right to break the law and steal from him?"

I blinked. How the hell had we gone from me walking across the road to stealing?

"I'm sorry, ah, Officer…" I trailed off. He was familiar, but how, I wasn't sure.

"Meyers. Officer Meyers."

"Sorry, I'm not following. I'll be sure to use the crosswalk next time."

He flipped open his book, and I stared at him in shock.

"You're going to write me a *ticket*? No one was around. Not a single car. I was in a hurry—I just wanted to get my girl some flowers." I stepped closer. "You understand, right? I just didn't think."

He shook his head, pulling out his pen. The motherfucker was going to write me up for crossing the road. Jaywalking.

Before he could start, Mack came out of the store. "Chase. Problem?" He looked between us.

"Nothing I can't handle, Mack," I said.

He looked at the police officer. "Dan? What's up?"

Dan.

Dan.

The reason he looked familiar was the fact that he was the guy who crowded Hannah on Saturday. The one interested in her. Suddenly, I wanted to laugh. He was pissed, and he was going to give me a ticket for jaywalking. Cause me some inconvenience.

I waved off Mack. "Don't worry, Mack. Officer Dan here is teaching me a lesson in civic duty. I was jaywalking."

Mack laughed. "Stop fooling around, Dan. Everyone walks across the road. You've done it yourself a hundred times. I've seen you."

Dan frowned, snapping the book shut. "Don't let me catch you doing it again." He stepped closer. "I'm watching you," he added in a low voice.

"I feel so much safer now."

He tugged down his glasses, glaring. "You shouldn't."

Then he stalked away, disappearing around the corner. I heard the slam of a car door, and a minute later, his cruiser tore out of the back parking lot, his tires squealing on the road. I watched him disappear around the bend, and I shook my head.

"What was that all about?" Mack asked.

I was honest. "He likes Hannah. Doesn't think I deserve her."

He laughed. "So he was gonna give you a ticket?"

I shrugged. "Can't give me one for stealing the girl, so that was all he could come up with, I guess."

Mack shook his head. "Always been a hothead that one. Went to school in Littleburn, and they moved away when he was in his teens. Bit younger than you."

"Yeah, name doesn't ring a bell."

"Anyway—ignore it and don't let it ruin your day. Enjoy your evening."

"You too, Mack."

HANNAH

I stirred the taco meat, inhaling the spicy aroma. I knew Chase loved tacos. He'd mentioned it once, and Charly had told me as well. They were easy and fun, and I wanted to do something nice for him today. He'd been so sweet the night before. I hadn't planned on crawling into his bed, but as soon as I was alone and the room was dark, the images from that awful day haunted me and I couldn't escape them. Tucked beside him with his arms around me, I felt safe and protected. I slept all night without a single nightmare. I'd been busy all day, enjoying puttering around the house. I had spent a little time in the garden out back, pulling weeds and tidying up the overgrown plots. At some point, it had been a well-laid-out garden, and I wanted to get it back to being usable. My mom and I had always lived in apartments, but whenever we could, we were part of community gardens, and I loved the idea of having my own to tend, being able to grow some vegetables and flowers. I was excited at the thought of sharing my bounty with my friends and Mom.

I heard Chase's truck, so I slid the shells into the oven to warm. He came in, and I grinned as I heard his keys being tossed into the bowl and his footsteps getting closer. "Cinnamon?" he called.

"In here."

He paused in the doorway. "God, supper smells incredible."

I turned and grinned. "Tacos."

His face lit up. "Awesome."

"You got the sour cream?"

He walked in, holding out the container. "Yep." Then from behind his back, he produced a stunning bouquet. It contained carnations, alstroemeria, hydrangeas, freesia, lilies, baby's breath, and the most perfect red rose in the middle. The ferns and leaves were lacy and pretty. It was incredible.

Chase looked shy as he held it out. "For you."

I took the flowers, burying my nose into the fragrant bundle. I shook my head. "I've never gotten flowers before."

He grinned. "I've never bought flowers before. See how perfect we are for each other?"

"I don't think we have a vase."

He laughed. "I have one. Charly gave it to Brett and me and told us every house had to have a vase. We kept it to appease her, but we never used it." He opened a cupboard and pulled out the large clear container. "It's a bit dusty. I used to use it for coins for a while, but she gave me shit."

I laughed and rinsed it out, putting the flowers in it. "Oh, they are so lovely." I set them on the table. "Look, how beautiful, Chase."

"I am," he said, but when I looked at him, his gaze wasn't on the flowers. It was on me. He touched my cheek. "The most beautiful thing I have ever seen."

"Chase," I murmured, awed by the intensity of his gaze.

"I want to kiss you."

"I'll kiss you right back."

"Yeah? I can?"

"You never have to ask."

He tugged me into his arms, his mouth covering mine. The kiss was sweet and sexy. Our mouths moved together, our tongues meeting and gliding. It was a kiss of hello and thank you. One that said I missed you and I'm glad you're here with me. He held my face between his hands, stroking his thumb in small circles on my cheeks. When he eased back, he stopped and kissed my forehead, then the end of my nose.

"I'm going to kiss you like that every day when I get home."

"I won't object."

"Can we have the tacos now? I'm starved."

I laughed. "Yes."

Chase sat back, pushing away his plate. "Those were incredible."

I grinned. "Really? You only ate six. I thought maybe you didn't like them."

He laughed, taking a drink of his water. "I've never had them with the cheese sauce before."

"I like queso."

"And you made it?"

"Yes. It's easy and tastes way better than the crap you get in a jar."

"I agree."

He stretched and smiled at me as I finished my taco, wiping my fingers. "How was the garage?"

"Busy. Maxx signed a deal a couple of months ago with a new company in Lomand. Delivery fleet. They handle all the shipments in about a three-hundred-mile range. We do the maintenance on the trucks. That extension he made to the garage is a boon for us since it can handle the bigger vehicles. Huge boost to the business. We have trucks scheduled all the time now. Maxx even hired a couple extra mechanics who do nothing but work on their fleet. Keeps the garage extra busy. Being commercial, they need a lot of maintenance paperwork. So, I'm constantly trying to keep up with that, as well as the rest of the front office stuff and do some of my upholstery gig."

"Sounds like you need help."

"Some days. It's easier when Brett is around, but when he is gone, Charly or Gabby pitches in, which helps. But they are pretty busy with the kids. Dom steps in, but he admits he hates the paperwork and computers. His talent is under the hood. So I do the best I can. When I get behind, I ask for help." He took another sip of water. "Maxx would hire someone if I asked, but so far, I'm okay."

"Good."

"You go back to work tomorrow."

"Yes." I sighed. "My days off go by fast."

"Not looking forward to it?"

"No, it's fine. I like my job. It's just—" I paused and took a sip of water "—I'll see Dan. I hope he'll be decent. He's a nice guy, so I think he will."

"Oh." He scratched his head. "About that."

I frowned. "What?"

Chase told me about his encounter with Dan, and I gaped at him. "He was going to write you a ticket? What the hell?"

Chase shrugged. "He was pissed about Saturday, and I get it. He knows we're together, and he's a little upset. It was his way of yanking my chain."

"I'll talk to him."

Chase shook his head. "Leave it. He'll think I sent you to fight my battles. He was being a dick, and I can handle that. After all, he lost you."

"He *never* had me. I told him I wasn't interested. More than once. I don't date fellow officers, and I had no desire to do so. He is a great guy but not the guy for me. I had zero attraction to him."

"Someone you are attracted to, Cinnamon?" Chase winked at me. "Anyone I know?"

I stood, shaking my head. "Seriously, Chase. What if he hassles you?"

"I can handle him, Hannah. He made his point. He's a cop. He can give me a jaywalking ticket, catch me speeding, whatever. Maybe he thinks if he shows you that I keep breaking the law, he looks like a better prospect."

I snorted. "Not likely."

He joined me at the counter, wrapping his arms around my waist. He kissed my neck, nuzzling the skin behind my ear, making me shiver. "Then don't worry about it, baby. It's all gonna be fine. It pissed me off but nothing big. I won't let him get under my skin."

"I don't want to be a source of aggravation for you."

He spun me, meeting my eyes. "You're not. And if he follows me around and writes me up for jaywalking every day, it's worth it to come home to you." He kissed the end of my nose. "You'd bail me out of jail, right?"

"Every time."

His mouth hovered over mine. "Then we're good."

CHAPTER FIFTEEN

Chase

We spent the evening simply doing nothing. She showed me the garden and the work she'd done. I offered to build her a couple of raised plant beds to make the backyard nicer. We sat outside, enjoying the fresh air, our hands linked, not saying a word, and enjoying every second of the silence. I liked the fact that I could be peaceful with Hannah. She didn't try to fill in the quiet with needless chatter or a thousand questions. The silence with her was tranquil.

When it got darker, we went inside, and I watched a baseball game on TV while she worked on knitting something. The sound of the needles clacking was surprisingly soothing. She told me she loved to knit and made a lot of blankets and booties she donated to the local hospital. *"I can knit without looking once I know the pattern,"* she explained. *"Especially simple blankets. Passes time in dispatch on quiet shifts, or I can watch a movie and knit at the same time."*

She was on one end of the sofa, her legs stretched out. I slid closer and propped her legs on my lap, wanting to touch her. I glanced at her, meeting her eyes, and she smiled at me but didn't say anything. After a while, the rhythm of the needles changed, then stopped, and I looked over, seeing she had fallen asleep. I watched her for a few moments, then stroked her calves. "Hannah, baby. Wake up."

Her eyes fluttered open.

"Time for bed."

"Oh," she mumbled. "Okay." She pushed off the sofa, bent down, and pressed a brief kiss to my mouth. "Night."

She wandered down the hall, and I waited for a few moments, then turned off the TV, checked the locks, and got ready for bed. I went to the kitchen and filled my jug with ice water, pausing at Hannah's door. I peeked in, seeing her sitting against her headboard.

"Okay, baby?" I asked.

"I'm fine."

"Okay, just checking. Night."

"Night."

I left my door open, so I could hear her. When she fell asleep, she made a soft whistling sound every so often, and I knew I wouldn't be able to sleep unless I heard it. But instead, I heard her toss and turn, the sound of her frustration quiet but evident.

I sat up, calling to her. "I'm right here, Cinnamon. I've got a big bed, and I'm waiting."

I tried not to laugh as the sounds of her hurried footsteps met my ears. I lifted the comforter, and she dove under, snuggling against me.

"I was trying not to bother you," she muttered.

I pressed a kiss to her head. "Not bothering. I like you here."

"Good. This is an awesome bed."

"Is it just the bed you like?"

She tilted up her head. "No, the sexy man waiting for me is the best part."

I lowered my head, capturing her mouth. Our lips moved together, and I deepened the kiss, our tongues tangling. Hannah whimpered, sliding her hands around my neck as I shifted, rising over her and pressing her down into the mattress. I slipped my hand under her, pulling her closer as our kissing became passionate. Deep and carnal. I groaned as she wrapped a leg around my waist, and I felt the heat of her. Dragging my lips down her throat, I licked and nipped at the skin. "We should stop, Cinnamon."

"No."

I felt her hand wrap around me, and I cursed as she cupped my balls.

"I want you, Chase."

"*Jesus*, Hannah." I was almost panting in my desperation for her.

"Please."

I didn't resist. I didn't want to resist. I had wanted her from the moment I met her. I rolled, taking her with me so she was straddling me. "Whatever you want, Hannah." I gathered her lacy gown in my hands. "But this has to go."

She helped me tug it over her head, and I stared at her in the dim light spilling in from the hall. Her breasts were high and tight, the nipples hard. She wore nothing else. I shook my head.

"So fucking gorgeous."

She leaned forward, kissing my jaw. "I want you naked too."

How I got my sweatpants off without moving her, I had no idea. But between us, we did, and then there was nothing. Nothing except her soft skin against mine. Her mouth pressed to my lips, our tongues tasting and dancing. We touched each other, discovering the hidden dips and valleys. She was ticklish under her ribs. She whimpered when I nuzzled the spot behind her ear. I found out how much she liked it when I pinched and sucked her nipples. The way she groaned when I stroked between her legs. The feel of her silky wetness was incredible on my fingers. I could only imagine how it would feel around my cock.

She stroked me, trailing her fingers along my length, rolling her thumb over the crown, and making me moan as she pumped me. I discovered I shuddered when she ran her fingers over my pelvis, the feeling incredible and arousing. We kissed endlessly, the taste of her addictive and heady. My body was on fire, awash with desire for her. Her little noises —the breathy sighs, low moans, and tiny whimpers—turned me on. I wanted to hear them every night.

"Make love to me, Chase."

I rolled over, hovering over her. "It's been a long time for me, Hannah. Years."

"Oh God, is it wrong I find that so hot?" she whispered. "It's like you're a born-again virgin."

I began to laugh, burying my face into her fragrant neck. "I think that's overstating it a little. My hand and my cock are best friends."

"I hate to break the two of you up."

"I'm good with it. Your pussy is going to be a major upgrade."

She wrapped her legs around me. "I'm on birth control. I'm safe. You're safe. Please."

I sank into her slowly. The heat, the intensity of the moment, the emotional impact this would have on us weren't lost on me. It was momentous. It meant so much to me, and I knew it did to Hannah as well. I flexed my hips again, sliding into her completely.

She groaned, clutching at my shoulders. "You feel so good. So good."

I had to shut my eyes. "So do you."

"Let go, Chase. I won't break."

"I want this to be good for you."

"It already is. I'm so close, please let go."

I pulled back and thrust forward again. And again. She met my movements, and it was as if the dam burst. The gratification was too incredible to ignore. She was perfect around me. I started to move faster, pushing her legs open wider so I could go deeper. Thrusting, pivoting my hips, listening to her cries of pleasure. I slid my arms under her, pulling her up my thighs as I sat back, surrounding her. I captured her mouth, thrusting hard, swallowing her groans. She tightened around me, yanking on my hair, screaming into my mouth. Blistering heat exploded, the flames of ecstasy raging under my skin. My orgasm burst, pushing sensations into every part of my body. I was a mass of quivering limbs and uncontrolled breathing. Hannah held me tight, and I rested my head on her shoulder, banding her close to my body.

For a moment, all I could do was hold her. Keep her close to me. Breathe her in. I felt her tremble, and I turned my head, speaking softly in her ear. "Okay, Cinnamon? Are you all right?"

"Aside from not being sure if I can walk tomorrow, I'm good. More than good." She met my eyes. "I know it's been a long time for you. Was it…" She trailed off.

"It was incredible. You were worth waiting for." I kissed her neck. "And not enough."

"Um, felt like enough to me."

I laughed, laying her down and hovering over her. "It will never be enough with you."

She traced her fingers along my jaw, cupping my cheek. "Chase," she whispered.

I turned my head and kissed her palm. Then bent and kissed her face. I rained hundreds of little kisses over her cheeks, forehead, nose, and neck. Everywhere I could reach.

She smiled, running her hands along my chest and neck, groaning as she felt me harden inside her.

"Again?" she murmured.

"Again."

HANNAH

I sat at my desk, looking over some reports and sipping a coffee. I stared at the papers in front of me, not seeing a word.

All I could see and feel was Chase. I swore I could still taste him in my mouth, feel his hands on my skin. Last night had been a time of simply being us. Spending time together. Enjoying each other. I hadn't intended on crawling into bed with him. But my bed felt wrong, and the room was too dark and too lonely. When I heard him call out and tell me he was waiting, I couldn't resist. I didn't want to. The thought of curling up beside him and feeling safe was too tempting.

I hadn't thought we'd make love. We had agreed on slow, and neither of us planned for it to happen.

But it did.

Being with Chase was intense and emotional for both of us. I knew it meant something special to him, and it did to me as well. We fit together so well, our bodies moving as one. For a man who hadn't been with someone in as long as he had, Chase was incredible. He was a giving lover, and I blushed just thinking about how many times he had made me come. I slept, wrapped in his embrace, waking up to his mouth pressing wet kisses to my neck, his cock hard between us. We made love again. Then this morning, he followed me into the shower and brought me to another orgasm with his talented tongue and fingers. I reciprocated by dropping to my knees and taking him into my mouth. He had groaned and hissed, his hand resting on my head, not pushing or directing, simply touching. He had begged me to stop, pleaded for more, then finally succumbed to his pleasure —loudly.

After, he insisted on washing every inch of me—some parts twice. We ran out of hot water, the last of the suds rinsed away with a lukewarm spray, but neither of us minded.

He kissed me long and hard before I left, promising me that he was going to grill dinner for us this evening.

I could hardly wait to see him.

A throat clearing made me look up, the smile on my face falling when I saw Dan standing by the desk.

"Hannah."

"Dan," I replied.

"I thought you were on patrol today."

"Things changed. I'm in the office today. Helping with paperwork."

I was good with paperwork and keeping track of files. I liked being organized, and I didn't mind the work. I had to admit, at times being out in the cruiser was boring. The people of the area were law-abiding. Often, my most exciting call was a cat up a tree, helping a senior, or the occasional speeder on the well-traveled road between Lomand and Littleburn. The last robbery call I got was a kid shoplifting a can of soda at the convenience store. He had done it on a dare and was so upset, the owner didn't want to press any charges. The kid had ended up pointing the finger at the boys who had dared him, and they were all spoken to by the police, with their parents sitting in. Then they spent a day picking up garbage around the town.

All of them now volunteered at the cleanup group every month.

Not a lot of crime happened here.

Dan shifted his weight, looking uncomfortable. I refused to say anything to help ease his discomfort.

"So, ah, the weekend. Sorry."

"Sorry?" I repeated. "That's all you got?"

"I thought I had read something that wasn't there. I misunderstood."

"I said no. More than once. Then you cage me against a wall, insisting we go out, not listening to a word I had to say..." I shook my head. "Never mind. Just leave me alone, Dan."

His face darkened. "I got the message when your so-called boyfriend showed up."

I lifted one eyebrow in derision. "*So-called?* Chase is my boyfriend." I lifted my chin, knowing I was speaking the truth. "And that is no excuse for your behavior. No is no.

You know that. We teach that at classes. We tell that to women all the time."

"I was a little drunk. I'm sorry. It won't happen again."

"Fine." I waved him off. "We are fellow officers and coworkers. That's it. Don't cross the line again."

He folded his arms over his chest, narrowing his eyes. "What about your roommate, Hannah? Your boyfriend—does he think dating a cop puts him above the law?"

I laughed. "Give it a rest, Dan. Jaywalking? You were really going to write him up for jaywalking? How petty."

"He told you, did he?"

"I told him I was worried you'd be a jerk today. He told me what happened. He was pretty sure you preferred being a jerk to him instead."

"I was being a cop. Doing my job."

"By harassing a citizen who was doing the same thing everyone else in this little town does. All because of who he is dating."

He leaned close. "All because of who he is. Do you know the person you're fucking?" he hissed. "He's a convict. Beneath you."

I drew in a long breath, counting to twenty. "First off, he paid for his mistake, and he is a different person. Second, who I date—or fuck—is none of your concern. And third, abusing your position by looking into his records?" I shook my head. "Bad move, Dan. I thought quite highly of you before. I see that was misplaced. Leave me alone. Leave Chase alone. If you don't, I'll go to the boss."

"I was concerned. I checked out his name. Imagine how shocked I was to see a fellow officer was living with a convict. I thought perhaps you didn't know, but obviously, you do. That is even more shocking to me."

"Chase is very upfront about his past. Unlike you, he is an honest person."

"Honest people don't go to jail."

I was done with this conversation. "People always deserve a second chance. And Chase has proven his integrity. Sadly, you have shown me the lack of yours." I stood, picking up my coffee cup. "From now on, we're coworkers, Dan. That is it. Have a good day."

I walked away.

By the end of my shift, I had a headache. After my run-in with Dan, the day went downhill. The station was busier than normal. Some files were missing. I kept spotting Dan, who seemed to make a habit of hanging around the part of the station I was working in, no matter how I tried to avoid him. I had never noticed how his laughter annoyed me or how condescending he was until today. I put it down to our interaction earlier and my annoyance at him for being such a jerk to Chase, so I purposely put a smile on my face and did my best to ignore him. I even waved and included him in my goodbyes for the day. I was grateful to leave and go home.

Chase wasn't home yet when I got there, but he had some steaks marinating in the fridge. I put together a salad, then decided to lie down and try to get rid of my headache. The pillow was cool under my cheek as I relaxed, letting the ice bag on my head and the silence soothe me. I slowly drifted, waking up to a low voice in my ear and a pair of strong arms holding me.

"Hannah," Chase crooned. "Wake up, baby."

I snuggled down, pushing back against his chest. He laughed quietly, tucking my hair behind my ear and resting his cheek against mine. "You okay?"

"Hmm. Headache. But it's gone."

"Headache? Why? Are you getting sick?"

"No, just a long day."

"Dan?" he asked.

"He was a bit of a jerk, but I think I nipped that in the bud." I told Chase about our conversation, and he chuckled at my words.

"So fierce, Hannah." He rolled me over, hovering above me. "So protective of me."

"I dislike people who want to prove they are more powerful. And thinking because you made a mistake in the past you should keep paying for it only shows how narrow-minded he is. Not very tolerant for a cop either."

He kissed me gently, his lips soft on mine. "Not everyone is as understanding as you, Cinnamon."

"You need to be understanding to be a cop. You have to show empathy at times. I remember once we were on a call, and I thought we were going to have to arrest a woman for her behavior in a bar. She was out of control and breaking things. My partner and I went in and talked to her, and she broke down and told me that her husband had left her that day, she lost her job that afternoon, and when she got to the bar, her best friend told her she was the reason her husband had left her. They were having an affair. By talking to her, I found out her story—she was normally a peaceful, kind person, but she'd had an epically shitty day and reacted badly. The owner didn't press charges, and she paid restitution for the damages. Ross taught me to ask first before assuming the worst about everyone. I try to do that on the job and in my life."

"Do you know what happened to her?" Chase asked.

"She got another job and found a new guy. She came to the station and dropped off cookies a few times. She found her feet and got back on track, but if Ross hadn't shown her some patience and empathy, she would have had a record that would have followed her around the rest of her life. He taught me to listen and watch. See things with your heart."

Chase leaned down and kissed me again. "I think your heart is beautiful."

I cupped his cheek. "Thank you."

"I think you're beautiful."

I smiled, lifting my head and kissing him. "If you're trying to butter me up, Chase, here's a hint. I'm a sure thing now."

He grinned. "Is that a fact?"

"Yes."

"And how's the headache?"

"Nothing you couldn't help with."

"Well then, let me take care of that. And you." His mouth covered mine.

Dinner was very late.

CHAPTER SIXTEEN

Chase

The entire week, the garage buzzed, busier than ever, and I could barely keep up. But the smile never faded from my face. I knew at the end of the day, I would see Hannah. I could hardly wait to get home every night to her. Her schedule changed due to a staff member being ill. Her boss had asked her to cover the office while her coworker was out, and Hannah had agreed, which meant she would be Monday to Friday regular hours for a while. I didn't react when she told me, except to acknowledge her change of shift. Even with the low crime rate of the area, I still worried about her as a police officer. You never knew what could happen during the course of a shift. Knowing she was in a more stable working environment made me breathe a little easier. I would never tell her that, although I had a feeling her mom agreed with me.

Thursday, I was deep into paperwork when a rap on the

door made me look up. Hannah was there, holding a bag. Her smile was warm, but she hesitated until I waved her in.

"What are you doing here?" I asked, standing and pressing a kiss to her cheek.

"I brought you lunch. I was out getting burgers for everyone, and I thought you might like one."

I was touched by her thoughtfulness. "Thank you. Wally's are the best."

"I should have got some for the others, but I had no idea how many were here."

"It's fine. They are talking about pizza for lunch. I'll eat this instead." I grinned at her. "But the best part is seeing you."

"I didn't want to disturb…" She trailed off.

"You never disturb."

"Um, can I ask a favor?"

"Anything."

"Mom was thinking of coming out this weekend. There is a craft sale at the town center on Saturday we were going to go to. Would you mind if she came out and spent the night?"

"Cinnamon, we've discussed this. It's your home too."

"I'll sleep on the sofa, and she'll—"

I cut her off. "Does your mom know about us?"

"Yes."

"Then you'll sleep with me, where you've been the last few nights. Not the sofa. Your mom can have the guest room."

"You mean my room."

I glanced behind her, but no one was looking our way. I pulled her close and kissed her. "I think of my room as our room now, so call it whatever you want. But you sleep with me. Got it?"

"Okay."

"There's a local band playing at Zeke's on Saturday. Maybe we could go and have a couple drinks? Would your mom enjoy that?"

"She'd love it."

"Great. We'll go and have dinner, then listen to some music." I pulled her closer. "Maybe do a little dancing."

"*I* would love that."

"Then we'll do it."

"Okay, I'll let Mom know. I have to get back to the station."

I nuzzled her cheek. "Thank you. And for the record, Hannah? I love it when you come see me. Never hesitate, okay?"

She smiled and cupped my cheek, pressing a fast kiss to my mouth. "Okay."

I watched her leave, thinking how hot she looked in her uniform. I wondered if she would be willing to play cops and robbers with me. I'd steal her clothes, and she could handcuff me. I might like that game. I had to shake my head to clear it and get back to work. I sat down, pulling the burger from the bag and taking a bite. I chewed and swallowed, enjoying the tasty lunch.

Dom walked in, grinning. "Your girl is looking after you, I see."

"She is."

"There's a part I need in Townshead. Anyone available to pick it up?"

I took another bite of burger. "Townshead?"

"It's back-ordered everywhere. Joe has one in stock he is willing to give me until we get one in to replace it. But he's alone today. I'm booked solid."

I glanced at the schedule. "Everyone is. Milt is in the opposite direction today, so he won't make it up to Townshead." I rubbed my chin. "I could go if Charly could look after the office for a couple of hours."

"Send a courier."

"That'll cost an arm and a leg."

"You're too busy."

"Hannah and Cherry are doing a craft fair on Saturday. I can come in and catch up."

He lifted his eyebrows, a smile playing on his mouth. "Cherry's coming for a visit?"

I grinned. "We're going to Zeke's to listen to the band Saturday."

"Isn't that interesting. I was planning on going myself."

"Oh? You like the Broken Owls, do you?"

"One of my favorites."

"Too bad it's the Frozen Tundra playing, then."

He threw back his head in laughter. "You got me. I don't give a care who is playing. It's who will be listening I'm interested in."

I laughed with him. "I never had this conversation with you."

"Nope."

"I'll go talk to Charly as soon as I finish my burger."

"I owe you."

"Yep."

I had the windows down as I drove back from Townshead. The sun was shining, and the breeze felt good. Charly was covering the office, and Mary was looking after the kids while I was gone. The trip up had been easy, the back roads I drove down mostly deserted. It felt like old times, driving to pick up a part. I thought about how my life had changed since the day I showed up at the garage, only planning on asking for one thing: forgiveness.

I got way more than I bargained for. I got a new life, a family, and that all led to this moment. A job I loved, a home, and a girl who made me feel as if I could do anything. Be anything.

The sudden sound of a siren and the flash of a red light in my rearview mirror startled me. I glanced at the speedometer and cursed. I had been so deep into my thoughts I hadn't noticed I'd gotten a little heavy-footed on the gas. But I was only ten kilometers over the limit and the road was empty, so I was surprised I was being pulled over. Regardless, I put on my blinker and slowed down, rolling to a stop and waiting as the officer climbed out of his cruiser. I hoped he'd lecture me, give me a warning, and let me go.

The hope ended when the officer appeared at my window.

"Going a little fast, Mr. Donner. Got somewhere important to be that you felt it was all right to break the law?"

I met the baleful stare of Dan Meyers, and I bit back my sarcastic retort.

"Sorry, *Officer*. I guess I didn't realize. Nice day out for a drive and all."

"Sunshine doesn't give you permission to speed."

"I was barely breaking the limit."

"I clocked you at over twenty."

I gaped at him. "It was hardly ten."

"You slowed down."

"But not enough for you."

"Not enough for the lawful limit."

I shook my head and narrowed my eyes. "What are you doing so far away from town? Are you *following* me?"

"We patrol a large area," he said, dismissing my query.

"And you just happen to be where I was driving," I reiterated.

"License and registration."

I held my tongue as I reached over and got the registration from the glove box. The bastard had followed me somehow. I dug into my coat pocket for my license, stopping at the sound I heard. I turned my head, seeing the gun Dan was now holding. "Remove your hand from that pocket slowly," he ordered.

"I am just getting my license."

"Slowly," he repeated.

I did as he requested, showing him my wallet. He lowered his gun, holstering it.

"Was that really necessary?" I questioned, refusing to let him see the anxiety that crept up my spine at the sight of him drawing his weapon on me.

"I had no idea what you were reaching into your pocket for."

I handed him my license and registration. "Exactly what you asked me for."

"Please step out of the car while I check this out."

My temper was beginning to grow, but I tamped it down and undid my seat belt, stepping onto the road.

"Place your hands on the vehicle and keep them there."

I wanted to throw a punch. Tell him what I thought of him and this stupid power play. But I knew what would happen. I'd end up in the back of his cruiser, handcuffed and on a trumped-up charge. So, without a word, I did as he asked.

I counted to a hundred in my mind over and over as I stood with my hands on my truck while Dan took his sweet-ass time verifying my information. Another car went by, slowing down to look at us, and I ignored them, resisting the urge to lift one hand and wave. I wouldn't put it past Dan to shoot me for it. He was doing this to cause me embarrassment, but the funny thing was, he was the one who should be embarrassed. I had done nothing except be a little heavy on the gas pedal.

He finally strolled back, indicating I could move. "I'm going to cut you a break, Chase."

"Is that a fact?" I snarled, taking my cards back. "What kind of break might that be?"

"I'm only writing you up for ten kilometers over the limit." He handed me a ticket. "Follow the instructions to pay the fine on the back." He smirked. "Or contest, if you prefer. I'll see you in court, then."

I took the ticket, seething. "Anything else?"

He narrowed his eyes. "Obey the law."

I leaned closer, glaring. "Maybe you should try to take your own advice," I spat. "Harassing me isn't going to get you anywhere with Hannah."

He shrugged. "I had no idea who you were when I pulled you over. I was doing my job."

I turned and walked away. "Right," I snorted under my breath. "Asshole."

In the truck, I snapped on my seat belt, watching him in the mirror. I waited for him to pull out, but he stayed in his car, waiting. I realized he planned on following me back to Littleburn—or at least as far as he could.

I rolled up my window and put on the air. I turned up the music and pulled away. I drove as slowly as I could without giving him cause to pull me over for going too slow. But he wanted me to abide by the law? He was going to get it.

I laughed as he eventually got tired and drove around me, leaving me in his dust. I flipped him the bird and sped up but set the cruise to exactly the speed limit as soon as he was out of sight.

I mulled over what to do, then decided to do nothing. Telling Hannah would only upset her. Fighting the ticket would give him ammunition. I would pay the fine and move on. But I knew I would have to be watchful for him now.

At the garage, I gave Dom his part and headed to the office. Charly smiled at me. "I was getting worried."

"I, ah, had a little trouble on the way back."

"What kind of trouble?"

I sat down and quietly told her. Her eyes widened, and she gripped my arm. "He drew his weapon?"

"Yeah."

"Chase, you need to report him."

"He was trying to scare me, Charly. Prove a point."

Her grip tightened. "What point? That he could shoot you?"

"That he is more powerful than me. Which, in this case, he is. He wasn't going to shoot me."

"Were you scared?"

"For a moment, yes," I admitted. "But he hadn't removed the safety. It was for show."

"You should still report him."

"No. He can argue he had just cause since I was reaching into my pocket, even though we both knew I was getting my wallet. And I'm not telling Hannah. She'll get in his face, and he wants to prove I'm scared of him. That I am not man enough for her."

She worried at her lip, her grip on my arm not lessening. "I don't like this, Chase."

I patted her hand. "It's okay, Charly. I'll keep my eyes open for the bastard now. He'll get tired of badgering me. Maybe he'll find someone else he's interested in and forget about me."

"I'm telling Maxx."

"No."

"Telling Maxx what?"

I groaned as Maxx walked in, looking between us. He frowned and shut the door. "Whatever it is you've said that has upset my wife, Chase, you are going to tell me. Now."

His tone brooked no argument.

I repeated my story to Maxx. He was silent for a moment, then nodded.

"I think he should report him," Charly said to him.

"I think, for now, Chase is right. Leave it alone."

"But—"

He held up his hand. "Listen first, Red."

She huffed, and I had to hide my smile.

"If Chase was speeding, however little, it was the asshole's right to pull him over. And Chase is right, he can argue Chase was reaching for something and, for his own safety, he drew his gun." He faced me. "Pay the fine and be done with it. Do not give him more ammo to come after you. No more road trips for a while without someone with you, Chase. Nothing. No bank runs, errands, even lunch. And watch your back. I've got some friends in the station, and I'll quietly ask about him. I don't think he's been here long."

"Hannah said about a year."

"Okay, he is pretty low in the pecking order, then. If you are suspicious of anything or he tries anything else, we go to his superior. Just don't give him any reason to. Including walking across the damn street like everyone else does. I agree he is doing this to be a prick, but we still have to be careful." He paused. "I do agree with Charly. Tell Hannah."

"I don't want to upset her."

"She'll be more upset when she finds out—which she will, Chase. They always do." He looked at Charly with a smile. "Right?"

"Absolutely. Holy moly, Maxx, you're actually learning."

He laughed and I joined in. Maxx adored his wife and told her everything. We all did. She only had to lift an eyebrow and put a hand on her hip, and we sang like canaries. It was a gift she possessed. There was no hiding anything from her.

"Fine. I'll tell her. But not until the weekend. I don't want her going in and running him over tomorrow. I'll give her a chance to settle down."

"You sure about that?" Charly asked.

I chuckled. "Yep. I'm sure."

"Okay."

Maxx clapped my shoulder. "We've got your back, Chase. You're not alone with this. Do not let him get to you and undo all the good you have accomplished since you stood up for my wife."

"I won't."

Maxx bent and kissed Charly. "Let go of his arm now, Red. Your boy is fine."

Charly looked shocked she was still hanging on to me. I grinned at her and squeezed her fingers. "Thanks, Charly."

Tears welled in her eyes, and I looked at Maxx, shocked. Charly never cried.

"I hate bullies," she muttered, wiping at her eyes. "I hate them."

Maxx tilted his head slightly, and I stood, leaving them alone. I looked back to see him enfold her in his arms. She always looked so small when he held her. An attitude and a heart the size of Texas encased in a tiny frame described Charly. And the fact that she was upset about me touched me in more ways than I could express. I was extremely lucky to have her in my corner.

I wouldn't do anything to jeopardize her faith in me.

No matter how much the asshole pushed me.

CHAPTER SEVENTEEN

Chase

F riday was quiet. Dom and I went to get lunch for everyone, and we didn't see OD, as Dom referred to him. He preferred Officer Dickface but shortened it. Maxx had told Stefano and Dom the basics, explaining why I was sticking close to the garage for a while. They were both pissed off, and Stefano had some creative ideas for getting even with him that made me laugh. They teased and made light of it, but I knew they had my back as much as Maxx and Charly did.

I finished the paperwork, silently blessing Charly, who had taken care of a bunch of it while I was gone yesterday. I helped Dom and Stefano since the garage was booked solid and we had a couple of emergencies that showed up, and Maxx liked to look after his customers. We also finished two jobs early, and that meant I could work on the custom upholstery on Saturday morning, which I was looking forward to. I drove home carefully, not seeing anything, and I relaxed a little, hoping that maybe OD had decided he'd yanked my chain enough. I doubted it, but I still hoped.

I opened the front door, knowing Cherry had arrived already. Her car was parked on the street, and I went to the kitchen to tell her to pull into the driveway and I would put my truck on the street.

She and Hannah were at the table, a bottle of wine open between them. Cherry hugged me, assuring me her car was fine on the street. Hannah's greeting was a little more reserved than the past few nights, but I still got to kiss her and hold her for a moment. I loved the feeling of her wrapping her arms around my waist and fitting herself to my chest. I hugged her hard and pressed a kiss to her head.

"Something smells delicious," I commented.

"We made spaghetti and garlic bread," Hannah said. "Probably not as good as Rosa's…"

I had to kiss her. "Better because you made it."

Cherry laughed. "Oh, you were right, Hannah. Your man is a charmer."

I leaned down. "Talking about me to your mom? Your man?" I teased.

"Go shower. You smell like garage."

"I had to help out front, we were so busy. Wanna come wash my back?"

She pushed me away. "No."

I snickered. She was trying not to do the same thing, and her eyes were sparkling with humor. I winked and sauntered down the hall.

"You can go, ah, *chat* with Chase," Cherry said, laughing. "I have headphones."

"Mom!"

I laughed loudly.

"Stop encouraging him," Hannah scolded.

"It's too fun," Cherry protested.

"Whatever."

"I'm all for a chat!" I called, smirking at their returned "Nos."

I chuckled as I took off my clothes, tossing them in the hamper. I stood under the spray, rolling my shoulders and letting the heat relax them. I had been tense all day, thinking about OD and wondering if he'd do something. But all my stress was for nothing. I was home, safe with my girl, and we had nothing planned other than some delicious spaghetti and a movie.

Life was good.

Hannah slipped under the comforter, immediately nestling beside me. I pulled her close. "It feels weird, my mom down the hall and me in here with you," she whispered.

I chuckled. "Would you rather it was your mom in here with me?"

Hannah giggled and slapped my chest. "You know what I mean."

"I kinda like it."

She snuggled closer. "I never said I didn't like it."

I slid my hand down her back, cupping her ass.

"Not tonight," she warned.

"I'm just hugging you."

"Your hand is on my ass."

I squeezed the full cheek. "I like your ass."

"I'm serious, Chase. My mom is a few feet away."

"And our door is closed. Her door is closed." I slid my hand under her nightshirt and between her legs. "And you're not wearing underwear."

"Chase…"

I covered her mouth with mine, kissing her. We slowly rolled so I was on top of her. "We can be quiet, Cinnamon. I can make sure you sleep well so you have a good day with your mom tomorrow," I murmured against her mouth.

She whimpered as I grazed my finger over her clit. She was wet and ready for me. She wanted me as much as I wanted her.

"Tell me yes," I begged, circling the nub.

"Oh God, yes."

I smiled as I kissed her again, settling between her thighs. She wrapped her legs around my hips, drawing me closer. I bent and sucked a taut nipple into my mouth, teasing it through the thin cotton. She bit her lip, a small sigh escaping her lips. I sat back, lifting her hips and sinking in, slow and deep, watching her expression as I did. The desire on her face the moment I was buried within the cradle of her body as far as I could go was wondrous. Her eyes widened, and she shivered. I gripped her hip, bending over her. "Quiet, baby." Then I covered her mouth and began to move. Hard. Fast. Rocking into her and feeling her clutch at me. Never releasing her lips from mine. Our tongues stroked together, mimicking the actions of our bodies until she tightened around me, her pleasure a silent scream in my mouth. My body responded, and my orgasm tore through me, the intensity of it hot and complete. I stilled, absorbing the aftershocks, then slowly withdrew, lying next to her. She rolled, once again nestled beside me.

"If that's any indication, tomorrow is going to be a great day," she muttered.

I chuckled and kissed her head. "Epic," I agreed.

Cherry smiled in delight as she looked around. "I love this place!"

I grinned at her. Cherry sat next to Hannah, and it was obvious they were related. I still thought they looked more like sisters than mother and daughter. Cherry was young-looking for her age. Hannah told me, growing up, Cherry was always mistaken for a sister or an aunt rather than her mother. She laughed when she told me about the boy in her class in grade ten who had a crush on her mother.

"I thought he liked me and was hanging out at our apartment for me. Turned out he had a thing for older women, and my mother was his fantasy."

"What happened?"

"He told her, and she was horrified. She informed him she was old enough to be his mother and she was friends with the woman who was. He told her that was okay, he'd handle it." Hannah grinned widely. "She handled it by taking him by the ear and dragging him from the apartment. She threatened to tell his mom if he ever mentioned it again. That was the last time he came over. He pretended we didn't know each other after that."

The bar was busy, the band getting ready to play. We'd come earlier and secured a good table, eaten some awesome burgers, and were getting ready to enjoy the music. I leaned close to Hannah, my voice low. "You like to dance, Cinnamon?"

She turned, meeting my eyes. We were close enough I could feel her breath wash over my skin as she spoke. "I do."

"Will you dance with me tonight?"

She smiled, closing the distance between us and brushing her lips on mine. "Yes."

I sat back, happy, keeping my arm around her shoulders. She smiled, picking up her wineglass and taking a drink. Cherry looked between us, a small grin on her lips. I scanned the bar, relieved not to see a familiar face in the crowd. OD didn't appear to be around this evening, which was a good thing in my book. I hadn't told Hannah what happened yet, but I planned to do so tomorrow after her mom left. The weekend was going too well to spoil it.

I saw Dom walking in, his tall figure easy to spot. He wore his leather jacket, the black cowhide well-worn and gleaming under the lights. His dark hair was brushed off his face, and his five-o'clock shadow looked more like ten o'clock. He looked every inch the bad boy Cherry thought him to be. He strolled to the bar, getting a beer, then turned and leaned against the wood, casually looking around. I covertly watched Cherry, knowing the second she noticed him. Her shoulders went back, her chin lifted, and she averted her eyes, looking anywhere but the bar area, the color on her cheeks darkening. I also observed her hand tightening on her wineglass. She shifted in her chair, tossing her hair over her shoulder in a defiant gesture. I hid my smile as Dom pushed off the bar and headed our way. Cherry made a small noise in the back of her throat, and I squeezed Hannah's shoulder. "Hey, look who it is."

Dom stopped at the table. "Chase. Hannah." He paused, focusing his attention on Cherry. "And Cherry Gallagher. What a pleasure to see you again."

Hannah grinned. "Here to listen to some music, Dom?"

He nodded. "I saw the flyers earlier this week when I was here."

"Hang around the bar a lot, do you?" Cherry asked.

Without waiting for an invitation, Dom pulled out the chair next to her and swung it around, straddling it. He sat beside her, angling his body her way.

"They have great food here. I was having dinner after looking at a couple of houses."

"Oh," she murmured.

"Enjoying your visit?"

"Yes."

He leaned closer to her and said something. Her cheeks darkened again, and she shook her head, replying to whatever his query was. Hannah watched them, fascinated. She leaned close to me.

"I can't tell if Mom is interested or appalled."

I chuckled. "I'd say both."

The band stepped onstage, and I focused my attention on them. Cherry and Dom were adults, and they could figure themselves out. I was going to listen to some great music and dance with my girl.

I couldn't recall the last time I'd had this much fun. Laughed so hard. Smiled so much. The band was great, getting the crowd on their feet fast. Although I wasn't a particularly good dancer, I pulled Hannah to the floor and tried to keep up with her. She was sexy, swaying her hips, shimmying to the beat, lifting her arms above her head as she moved. She sang with the band, her voice slightly off-key but sweet. We danced close during the slow songs, kissing endlessly at times. I never wanted the night to end.

I caught sight of Dom and Cherry dancing a couple of times, often sitting at the table, their heads close together, talking a lot. Cherry used her hands a great deal when she spoke, and more than once, I saw Dom grab her hand and kiss the knuckles. She'd yank her hand away, but I noticed her smile more than once. The last I had seen, he was at the bar, and she had headed to the ladies' room.

Hannah leaned her head on my shoulder. "My feet hurt, I'm thirsty, and I have to pee."

I laughed. "Come on then, Cinnamon. You go join the line, I'll get us drinks. I'll give you a break for a while, and when we get home, I'll rub your feet."

She smiled up at me, slightly tipsy. I was much the same, and I already knew I would be leaving my truck here and we would walk home or grab a cab. I moved us close to the hall for the ladies' room and headed to the bar, pleasantly surprised when I got served right away.

"Good timing," the bartender acknowledged. "The band is taking a break in ten, and the line will be crazy."

I got a tray for the drinks and ordered some nachos and wings. I was starving after all the dancing. I headed back to the table, sitting down. Hannah appeared a few moments later, shaking her head.

"What?" I asked.

"Your friend is a piece of work. He was dancing with my mom earlier, and I just saw him at the end of the hall, kissing the hell out of some woman. Her legs were around his waist, and I'm not sure I want to know where his hands were. They were going at it pretty hard." She sighed. "Mom thought he was a player. I guess she was right."

I glanced over her shoulder, biting back my smile. "Um, Cinnamon."

"What?"

"Look."

She turned and gasped. Dom was walking through the crowd, his hand firmly clasping the waist of a very disheveled Cherry Gallagher. Her hair was a mess, her lips swollen, and as they got closer, I saw the red mark on her neck. His hair was everywhere, his shirt untucked. The look on his face was intense and serious. He stopped at the table, grabbing her purse and his jacket.

"We're going for coffee," he said, his voice deep and rough. He looked at Hannah. "Don't wait up."

Cherry looked at her daughter, wide-eyed and blushing. "Just coffee," she called over her shoulder. "I'll be home soon."

Dom's laugh bellowed out loudly. "Don't count on it."

And they were gone.

Hannah turned around and blinked. She looked at me, the door to the bar, then back over her shoulder to the hall.

"That—that was my mom he was manhandling."

"Woman-handling, I'd say," I drawled, lifting my beer to my mouth. "But it's just coffee—you know, Hannah. *Chatting.*"

"Her legs around his—" She swallowed. "He's going... They're going..."

I nodded.

"My mom. Oh God." She met my eyes. "Chatting."

"From the look of the two of them, I'd say some pretty *intense* chatting."

She covered her face. "Oh God."

"I think the only playing happening for Dom tonight is the age-old Italian game of hide the salami. I think Dom's an expert."

Hannah slapped my shoulder. "Stop it! That's my mom!"

I grinned. "We can go home and play too if you want."

"Do we know if she's safe with him? What if he's a degenerate?"

"What if Cherry wants a degenerate?"

"Chase! Stop it!"

I laughed and tugged her chair close, kissing her. "Dom is a great guy. Rough around the edges with a heart of gold. Stefano has known him for a long time. Maxx likes him. I think he is awesome. Your mom is in perfectly safe—and probably very capable—hands." I winked.

"I can't even think about my mom having sex."

"Then think about us having sex. Loudly. Until she comes home—then we can tease the hell out of her."

She fisted my shirt. "We should go now."

"Oh. I ordered nachos and wings."

Her eyes widened. "Ooh. Nachos."

"With extra cheese."

"Okay. Eat. Then home. Sex." She grinned. "Lots of sex."

"Perfect."

CHAPTER EIGHTEEN

Chase

We stumbled from the bar, laughing. I had my arm slung around Hannah's shoulder, and her hand gripped my waist. I was pretty sure we were holding each other up. I looked up and down the street, surprised not to see any cabs waiting. She shivered, nestling closer. "We can just walk."

"Where is your jacket?"

"In the truck."

"Let's get it. Then if no cabs show up, we'll walk."

We headed to the truck at the back of the bar, slightly weaving. I pulled the fob from my pocket, opening the door. I slid into the truck, looking around. It was colder than I expected it to be outside, and I decided we could sit in the truck and Hannah could get warm while we waited for a cab. I started the truck, and finally spotting the jacket on the floor behind the seats, I leaned over and grabbed it, rolling down the window. "Come get warm, and we'll call a cab and wait here," I instructed. Before she could move, bright lights hit my eyes, and I shielded them with my hand.

I cursed as I saw the police car in front of the truck. Hannah stopped walking, frowning. I turned off the truck, got out, and handed the jacket to her. An officer got out of the car, sauntering over, holding up a flashlight. There was no doubt who it was. I recognized the swagger.

He stopped in front of us, and Hannah waved her hand. "Get the light out of my face, Dan."

"Where you two kids off to?"

"We're heading home," I informed him.

He tsked under his breath. "Driving while under the influence? Not a good idea."

"I wasn't driving," I pointed out.

"You were in the truck. The engine was running."

"I was getting her jacket and warming the truck so we could sit in it until the cab came. Not driving."

"So you say."

"It's the truth."

"From where I stand, looks to me like you were planning on driving."

"We were waiting for a cab," Hannah protested. "Just like Chase said."

"You ordered one?"

"I was about to."

He nodded, looking smug. "So you haven't ordered a cab. You've been drinking. You were sitting behind the wheel of a running vehicle, and you expect me to believe it was to warm up."

All the euphoria of the evening vanished. The slightly hazy feeling evaporated, and I was clearheaded and sober. Angry. "Yes," I snapped. "Because it's the truth."

"I'm going to need you to step away from the vehicle, sir. I'm going to conduct a sobriety test."

"There is no need to do that. I admit I've been drinking. I wasn't going to drive." Inwardly, I was cursing. I should never have started the truck. I had just given him the ammo he was looking for.

Hannah stepped between us. "We were going to walk, but it's colder than we expected. Chase came to get my jacket and decided we should call a cab and sit in the truck to wait. That is all. I give you my word, Dan. He wasn't going to drive. I wouldn't let him do that."

Dan looked at her, his voice scathing. "Given the fact that you fuck him, I can't really take your word for it."

I reached around her, pushing her behind me and getting his face.

"Watch yourself, asshole."

"That's Officer Meyers to you."

"Keep pushing me, and I'll forget you're a cop."

"You gonna hit me?" he taunted.

I curled my hands into fists, but Hannah gripped my arm, stopping me.

"I wouldn't give you the satisfaction, no matter how much you goad me. If you're going to arrest me, do it. Or write me another ticket—whatever makes you feel better. At least this time, you didn't pull your gun."

I heard Hannah's low gasp, and I cursed internally. I hadn't meant to say that.

"Do whatever you need to, *Officer*." I indicated the truck. "Hannah, wait inside. It's cold."

"I don't think so," she replied.

Dan narrowed his eyes, looking between us. "I'll let you off with a warning, Mr. Donner. But I'll be watching."

He turned and headed to his car, calling over his shoulder, "And I'll be waiting until your cab comes."

He got in his cruiser, and I tugged Hannah with me. "Let's go wait in the bar."

Back out front, a cab was idling at the curb, and we slid in. I didn't know the driver, so I gave him my address, still fuming. Hannah was quiet during the short ride, Dan's cruiser following us all the way. I handed the cabbie a twenty, muttering my thanks, and we walked up the steps and into the house. Inside, I turned and watched as Dan sat at the end of the driveway for a minute, then slowly drove off. He flashed his lights before he drove off, making sure the neighbors knew I had been followed by a cop. The bastard.

I shook my head, relieved and still angry. Turning to Hannah, I met her eyes, knowing what was about to happen.

"He pulled you over already?"

"Yes."

"When?"

"Thursday."

"And you didn't tell me."

I sighed, dropping my head. "I didn't want to ruin the weekend. Trust Danny boy to do it for me."

She stepped closer. "He pulled his gun on you?"

I tugged her to the sofa, grateful she wasn't furious with me. I told her what had happened. She listened with a frown on her face. "He has overstepped."

I laughed, the sound bitter. "Yes, he has. And I can't do anything about it."

"I'll talk to my boss."

"No. He is being a prick, but it's his word against mine. The guy with the record against a police officer. I was speeding— even if it was barely over the limit. I was drinking, and I should never have started the truck. All I was thinking about was getting you warm." I scrubbed my face. "He was doing his job. Just zealously."

"Because of me."

"He's jealous." I dared to wrap my arm around her. "I don't blame him."

"I hate that he is doing this. I'll talk to him."

I shook my head. "You sticking up for me will rile him up more. Let it alone. I'll watch myself, and he'll get tired of pissing me off."

"I am hardly worth all this trouble."

"I disagree."

She rolled her eyes. "Chase."

I shifted closer. "Hannah. He's pissed. He doesn't like me."

"He's abusing his position."

"I know. There were guys like him while I was in jail. They'd push me around, showing me they had the power.

Try to get under my skin. I ignored them, and they got bored. Let him get it out of his system."

"If it doesn't stop, I'm going to my boss."

I slid my hand around her neck. "Fine. Enough about him. We had a plan."

"A plan?"

"Dancing, drinks, food. Then home for sex. We did the first three." I pulled her close, ghosting my mouth over hers. "I was really looking forward to the last one."

"Oh. *Oh.*"

"Oh," I repeated back. "I want to hear you cry that out. Loudly."

She wrapped her arms around me, and I pulled her onto my lap so she was straddling me. I covered her mouth with mine and kissed her until she was breathless. Moving her hips restlessly. Feeling the way I wanted her.

"Here or the bedroom, Cinnamon?" I murmured into her ear, tugging the lobe with my teeth.

"Yes," she replied, her voice raspy. "Both."

I grinned against her skin. I could get on board with that.

The sun slanted through the blinds as I walked into the bedroom, carrying mugs of coffee. Hannah sat up, leaning against the headboard, the sheet barely covering the swells of her breasts. Her hair was chaotic, she had little smudges of mascara under her eyes that she'd missed when washing her face last night, and her neck and shoulders had scruff marks scattered on them. A tiny mark glowed red on her neck. Her mouth was still swollen, and she looked tired. She was fucking gorgeous.

"Jesus, you are sexy," I said with a wide grin. "I love how you look in my—*our*—bed."

She laughed, taking the mug I offered her. "I'm a mess."

I leaned over, kissing her. "You're my mess."

She smiled. "What do I smell?"

"I went to go get cinnamon buns at the bakery, and I picked up the truck."

"Was it okay?"

"It was fine." I didn't mention the scratch I had seen down the side, no doubt courtesy of a key. I'd buff it out at the shop. I was pretty sure who put it there, but if I told her I knew, she would freak out.

"I'm sorry that Dan—"

I put my finger on her lips. "Never mention his name while you're in our bed. His behavior is on him, not you."

She pushed her lips against my skin, kissing the finger. "I still hate it, and I'm sorry."

"Forget it. Let's have a cinnamon bun and lie in wait for your mother and Dom. I bet he brings her home. I want to see what he has to say for himself."

Hannah groaned. "I don't think I can handle this."

I chuckled. "Come on, it'll be fun."

She took a long drink of coffee. "Fine."

She got up, and I headed to the kitchen, pulling the cinnamon buns from the oven. Despite OD's appearance last night, I was surprisingly chipper. I decided it was the incredible blow job Hannah gave me in the living room, plus the intense sex marathon we had in our room afterward. She'd cried "oh" more times than I could count. I especially liked it when it came out sounding breathy and hot.

I poured us more coffee, and Hannah appeared, her hair neatly braided, her skin glowing. She was dressed much the way I was, in sweats and a shirt. I narrowed my eyes at her. "Is that my shirt?" I asked, indicating the too-large T-shirt she sported.

A grin played on her mouth. "Maybe."

I leaned over and kissed her. "I like it."

We munched on the warm rolls, sipping coffee, not saying much. The sound of the front door opening made me grin,

235

and I met Hannah's wide-eyed gaze. "Showtime," I mouthed. I stood and looked down the hall. Cherry was in the doorway, Dom on the step. He was saying something to her in a low voice, and she was shaking her head. I tried not to laugh at her outfit. The shirt she was wearing did not belong to her. Obviously, mother and daughter liked to borrow their man's clothes. I had a feeling Dom was as okay with it as I was.

"Morning, kids!" I sang out, startling them. "We got breakfast on the table. Come on in, Dom. No need to stand outside like a degenerate or something."

"Dom was just leaving," Cherry protested, the color on her cheeks high.

"Breakfast?" Dom said at the same time.

"Fresh cinnamon rolls from Lulu's."

"He'll take one to go."

Dom shook his head. "I'll eat in."

Cherry huffed an impatient sound and brushed past me, hurrying into the kitchen. She looked like she'd been worked over good. Hannah was going to be horrified. I met Dom's calm gaze with a grin. "Good night?"

He came in, shutting the door. "Be respectful. I'm trying to win her over."

"Scout's honor."

He hung his head. "Well, I'm fucked."

Laughing, I clapped him on the shoulder. "It's all good."

In the kitchen, I grabbed two more cups and the coffeepot. Cherry and Hannah were talking, quiet and fast, their heads bent together. They were both gesturing, their hands flying around as they spoke, the gestures similar. Cherry looked flushed and nervous. Hannah looked as horrified as I thought she would.

"You're looking at your future," Dom muttered. "Good Lord, that woman can talk. I had to get inventive in order to keep her quiet."

I almost choked on my coffee. I side-eyed him, and he winked, not looking embarrassed. "Shut up, yourself," I muttered, pushing the buns his way. "Fill your mouth with one of those instead."

He grinned, taking a bite. "Not as sweet as what I filled it with earlier."

Cherry heard him, her head snapping in his direction. He winked at her. "Yes, Cherry G. I'm talking about you."

"Well, stop it," she and Hannah said at the same time. I tried not to laugh but failed. They looked so alike, acted the same, and Dom was correct. Hannah was a younger version of her mom. I was more than okay with it. "Sweet buns?" I asked Cherry, lifting the plate. "Or did you get enough of Dom's?"

Cherry's eyes widened. Dom chuckled, and Hannah glared at me. Cherry took one, primly thanking me. Then she and Hannah began talking again, ignoring our presence. Dom and I sipped and chewed in silence for a moment. Keeping my voice hushed, I told him about our run-in with OD. He blew out a low whistle. "He's got a hard-on for you."

"Sadly."

He reached for the pot and filled his cup. "We need to keep an eye out. It sounds like he's following you."

"Great," I muttered. "A police stalker."

"We'll figure this out, kid. Just stick close to home and keep your nose clean. He'll get tired."

"That's what I'm hoping."

Cherry tossed her hair at something Hannah said, and I bit back another laugh. Cherry had a bite mark at the base of her neck, and Hannah's eyes focused on the mark before she met my gaze with a WTF look. I winked at her, and she bit her lip, holding in her laughter.

"What?" Cherry asked.

"Ah, you have a little, um, mark," I said. "On your neck."

She brushed at her skin. "Where?"

"The spot I sank my teeth into," Dom said calmly. "It'll fade. Until next time."

Cherry's eyes widened, and she looked at Hannah.

"Mom…" Hannah choked out.

Cherry stood. "I'm going to get ready to head home. I have a million things to do." She practically ran from the kitchen. Hannah began to stand, but Dom waved her off.

"I'll go talk to her." He paused at the door, turning to speak. "I like your mother, Hannah. She's incredible. You should come have lunch with me. Get to know me. I plan on being around a lot." He glanced down the hall. "If that stubborn woman will let me." He flexed his shoulders. "I'm going in." He flashed a smile. "If you hear screaming, no one is being hurt. Trust me. Don't come in."

Hannah and I looked at each other across the table.

"If I had known how interesting it was going to be having a roommate, I would have gotten one sooner," I observed. "Brett was positively boring compared to you." I winked at her so she knew I was teasing.

She picked up another cinnamon bun. "You ain't seen nothing yet, Chase Donner."

I grinned. "I'm counting on it."

CHAPTER NINETEEN

Hannah

Monday morning, I was in a good mood. The station bustled, I went through reports and schedules, spoke with some people, and put everything on the chief's desk to approve. I was pleased to see that Dan had nights again for a while, and he was on a three-day-on, four-day-off rotation. I wondered if he'd requested that so as not to run into me during the day while I worked from the station or if it was coincidence. Either way, I liked it. The nice guy I thought him to be no longer existed. He was acting like a petulant child who didn't get his way, and I wasn't fond of his actions or attitude.

I had lunch with some of the girls in dispatch and the 9-1-1 center. Things ran differently in a small town. Everything was in one place here, and there were fewer officers, people, and department heads, and the protocol was less severe. We were considered peacekeepers, and the RCMP was the main law enforcement. The fire station was right next door, and we shared staff rooms. The woman I was subbing for was like a regular office manager but with access to files and experience with the criminal system. Utmost discretion and privacy was upheld.

I had taken some business courses to please my mom before I became a cop, so that helped me understand the job and one of the reasons I was asked to help out. I found myself enjoying it. There was enough to do without being overwhelmed. I got to be with cops and other first responders, and I was still contributing. I didn't want to admit it, but being behind the scenes, I felt safer than I did when out on patrol, even here in the small area.

I knew Chase and my mom liked the fact that I was working inside the station rather than out, although they had both been very circumspect with their comments. When I told Chase I was doing it again this week, he had smiled widely before schooling his features and telling me it was good of me to agree. Mom hadn't hidden her relief quite as well, but she was also not really herself.

In Chase's words, she'd been "Dom-inated."

I wasn't sure how I felt about my mom and Dom. The events of the weekend kept flipping through my head as I sorted some reports, getting them ready for filing. Her reaction to Dom was interesting. She admitted to me that despite trying not to, she liked him. A lot.

"He is so incredibly hot," she whispered to me when I went to check

on her after he had left on Sunday. She was sitting on my bed, her lips once again swollen, her hair a mess, and a dazed look on her face.

"Did you sleep with him?" I asked.

She blinked and looked at me, straight in the eye. "Not a lot of sleep happened, Hannah."

I found myself laughing at her admission. "You like him."

"He's not my type," she insisted. "He's a reformed bad boy who hasn't completely given up that edge," she mused. "He's bossy and determined. Dom is the right name for him. He gets what he wants." She paused. "Everywhere."

"I see." I wasn't sure what else to say. Mom and I had always been close. She hadn't started dating for almost ten years after my dad passed. She'd tell me about failed date after failed date, laughing with me over some of the men she'd go out with. Boring. Dull. Too much. Too fast. They ranged in their differences, with one thing in common: Mom wasn't interested.

I had a feeling even though she was fighting it, Dom was different.

"But he is so sweet," she murmured. "Thoughtful. Giving. I haven't felt like a sexy woman in years. Since your dad. Last night, I was reminded of the fact that I was." She swallowed. "Several times."

"Um…"

She kept talking. "And he came in here and reminded me again."

At what was my no-doubt horrified expression, she waved her hand. "We didn't. But the man can kiss. And what a dirty talker." She fanned herself. "My, my, my."

I laughed again. "If you like him, and he likes you, why are you fighting it?"

"He lives here. I live in Toronto. I am too old to be in a casual hookup, whenever-you're-in-town woman. I don't want that."

"Is that what Dom wants? He seems pretty steady."

"Long-distance relationships are too hard, jellybean."

"Not if you really want them."

She shrugged. "I'm not sure I do."

I thought she was full of it, but I didn't push her. I wanted her happy. I almost pointed out there were salons here as well. That she could move here and be close to me, but it was too early in the relationship to push that angle. I had to let her figure it out the same way she stepped aside and let me figure out my life. But I did plan on getting to know Dom a little more. I intended to take him up on his lunch offer. And if everything went according to plan, he'd be at the house this weekend to work on the roof. Maybe I would get Mom to come back out so we could work on the garden at the same time.

I grinned at my thoughts. I was sure Chase would agree to help me. I knew he admired Dom a lot, and I was certain he would like to see them together.

I'd discuss it with him tonight at home.

I moved on to the next set of files with a smile tugging on my mouth.

Chase.

I hadn't expected him. I hadn't expected us. I had hoped to get to know him. To discover if he liked me the way I liked him. I never thought the inferno between us would be so fast or so intense. Not long ago, I had thought it had been a mistake to even try—that I needed to move out and forget my fledgling feelings. Now, I was in his bed, wrapped tight in his arms every night. I thought about him all the time. He admitted he felt the same about me. He was protective, caring, sexy, and funny. The whole package.

And he was mine.

Yesterday after my mom left, I washed the sheets and made up the bed. Chase watched me, trying to help with his clumsy attempts. I had seen him dismantle an engine. Watched him work a pattern in leather that was intricate and perfect. But tuck in a sheet? He was helpless.

"She only slept in the bed one night," he said. "You could have just made it up for her for next time."

"I prefer clean sheets." I shrugged, tugging on the blanket to straighten it out. Chase was behind me in an instant, spinning me in his arms.

"You aren't sleeping in here tonight. Or tomorrow."

I blinked up at his vehemence. "I'm not?"

"No. You sleep in our bed, down the hall, with me. I decree this the guest room now, unless you're pissed at me."

"You decree? Like a king or something?" I laughed, teasing him. His words made my heart soar. I wanted to sleep with him. I felt safe and protected. Wanted and adored.

"Damn right. King of this castle." He swept me up in his arms. "And you are my freaking queen. You sleep beside me. End of story."

He tossed me on his—our—bed and crawled on top, hovering over me. "You hear me, Cinnamon?"

"Shouldn't that be Queen Cinnamon?" I murmured, running my finger along his jaw.

His eyes darkened, becoming heated.

"You are," he agreed. "So I am going to worship you."

I felt my cheeks flush as I recalled how hard he had worshiped me. A throat clearing startled me, and I looked up into the eyes of the chief. He smiled at me. "Catching up on the filing, Hannah?"

"Yes."

"Martha will appreciate all your efforts. She hasn't been well."

"I'm sorry to hear that."

He nodded. "She'll be back soon, but to be honest, I don't know if she'll stay. I think her husband wants her to retire."

"Oh, that's too bad. She keeps this place organized."

He scratched his chin. "You interested in the position?"

"What?"

"Running the office. Straight days. Benefits are good—even better than you have now. Steady pay, steady hours, great holidays." He met my gaze. "Safer, easier on the nerves."

The chief knew my history. We'd talked about it in depth when I came for the interview. He asked me point-blank if I was going to be hiding here. I guaranteed him I wouldn't. I still wanted to be a cop but admitted the less-dangerous aspect appealed to me.

"But I can still perform my duties effectively." I had assured him.

He had nodded, and I was grateful he'd given me a chance.

I frowned at his offer. Two years ago, I would have said no. Before the incident, I would never have considered coming to a small town, working in an environment so different from what I was used to. Now I was actually contemplating not being a cop. It startled me.

"Um, I'm not sure. I would have to think on it."

"Of course. Martha isn't a hundred percent sure yet. But if she decided to leave, you are the top candidate for the job. You can do it easily. Maybe help in other ways with your experience. You're smart and clever. You think it over, and we'll talk."

"All right."

He walked away, and I mulled over his words. I looked around the office. Unlike the building in Toronto, it was small, housing only a dozen people maximum at any time. Dispatch was located down the hall. We serviced half a dozen small towns, located close together. The front main desk was staffed by one person. The waiting room had four chairs. Most days, there were two cruisers out, three if the towns were busy, but that was rare. Only two officers were in-house all the time for walk-ins, and one worked the front desk. The fire department and EMS were equally as small. But it was well-run and organized.

If Martha left and I took the job, I would no longer be a cop. I wasn't sure how I felt about that. I needed to think about it. Discuss it with Mom. Chase. I was already certain what their reactions would be. I had to weigh the pros and cons myself and make sure I was doing what made me happy.

Oddly enough, I wasn't sure if it was the same thing I thought made me happy before.

I tucked the information into the back of my mind and concentrated on the task at hand.

The week went by fast. Chase was in a great mood, excited about the roof project on the weekend. There were no Dan sightings—even at work. I was grateful and decided he'd gotten over his tantrum and moved on. Friday, Chase and I went shopping and bought food to feed everyone for the next couple of days. It would be all hands on deck, so to speak, with all the projects. Mom was coming out in the morning. Rosa and Mack were minding the kids, and Maxx had a couple of junior mechanics at the garage, so we were going to be going at it early and hard. When I said that to Chase in the store, he had grinned and grabbed me, yanking me close.

"That's what I plan to do before they all arrive in the morning."

He made me laugh, kissing me hard before letting me go so we could finish shopping.

The supplies had arrived, and during the week, Chase and Dom had taken the small deck off the back and had begun the removal of the roof shingles. Dom was sure with everyone helping, they would get the roof done and start framing the deck. The weather promised to be perfect, and Chase was looking forward to the weekend. We got home and unloaded the groceries, eating some Chinese food we'd picked up. We sat on the sofa, eating with chopsticks, sipping pop from a can. Relaxed. Easy. I loved how easy it was with him.

Chase's phone buzzed, and he looked at it with a wide grin.

"Dom's bringing a couple of friends who have experience with roofs. That'll make it go even faster. We can split up and do the deck supports and the roof at the same time."

"Awesome," I agreed.

"I hope the neighbors don't get upset at all the bikes parked in front of the house," he mused. "I'm sure Maxx and Stefano will be on theirs too if the weather is going to be good."

"You don't have a motorcycle."

"No." He chewed and swallowed a mouthful of noodles. "I don't like them. I mean, they're beautiful to look at, fun to work on, but not for me."

"Really?" I said, surprised. "I would have thought, surrounded by them, you'd ride one."

He finished his dinner, wiping his mouth. "I watched a friend of mine die from a motorcycle accident. I've never had the desire to climb on one."

I reached over, grasping his hand. "Chase, sweetheart, I'm sorry."

He smiled ruefully, looking down at our hands. "I know Maxx and Stefano are careful. Dom too. They respect the machine and the power. They wear the safety equipment. Obey the laws. But I've never been able to get past what I witnessed. I tried. I signed up for lessons, thinking if I could ride one, I would get over my anxiety. But I couldn't. Every time I was on the bike, my fear kicked in, and I froze. My instructor told me I would never be safe driving with that sort of worry on my mind all the time—and he was right."

Chase sighed. "I think there are some fears you simply cannot get over. You accept that and move on. Riding a motorcycle is one for me."

I squeezed his hand, and he looked up at me, the sorrow in his expression tugging on my heart. "It's okay," I assured him. "I think it takes a great deal of strength to admit your fear. How old was your friend?"

"Eighteen. His dad gave him the bike. It was too big and powerful for him. He was showing off, going too fast, not wearing his helmet. I told him to stop, but he laughed and told me it was a dirt road. Grass. Nothing could happen. He was trying to impress a girl. He skidded, flew off." He swallowed. "That dirt road and grass were hiding some rocks. He smashed his head and died two days later in the hospital. His dad never forgave himself. He moved away, and I lost my friend and the only adult figure I admired. Wes had even more influence on me, and I let him. I was grieving, and I didn't care."

"This was before you met Ellen?"

"Yes."

I set aside my dinner and crawled onto his lap, embracing him. He wrapped his arms around me, holding tight. He had suffered so much growing up. He was abandoned, alone, and lost. That he was such an amazing human being was a miracle.

"I'm sorry about your friend. I didn't mean to bring up such a bad memory."

He held me closer. "Thank you for listening. I rarely talk about him."

I sat back, holding his face between my hands. "You can talk to me about anything, Chase."

He smiled, turning his face to kiss my palm. "Will you call me sweetheart again?"

"If you want."

"I liked it."

"Then I guess you have a new nickname. Cinnamon and sweetheart."

He laughed. "I like that too." He paused. "Can I really tell you anything?"

"Yes."

He met my eyes, his anxious but determined. "I'm falling in love with you, Hannah."

My breath caught.

"I can't imagine my life without you. I know it's fast, and I know you don't feel the same way. But I hope you do one day. I thought maybe if you knew, it would help somehow." He shrugged. "Maybe I'm being stupid, but—"

I silenced him, pressing a finger on his mouth. "You aren't stupid, Chase. I'm falling for you too. So hard."

For a moment, there was silence. I watched his eyes change. The anxiety left his expression, and joy replaced it. Wonder. A smile broke out on his face. "Really?" he whispered.

I smiled back at him. "I would say I'm beyond falling."

"Say it, then, Hannah. Please say it."

"I love you."

He crushed me to him, burying his face into my neck. "I love you too." He kissed me, trapping my face between his hands. He kissed me again. "So much, Cinnamon. You mean so much, I can't even begin to express it. And it's going to grow. I know it. You're already my world. You're going to become my universe."

He kissed me again and held me. I felt the dampness of his tears on my skin, and I clutched him close. I liked the fact that he was emotional and not afraid to show me. To express his feelings. He wasn't alone now, and he never would be again.

I wasn't going anywhere.

Ever.

CHAPTER TWENTY

Chase

The sounds of laughter and the constant thud of hammers pounding and saws buzzing filled the air. Music played, the beat drifting across the yard. Men were on the roof, working hard. Dom and I had been pleased to find no damage under the old shingles we'd stripped off. The new membrane had been easy to install, and the shingles I had chosen were being fitted. His crew were old hands at this, and I was enjoying learning. Manny and Bruce were good people, even if they looked like hard-core bikers. Covered in tattoos with beards and dressed in their leathers, they could appear intimidating, but they were soft-spoken, articulate, and friendly. Knowledgeable. They sat down, having a cup of coffee and a bagel before starting the job, offering advice, and talking cars with Maxx, Stefano, Dom, and me. They liked Charly, calling her a little spitfire and making her laugh. They were respectful to Gabby and thanked Hannah and Cherry for their breakfast before starting to work, strapping on tool belts after discarding their jackets.

At the back of the house, Maxx and Stefano were pouring the footings for the new deck. The building permit I had obtained hung at the door in case I was questioned. Since we were adding to the deck, it was required. It went through fast since I knew the woman at city hall and she was a good customer, and the deck was simple and the plans accurate. I was still waiting for some of the supplies, but getting the footings done today and maybe some of the framing would make the rest of the job easier.

I glanced down at the backyard. Hannah and the other women had been working on the gardens, planting some new crops and filling the raised beds I had made with flowers. The barbecue was lit, and I knew lunch would be made shortly. We had burgers and sausage to grill. Potato salad and coleslaw. A huge pizza Rosa had sent over with Charly when she'd dropped off the kids with the older folks to care for while we worked. Cherry had brought a cake. Hannah had made cookies and muffins. Gabby brought a pasta salad.

No one would go hungry.

I watched Hannah bend to plant a colorful pot of flowers. Her ass looked particularly curvy in the shorts she was wearing today. I wanted to be as close to her as I could be every moment, and the yard separating us felt like miles not feet. She straightened, brushed off her hand and turned, catching me looking in her direction. She shielded her eyes. "Get to work, Donner. Enough ogling," she called, teasing.

I laughed. "Making sure you're doing it right, Cinnamon."

"Whatever, sweetheart," she replied.

My heart swelled. I loved it when she called me that. It was still so new. This feeling inside me was still so new. She loved me. Me. Chase Donner. And I loved her. Everything about her. All the wonderful things I knew to be Hannah Gallagher enchanted me. I looked forward to all the things I had yet to discover.

I bent, shifting another shingle into place. I looked to my right, catching Dom staring down, and I followed his gaze. Cherry was at the barbecue, cooking. Her hair was bright in the sunlight, a different red from Charly's or Hannah's. More rust. She was dressed in shorts and a T-shirt like Hannah, and I had the feeling Dom approved of her attire.

He was staring at her with intense focus on his face. She looked up toward the roof, freezing when she saw him. He laughed quietly when she turned her head, lowering her eyes.

"Stubborn woman," he murmured. "Keep it up." He looked at me, winking as he stepped closer. "Makes victory all that much sweeter."

I shook my head. "Maybe she doesn't want to be your victory."

"Not what her mouth was saying this morning. Or last week when I took her out to dinner."

"You took her out to dinner?"

He nodded. "I couldn't wait a week to see her. I went into Toronto, and we had dinner. I came back the next morning." He winked. "I left her satisfied."

"TMI, Dom. TMI."

He chuckled. "She's still fighting it, though. Lots of BS about long-distance relationships and our age, blah, blah, blah. We'll figure it out. We're too compatible not to."

"You serious about her?"

"Totally."

"Huh. Must be the Gallagher effect."

He clapped me on the shoulder. "Yep. We've been Gallagher-ized."

I laughed. "I told Hannah her mom had been 'Dominated.'"

He burst out laughing, the sound loud and carefree. Hannah and her mom glanced our way, and Cherry said something to Hannah, tossing her hair the way she did when annoyed. I noticed she tossed her hair a lot around Dom.

"What are you two planning?" Hannah called out.

"Wondering when lunch is gonna be," I called back. "I'm starving, Cinnamon."

"Keep your shirt on, Donner," she replied. "It's coming."

I chuckled and set another shingle into place. I wiped my hand across my forehead. It was hot, sweaty work. Dom and I labored for a bit, smelling the aroma of meat grilling, both of us thrilled when lunch was announced. We got cleaned up and gathered around the tables the women had set up. Maxx had brought extra chairs, and the large tree provided a decent amount of shade for everyone to sit under and enjoy their food.

The only sound for a while was the music playing on the speaker, the rough perfection of Creedence Clearwater Revival drifting through the air, and the muffled sounds of people eating. Chewing and swallowing. Muttered compliments, muted groans of appreciation. Sighs of satisfaction when plates were empty and stomachs full.

I surveyed what had been accomplished. The small group gathered to help. I felt the appreciation well inside me for their help. Intense pride filled me at the thought of improving my own place. Making the house better for me and Hannah. Happiness that I had the chance to experience all this camaraderie.

And then a man appeared, looking far too official to be lost. He was short, bald, and rotund, wearing a suit and carrying a tablet under his arm and a measuring tape clipped to his pocket. I stood with a frown. Dom, Maxx, and Stefano all stood beside me. "Can I help you?"

He approached me, handing me a card. "I was called about an unlicensed build happening."

"No, sir. I have a building permit."

He walked with me, and I got the permit, showing it to him. He checked it over, made some measurements, asked a couple of questions, then nodded, and closed his tablet. "All looks in order. I think maybe one of your neighbors took exception and made a call. I'll make my report as passed." He handed me a card. "Thanks for your cooperation." He shrugged out of his jacket, wiping his head. "Now I'm off for the day."

"Can I offer you a burger and a soda?" Hannah asked beside me. "Since you're off the clock and all? We're about to have cake."

His eyes glowed. "Cake?"

She nodded. "Pound cake with fresh strawberries."

He hesitated. "I did miss lunch because of this call."

Charly linked her arm with his. "Come join us for a bite, then."

They walked away, and I glanced at Dom. "Neighbor, my ass."

"Exactly my thoughts."

Just then a cop walked around the side of the house. I cursed under my breath. He approached us with a nod, removing his hat. It wasn't Dan, but I didn't recognize him.

"Sorry to bother. We had a complaint about a noise violation and a loud party of bikers going on at this address." He looked around. "Looks more like a bunch of friends helping out to me."

Hannah returned, looking surprised. "Ben, what are you doing here?"

He smiled at her. "Hannah." He repeated what he'd told us. Maxx walked over and shook his hand. "Ben. What brings you here?"

"Bullshit is what brings him," Hannah muttered. "A bogus call." She met my gaze.

"Why would someone do that?" Ben asked.

"Spite," I muttered.

"The same reason someone sent a permit inspector. To embarrass us in front of our neighbors," Hannah said, sounding furious.

"You live here?" he asked.

She wrapped her arm around my waist. "Yes. Chase and I live here."

"Well, congrats. Sorry to spoil the party. I had to check it out. Obviously, someone had the wrong address. I'll have

the call checked. Nothing but friends helping friends here."
He inhaled. "And sharing some great food."

"Come have a burger and a soda," I offered.

"I couldn't."

"Sure you can. Take it to go if you have to. There is plenty."

"I could radio in I'm taking a break."

"Do that," Hannah urged. "Come sit for a few minutes."

He agreed, and soon the group had two more guests. The cop and the building inspector, no doubt sent by OD to piss us off and hopefully stop what we were doing.

Listening to the two men laugh and watching them eat the food we gave them with gusto, I was sure we'd spoiled his endeavors.

The satisfaction I got from that made me smile.

Later that night, Hannah snuggled into my side, laughing as I groaned and wrapped my arm around her. Or tried to.

"I can't tonight, Cinnamon. My body is killing me."

"You were so hot today, working on the roof, sweating, your muscles rippling," she murmured.

"I have no idea how the rest of the guys feel. They all seemed fine. I am way out of shape, I guess." I ached everywhere, but the roof was done. Many hands made it go fast. The deck was framed. It had been a productive, and exhausting, day.

She shook her head. "Everyone was sore, I think. Even Dom was off his game. He kissed Mom goodbye and didn't attempt to drag her with him."

"He'll be back in the morning. Did you know they had dinner last week?"

"Mom mentioned it today."

"I think Dom is pretty serious about her. You Gallagher women are hard to resist."

She smirked, kissing my chest. She trailed her fingers down my torso, light and teasing. "It's futile."

I pressed a kiss to her head. "I'm not trying."

She hummed and was quiet for a moment. "I'm talking to my boss."

I knew what she meant. "We don't know it was him. There's no proof."

"Far too coincidental. He knows where we live. I told him to stay away, and he doesn't want me ratting on him. He thinks I'm too stupid to figure out that a cop and building permit inspector show up? A noise violation? Seriously. None of your neighbors would do that. They all love you."

"I agree it was OD, but we have no proof. Going to your boss now isn't a good plan."

She sat up, looking down at me with a confused look. "OD?"

"Yeah. Officer Dickface. OD for short."

She blinked, then began to laugh. Her shoulders shook with the force of her merriment. "Oh my God, that's priceless."

"Dom made it up."

She settled against my chest again, her cheek pressed on my skin. I ran my fingers through her thick hair, enjoying the silkiness of the waves. We were quiet for a bit, and I thought she had fallen asleep. She'd worked hard all day as well. But she glanced up, our eyes meeting. Her gaze was soft and warm. I stroked her cheek.

"There's a music festival next weekend in Townshead. I saw the poster when I was there last week. You wanna go? Some great bands lined up. There's a fair too."

"I'd love that."

"Okay. We'll head up after I close the garage."

"Sounds perfect."

She was quiet again. She traced her fingers over my chest, slowly stroking. Lower and lower she went, until her hand slipped under my waistband. "Someone isn't that tired," she whispered.

"Baby, he is always ready for you, but I don't think I can."

She moved, straddling me. I groaned at the feel of her heat even through the material that separated us. As usual, she wore no underwear, and her desire was evident. "What if I do all the work?"

"Jesus, you really want me," I hissed.

"Seeing you today? All manly and wielding a hammer? Using the saw? All sweaty and hot? You were so...*virile*. I wanted you then, and I want you now. You lie there, and I'll take care of you for a change."

"I want it to be good for you," I protested.

She hovered over my lips, her breath tickling my skin. "Trust me, it will be."

"Then I'm all yours."

She grinned as she pulled her pretty nightgown over her head then tugged my sleep pants off, pushing them down my legs and straddling me again.

"Yes, Chase Donner, you are."

She dropped, her heat encasing me. I arched my back with a groan that was part pleasure and part pain. The pleasure was rapidly winning out, though. Especially when she began to move.

"All mine."

CHAPTER TWENTY-ONE

Hannah

As the week passed, I grew more determined to do something about the situation. Dan wasn't around much, yet somehow his presence permeated the station. I saw him talking to some of the EMS guys, yet when I went into the room, he was gone. He walked past me into the locker room on Wednesday afternoon, and as soon as I finished with the phone call I was on, I hurried in, only to find it vacant.

The bastard knew I had something to say to him, and he was avoiding me. Luckily, there had been no other interactions between him and Chase, and he knew better than to try to pull something on me. Thursday, I was handing out paystubs, and I heard Dan radio in to dispatch the fact that he was taking a break for dinner. He gave his location, and I informed the other woman in the office that I was leaving early to run an errand. I hadn't taken a break all day, so she smiled and waved me off.

I found Dan sitting on a picnic bench behind the local drive-in burger stand. He was eating his dinner, not paying much attention to what was going on around him. When I slid across from him, he looked up, surprised. He frowned and picked up his burger. "What?" he asked shortly.

"Stop it, Dan. Stop all this nonsense. Trying to catch Chase doing something illegal. Sending cops and inspectors to the house. Just stop it." I shook my head. "It's beneath you."

"I don't know what you're talking about." He denied my words, but the tips of his ears turned a dull pink.

"I always thought you were a nice guy. We got along well. I thought we were friends."

"I thought we were more than that," he snapped.

"Why?" I asked, bewildered. "Because we had coffee? Because we talked?"

"You gave me signals."

"Signals?" I questioned.

"You were friendly. Overly so. You brought me coffee. You always stopped to say hello."

"I'm always friendly. I brought a lot of people coffee. I brought the entire station pizza one day. No one took that for anything but what it was. And I say hello to everyone. It's not a big station, Dan. It's not my fault you read something into it that wasn't there. When you asked me out, I said no. I made it clear I don't date fellow officers and that I wasn't interested. You're the one who refused to see the truth."

He didn't respond, stuffing fries into his mouth.

"Don't make me go to the boss."

"You have no proof."

"I'll tell him what has happened. I was there the other night. It was uncalled-for."

He slammed his hand on the table. "He's an ex-con, Hannah. He's been in jail. A lowlife. That's what you want to date? To live with? You chose him over me? A criminal instead of a cop?"

I stood, looking down at him. "Chase did his time. He accepted the consequences of his actions, and he paid the price. He's not the boy who went to jail. He grew up and learned his lesson. Sounds to me like you're still stuck in high school. You have no claim on me. There was never a relationship. I didn't choose him over you, because you were never in the picture except as a friend and a coworker." I paused. "Where is your empathy? The idea that people get second chances? I always assume the best in people."

"You're naïve."

"You're jaded and angry. Take that somewhere else, Dan. Leave Chase and me alone."

"And if I don't?"

"I'll make a formal complaint. You should know I would have already, but Chase asked me not to."

"Wasn't that sweet of him," he spat. "He didn't let his girlfriend fight his battles."

"I love him," I said. "So, you come after him, you come after me."

He gaped at me. "You *love* him? That—that *degenerate*? Are you crazy?"

"That degenerate, as you call him, is warm and kind. Treats me like a queen. Respects me. He is someone you should strive to be, not someone you should try to destroy."

He stood, shutting his takeout container. "If you're done with your lecture, I'm leaving."

I laid a hand on his arm to stop him from leaving. "Dan. Please. For the sake of our working relationship and the friendship we had, stop this."

He looked down at my hand and shook it off. "There is no friendship. You made your choice."

His cruiser shook with the force of his slamming the door. Dust and gravel were kicked up as he tore out of the parking lot and disappeared around the corner.

I blew out a long breath. I thought I could appeal to the good side of Dan. The one I thought he had. Appeal to him person-to-person—even cop-to-cop. That blew up in my face.

I had a feeling I'd just made it worse.

Chase looked thoughtful when I told him later what had transpired between Dan and me. "I shouldn't have done it. I thought I could reason with him." I met Chase's understanding gaze. "I had no idea he felt so strongly for me." I sighed. "Or his level of contempt. We're taught that everyone can turn over a new leaf. Ex-cons deserve our respect as much as someone with a clean record, unless they prove themselves to be unchanged. A repeat offender." I ran a hand through my hair. "And you have changed. I know it. I know the man you are. I don't understand him."

"He's angry. Angrier than I expected. You might not have seen it, Hannah, but he obviously had feelings for you. What you thought of as a coworker and friendship, he put more significance on. He's furious you didn't return his affection and that you chose someone he feels isn't worthy of you."

"And he is?"

Chase shrugged. "In his mind, yes."

I sighed, and Chase pulled me into the crook of his arm. I nestled against him, resting my head on his shoulder. It amazed me how right it always felt to be close to him, how natural and at home I was. "When did you get so smart?" I asked.

He chuckled, pressing a kiss to my head. "Charly taught me."

I laughed. "She is clever."

He nodded, his voice becoming serious. "Be careful around him, Hannah, okay? I don't want him to turn his anger on you."

"I will."

He pressed a kiss to my head. "Good. Just avoid him. Maybe now you've told him we're serious, he'll back off."

"I hope so." I yawned.

Chase smiled. "Tired, baby?"

"I am."

"You go back to patrol next week?"

"Yes. With holidays, the shifts have changed. I'm on two to ten."

He frowned. "I'll hardly see you."

"It's not for long."

He shifted. "I don't like the thought of you working at night."

"I'll be fine, Chase. Trust me, it's fairly boring. Even more so than days. The occasional call, but not much. And if it's a serious call, two cars are dispatched. I have backup."

"I still don't like it."

"It's what I do," I reminded him gently.

"I know. But I'll worry."

I turned and ran my finger over the crease in his forehead. "I'll be fine." I paused. "I have something to tell you."

He frowned and grabbed my hand. "What is it? Are you okay?"

I told him about Martha. The possibility of being the office manager for the building.

"Are you interested?" he asked.

"I don't know."

"Is it normal to have a manager in a police station?"

"We're run a little differently here. They have everything together in one place, under the same umbrella, so to speak. Some small towns only have a station, very few officers. We service a larger area, so we have more staff and items to manage. Martha is a civilian, so I wouldn't be a cop anymore."

His shoulders dropped. "So that's a no."

"I didn't say that. I haven't decided yet. I don't even know if Martha has made up her mind. I would have to get all the particulars once she does and talk to my boss." I studied his face. "You want me to take it, don't you?"

"I want you to be happy."

"Chase, be honest."

"Yes, if you took a clerical job where you'd be safer and came home every night, I would like that. But if it makes you miserable and unfulfilled, then no. I think you'd be great at it, given your business degree, and I agree with your boss. You might bring something extra to the job. Maybe you could work with the cops on how to improve the way it is run." He shrugged. "Or I can just shut up and know you'd be happiest as a cop and accept it."

I leaned close and kissed him. "Thank you. The way you worry is rather sweet."

"I do worry. I'll always worry. No matter how safe the area is, there is always a risk. But I won't be the guy who asks you to stop being who you are. I love you too much for that, Hannah."

I threw my arms around his neck and kissed him in gratitude. His support and love meant everything to me. I knew he worried. So did my mom. But he was right; I had to do what was best for me.

"I'll think about it once Martha decides, and we'll talk again."

He held me close. "Okay, Cinnamon. Okay."

CHASE

Hannah swayed to the music, lifting her arms in the air. I linked my hands around her waist, pulling her close and swaying with her. It had been the perfect day. After I closed the garage, we jumped in the truck and headed to the music festival. It was packed, and we had to park on the edge of a farmer's field with some other latecomers. I had a feeling when we got back later that night, it would be even fuller with the people who only came for the evening concert. We strolled to the festival and spent the afternoon listening to the free music, visiting the stalls and buying some local crafts, and eating our weight in food. Sticky ribs from the barbecue place, handmade chips from another stall. A spicy turkey leg from a Middle Eastern vendor who assured me it wasn't "too" spicy. It took two lemonades and a cold beer to put out the fire. Hannah laughed her ass off at me. We ate mini donuts and an apple dumpling doused in caramel sauce. We trekked back to the truck twice to toss the bags with the purchases from the stalls into the rear seat. As I thought, the field was fuller now, the cars and trucks parked everywhere. I looked again for someone to pay but never saw anyone. The truck was under a tree, and I put down the tailgate and Hannah and I sat in the shade, sipping on lemonade and eating the last of the donuts. Hannah licked her fingers and groaned.

"No more food."

I laughed. "Okay, Cinnamon. But you were eyeing the brisket and pulled pork sliders earlier."

"Maybe after the concert."

I kissed her head. "Whatever you want."

"Those pictures will look so good in the hall," she said enthusiastically. "And the place mats so good on the table."

"Yep."

She sighed, leaning her head on my shoulder. "Such a great day, Chase. It's been so much fun."

She was right. It had been great.

The band revved up for their last number—a rock ballad that had been huge in the eighties. I spun her in my arms, and we swayed to the music, kissing under the stars and not caring who saw us. The song ended, and the applause was loud. We waited patiently as the crowds dispersed, surprised when we bumped into Stefano and Gabby.

"I didn't know you were here," I said.

He grinned. "We love these festivals. Maxx and Charly are here too somewhere."

"I assume Mack and Rosa have the kids?"

"Yep." He glanced at Hannah. "I think I saw your mom and Dom too."

Hannah's eyebrows shot up. "Really?"

"I was sure it was them, but I lost them in the crowd."

"Huh," I muttered. "He never mentioned it earlier at the garage."

Hannah pouted a little. "Neither did Mom when I spoke to her yesterday."

"Ah, those crazy kids," Stefano chuckled.

I had to laugh. "Yep."

"Where're you parked?"

"The field at the edge."

"We're going for sliders first," Hannah interjected.

"Oh, sounds good."

"Come join us."

"Join you for what?" Charly appeared at my elbow.

I laughed, dropping my arm around her shoulder. "Sliders."

"Ooh, good idea."

"No curfew tonight?"

She smiled widely. "Nope. Rosa and Mack have all the kids tonight. Mary and Larry were there for the day. We're going over in the morning for brunch and to pick up the kids."

Stefano laughed. "Theo won't want to come home. He never does."

Maxx chuckled. "Ours are the same. They get spoiled."

"So, sliders for six, then?" I asked.

"Let's go!"

The crowds dwindled as we ate our late snacks. We ordered a bunch of items, creating our own little buffet of delicious messiness. We ate sliders and cheese fries. Chicken bites and burnt ends. More mini donuts Hannah simply had to have. All were eaten with our fingers, with plenty of napkins to wipe up the gooeyness. We sat at two picnic tables, watching as the fair began to shut down and the late-nighters walked around, enjoying the benefits of the quieter grounds. Music still played, and the rides were running for at least another hour. We talked about the concert, the crafts, and the day. It felt great to be part of the conversation, sharing the time I spent with Hannah instead of being on the fringes of the day. Tagging along with one of the couples. Today, I was one of them. I slipped an arm around Hannah, tucking her to my side and pressing a kiss to her forehead.

"What was that for?" she asked, a donut held between her fingers and cinnamon-sugar on her lips. I bent and kissed her again, tasting the sweetness on her mouth.

"For being you."

She smiled at me. "Carry on, then."

"I love you," I murmured. "You make me so happy."

"I love you too."

"You ready to go home?"

She put her lips close to my ear. "You gonna sex me up when we get there?"

I turned my head, meeting her beautiful eyes. "Definitely."

"Let's go."

I hopped off the table, holding out my hand. "We're off."

Stefano stood. "We're parked in the field too. We'll walk with you."

Maxx looked over at Charly, slinging his arm around her shoulder. "Come on, Red. Let's walk the kids to their car."

We laughed, strolling toward the vehicles, acting like goofballs. The girls laughed as we played tag, using them to shield us as we tried to avoid being "it." The game was silly and juvenile and fun. Maxx stopped walking as we got close to the spot my truck was parked, staring ahead. "You park on a hill, Chase?"

I frowned. "No, I don't think so."

Stefano tilted his head. "The angle is odd. You must have."

We drew closer, and my stomach twisted as Hannah gasped. "Did a tree branch break?"

Across the hood was a big branch, broken and twisted. My windshield was cracked, a large dent in the metal and the paint destroyed.

"Fuck," Maxx muttered.

"Holy shit," Stefano added, walking closer. "Your tires are blown out. That's why the angle is off."

I stared at the truck and walked around it. Nothing else was damaged. It appeared the huge tree limb snapped off and fell on my hood by accident.

But when I lifted my phone, using the flashlight to inspect the tree limb, I had my doubts. Stefano stood beside me. "Would a tree limb falling really blow out the tires?" I asked quietly.

"Highly doubtful."

"Does some of the end of the tree look as though it was cut?" I wondered out loud. "Deliberately?"

"Hard to tell in this light, but I would say yes."

Maxx joined us. "I phoned the tow truck company and called in a favor. They'll be here shortly."

Stefano spoke up. "You head home, Maxx. Hannah and Chase can catch a ride with us." He kept his voice low. "We're taking the damn tree limb with us."

Hannah came over. "Chase, I'm so sorry!"

I didn't want to worry her. I pulled her close. "I'm glad we weren't in it when it happened. We'll get it towed and go home with Stefano and Gabby."

Charly joined us, staring at the vehicle. "Aren't those new tires?"

"Yes."

She looked up. "The tree looks pretty healthy to me."

I nodded grimly.

Hannah frowned. "You mean this wasn't an accident?"

"We don't know that," I assured her.

"But how? Why?" she said, then covered her mouth. "No."

I sighed. "Let's not jump to conclusions."

"But it's what you think. That Dan did this. That he is responsible. How would he even know we were here?"

I shrugged. "He could have seen us. Overheard you talking at work. Been here himself. Or followed us. I have no idea. We don't know for sure if it was on purpose or just a freak accident."

I looked at the truck.

"But I'm going to find out."

UNDER THE RADAR

Maxx and Stefano were already bent over the truck when I got there on Sunday morning. I left an exhausted Hannah asleep in our bed. She'd had nightmares all night, even with me holding her. At one point, she'd confessed she was afraid I was going to leave her because of what Dan was doing, and that was playing on her psyche.

"I'm not worth it," she sobbed. "If he did that, if he keeps doing things, you'll get tired of it."

I held her close, murmuring comforting words into her ear. "No, Cinnamon. He is not going to win. I will never let you go."

She'd finally fallen asleep, and I'd slipped out of bed, leaving her a note, and headed to the garage.

In the light, the damage was even more than I had thought the night before. The windshield was a given, but the hood was dented and damaged to the point I knew I would have to replace it. Luckily, nothing mechanical was impaired.

I hunched down, looking at the heavy limb we'd brought back to the garage. I ran my fingers over the edges. "I don't see saw marks."

"No," Stefano agreed, tracing his finger along the torn limb. "It has a split here and here." He ran his hand over the trunk. "These depressions bother me."

279

Another truck pulled up, and Dom swung out of the driver's seat, frowning. He joined us, rubbing his chin. "Wow."

"What are you doing here?"

"Hannah called her mom. I just dropped her off at your place. I came to see what I could do to help."

"Were you there last night?"

"Yeah, we were." He looked at me. "So was your friend."

"You saw Dan?"

He nodded. "Briefly."

"Fucker," I cursed.

Dom studied the branch, looked at the hood, and joined Maxx, who was checking out the tires. They stood. "Those tires were tampered with."

"So was the branch," Dom stated.

"How can you be sure?"

"I worked landscaping in my teens. Sometimes if a branch was broken enough, it simply needed encouragement to give way. I used to hang on to the limb above it and bounce on the broken one below until it snapped. When it gave way, I was safe, but the branch on the ground. I'd climb down." He shrugged with a grin. "Funner than using a saw."

"And no noise for people to notice last night."

"The tires were purposely cut. Probably a drill, used fast and sloppy to make it look like it blew. But these holes are deliberate."

"And I have zero proof."

My friends all nodded.

I tore off my beanie and scrubbed my head. "I'm getting sick and tired of this asshole. What was the point?"

"To inconvenience you," Maxx muttered.

"Annoy you," Stefano added.

"Cost you money. Piss you off," Dom mused.

"Mission accomplished on all the above. Thank God you guys were around."

Maxx laughed. "He hadn't counted on that. He thought you'd be stranded."

"I can't prove it was him."

"No. He's good. But I'm afraid we can't buff this one out, Chase. You'll have to drive a company truck for a while."

"Hannah wants to go to her chief with her suspicions."

They looked at each other, then Stefano spoke. "It could backfire."

"I know. I am hesitant."

Dom rubbed his chin, looking thoughtful. "She could just go with the facts. Your run-ins. Him abusing his position."

"But is he really? He's a cop. I'm a convict. His word against mine."

"You're not a convict," Maxx growled. "You made a fucking mistake, and it's in the past. Stop letting him throw you back there. If Charly hears you talking like that, she'll kick your ass."

I smiled ruefully, knowing he was right.

"And he was purposely following you. Anyone else doing ten over the limit on that road would have been left alone. Same with you in the parking lot. He was trumping things up."

"I'll see what happens this week. If anything else odd occurs, I'll go with Hannah and see her boss." I was getting weary of this asshole ruining everything Hannah and I did together. Inserting himself without even being there. Destroying the memories of what should be happy days. It was getting on my nerves, and I wanted it to stop. I hated that it upset Hannah. I hated that it made me angry, and I worried about losing it and doing something I regretted, which I knew was what he wanted. He thought if he pushed me enough, I would make a mistake and blow up and somehow give him what he needed to show Hannah I was nothing but a screw-up. That he was the better guy for her.

But he was wrong. I was the right man for Hannah, and for her, I would remain calm. But it didn't mean I wouldn't fight back if I had the chance.

Maxx met my eyes. "We'll be your character witnesses if needed. We've got your back, Chase."

Stefano and Dom nodded in agreement. I had to swallow the lump in my throat before responding.

"Thanks."

I glanced at my truck, hoping they wouldn't be needed. That I wouldn't have to go and talk to anyone. That the asshole didn't have anything else planned.

Even though, deep in my heart, I knew he did.

CHAPTER TWENTY-TWO

Hannah

I carried my lunch outside, sitting at one of the picnic tables set up at the back of the station. Last night, Chase had been in charge of making lunches, and when I opened my container, I saw he'd added an extra something. I opened the slightly oddly shaped heart, reading his little note.

> *Have a good day.*
> *Can't wait to see you at home later.*
> *Love you, Cinnamon.*
> *Chase xx*

I smiled, tucking the note into my pocket. He was sweet and wonderful. I picked up my sandwich, taking a bite and chewing it slowly. I had to admit, I wasn't looking forward to going back on patrol tomorrow. But Martha was back, at least for now, and that was my job. I stared at the trees swaying in the wind, wondering if I had always wanted to be a cop because of my dad and keeping his memory alive somehow, rather than wanting to really be a cop. My passion had waned, and I wasn't sure if it was still the lingering effects from the trauma or the fact that my life had changed so much.

Annette joined me at the picnic table, opening her lunch and chatting. "Hey, you. How's it going?"

"Good."

"How is that hunk of heaven you left the bar with? Still seeing him?"

I smiled. "He is actually my roommate, but yes, we're a couple now too. He had just stepped in to get me away from Dan. It sort of changed our dynamic."

Her eyebrows lifted. "I bet Dan didn't like that, did he?"

"No, he didn't."

We were quiet for a moment, eating. I leaned forward. "Can I ask you some advice?"

"Of course you can."

I paused, sorting out my words and how much to say. Then I told Annette about Dan. The things he'd been doing. The suspicions that he was behind the truck damage. She listened, looking thoughtful when I finished.

"I think I should tell the chief. But Chase is worried it'll cause more trouble or the boss will side with Dan."

She nodded, finishing her salad. "Dan transferred here about six months before you did. He came from Ottawa." She met my eyes. "I heard rumors the transfer was not something he wanted but had no choice other than to accept. I also heard there had been complaints against him."

I felt my eyes widen. "Oh."

"After he got here, there was another female officer who was new as well. Gail. They dated, and she ended it. She transferred out about a month after they broke up. I heard her tell someone she didn't want to be around Dan anymore —he was 'too much,' were her words. 'Over the top' and 'crazy-possessive' were other phrases I understand she used." Annette met my gaze. "I think Dan has a habit of holding on too tight, if you catch my drift."

I nodded.

"I don't think the chief would take Dan's side. I think you should tell him—even if it's off the record. Then if it escalates, he has something to go on. If nothing else happens, no harm done." She took a sip of her water. "My boss would want to know. He's very supportive, and he and your boss work well together. They're on the same wavelength."

Annette's boss was the fire chief, and she was right. Jed, her boss, and Henry, my boss, were both great leaders and had open-door policies. They ran the building as a unit, and it was a positive environment to work in.

I sighed. "You're right. I should."

"How is Chase handling it?"

"Better than I am, I have to admit. He's being coolheaded. I want to yell and tell Dan to stop being such an ass. He seems to be escalating."

"If he was responsible for the truck damage, I agree. You should talk to your chief ASAP."

"I will. This afternoon."

Henry sat back, regarding me thoughtfully. "I don't like the sounds of any of this, Hannah."

"I'm sorry."

He held up his hand. "Not what I meant. No one in my station should be harassed or have some personal vendetta played out against them using the badge. Chase should have made a complaint."

"He didn't want to." I drew in a deep breath. "He has a record."

He nodded. "I'm aware of who Chase Donner is. I was around when he was causing his mischief. I also know he's a changed man." He smiled kindly. "I was only an officer then, but he and his brother were holy terrors around here. I'm glad he got his life on track."

"He is a wonderful guy now. He left that life behind him."

"I'd like to talk to him." He held up his hand. "Off the record, as you requested."

I worried at my lip. "I'll ask him to come in."

"You do that. Until then, I'll stay quiet unless Dan steps out of line again." He frowned as he tapped a pen on his desk. "Obviously, I can't do anything about the truck unless there were witnesses."

"I don't think Chase wants to press charges of any kind. He just wants Dan to stop harassing him." I paused. "I heard maybe this isn't the first time Dan has overstepped."

Henry sat back, contemplating me. "Sometimes being a small station, you inherit problems from larger ones," he said slowly, neither confirming nor denying my statement.

"Like me."

He shook his head. "You were not a problem, then or now. You have an exemplary record. I consider you very brave, Hannah. Many officers, even seasoned ones, would not have returned after experiencing what you went through."

"Thank you."

He nodded and stood, indicating the meeting was over. "I will wait for you to talk to Chase. I'll be keeping an eye on Dan. And you."

"Thank you, sir."

I left his office, rounding the corner. Deep in my thoughts, I bumped into someone and stepped back, automatically apologizing. "I'm sorry, I…" I trailed off when I saw it was Dan. He looked at me, then glanced over my shoulder toward the chief's office. He narrowed his eyes.

"Telling tales, Hannah?"

"Nope. Meeting about schedules."

He obviously didn't believe me, but I met his gaze, keeping mine open and steady. He brushed past me roughly, pushing me out of the way, muttering under his breath. My shoulder hit the wall, and I gasped at the sudden sharp pain. The chief came out of his office.

"Officer Meyers!"

Dan stopped, glowering at me. The chief looked between us. "Although I'm certain you didn't mean to run into her, I believe you owe Officer Gallagher an apology for doing so."

"Sorry, Gallagher," Dan almost spat. "I didn't see you."

"Of course." I smiled at him. "I accept your *sincere* apology."

He turned and stormed off. The chief met my eyes.

"Watch yourself. And get Chase to call me."

I nodded and headed to my desk. I had a feeling Chase wasn't going to like the message.

CHASE

Hannah was jumpy all evening. She barely picked at her dinner, making an excuse of a big lunch, which made me laugh. It had been my turn to pack lunches, and I knew exactly what had been in her container. A sandwich, some carrots, and an apple were hardly a large meal. But I let it go, wanting her to tell me what was going on. After dinner, she was on the move, changing things around, swapping out knickknacks from one place to another, only to change them back. I heard her go into her old room and shut the door, calling her mother, I assumed. She looked resigned when she came out, sitting beside me on the sofa. I offered her some popcorn, and she took a handful, staring at the screen.

"The rest of the composite is arriving on Thursday. Dom and Stefano are going to come on Saturday, and we'll do the deck. His friends are going to come too, so it should go fast. One measuring, one cutting, two installing. We should get it done in a day," I informed her.

She nodded. "Okay. Good."

"As long as we don't have any surprise inspectors," I teased.

She looked at me, her eyes wide with anxiety.

"Hey." I leaned closer and brushed my knuckles down her cheek. "I was joking. We're all good."

"I did something you aren't going to like," she burst out.

I sat back with a frown. "Okay?" I questioned her, my mind going a thousand miles an hour. "What did you do? Order a new kitchen? Decide to hang pink curtains in here?"

"I talked to the chief about Dan."

That startled me. "Oh."

She turned, her shoulders tense, her voice thick. "Off the record. I talked to Annette, and she'd heard Dan might have done this before. She thought I should say something."

I blew out a breath. "Yeah, I suppose she was right." I took her hand when I realized she was still holding popcorn in her fist and massaged the knuckles. "Relax, Cinnamon. I'm not angry."

"You're not?"

"No. If Dan has been a pain to someone else, then Annette was right. And if you felt you could trust the chief and talk to him, then I trust you."

"Oh," she whispered, her shoulders dropping in relief.

"Hannah, did you really think I would be angry at you? I know you're trying to protect me."

"I was worried. I know with your record, you're sensitive. Henry—the chief—says he knows who you are."

I offered her a rueful smile. "I'm not surprised. I remember him as well from when he was only an officer. He was always fair."

"He says he's glad you turned your life around, and he just wants to talk to you off the record too, in case."

"Okay. I'll arrange to talk to him—outside the station if I can. The next two days are crazy. That delivery company Maxx has the new contract with is bringing in two dozen more vehicles the guy just purchased over the next couple of days for service. It'll be all hands on deck. Maxx wants to impress the owner, who is apparently a bit of a hardnose to deal with. But the contract means a huge boost to the bottom line for the garage. Maxx thinks if he goes above and beyond, this guy will give him another contract for a second business he is planning."

"That's great."

"It is. Maxx has accrued a lot of expenses to get this job. More tools, more staff, some specialized machines that were a huge cost, in order to work on their vehicles. But it will pay for itself in six months after Charly crunched the numbers—even faster now he has added more vehicles. So we'll all make sure this guy—Jim Albright—is impressed. So far, there have been no complaints, so I hope it continues. But I have to be around for the paperwork and oversee the guys."

"Okay. I'll tell the chief."

I shifted closer, draping my arm around her shoulders. "Relax, Cinnamon. I'm not upset. Everything is okay, and we're going to get through this."

"Any news on your truck?"

"Well, I found a hood in a junkyard on the other side of Toronto. It will be here next week. The windshield is ordered, and Stefano decided while it was being repaired to do some cool airbrushing on it. Until then, I'll drive the company truck, which I'm good with."

"Okay." She leaned her head on my shoulder.

"Are you worried about going back on patrol?"

"Not really. I'm surprised how much I enjoyed the office work, though. Learning more about how the station runs in conjunction with EMS and fire."

"Are you thinking of going for the job if Martha decides to retire?"

She sighed, glancing up. "Maybe. I keep wondering if I would regret it."

"Why don't you ask your boss if you could take a leave of absence for three months and try it? If you regret it, you can go back to being a cop. If you like it, you can stay."

She frowned. "That's a good idea. If he brings it up again, I'll ask."

I kissed her forehead. "You wanna have a bath and go to bed early?"

"Will you wash my back?"

"Yep. Anything else I think needs a good rubbing too."

She laughed, the sound light and sweet. I bent and kissed her mouth. "Go fill the tub. I'll be right behind you."

She stood, and I chuckled, holding out the bowl. "Drop the popcorn, Cinnamon."

She shook her head, stuffing it into her mouth and hurrying away. I watched her go with a smile.

I leaned my head back, wondering how a talk with Henry Harper would go. He'd always been decent with me. Tried to advise me more than once to get my life on track. Unlike some of the police I'd had interactions with, he had never been obnoxious or talked to me as if I was some lowlife. I was surprised he remembered me, but I was glad he seemed open-minded about this situation.

I heard Hannah's voice humming down the hall, and I stood. I would deal with that in a couple of days. I had skin to wash.

Thoroughly.

So thoroughly that Hannah forgot about the day.

It was good to have a goal.

CHAPTER TWENTY-THREE

Chase

I wasn't in a great mood the next morning. The night before, Hannah had candles burning when I joined her in the tub, but earlier today, in the morning light, I saw the bruise on her shoulder when she was getting dressed. I stilled her movements, brushing my fingers over the darkened skin.

"What happened?"

"Nothing. I was just clumsy."

I shook my head. "You're never clumsy."

She sighed and told me how Dan had pushed her into the corner of the wall where a steel case was located. "It's fine. It doesn't hurt. The chief made him apologize," she assured me.

I was furious that he would even be close enough to her to touch her. That he would pick on a woman because he was angry she wasn't in love with him.

"He needs to be taught a lesson."

Hannah gripped my arm. "Not by you. Do not seek him out, Chase. Promise me."

I was still mulling it over when I arrived at the garage. It was already bustling with our regular clients. I grabbed a coffee and sat at my desk, pulling up the schedule, pleased to see we were on track with everything. Charly wandered in, dressed in red overalls and a lacy white T-shirt. She'd tied up the shoulders with ribbons and rolled the cuffs of the pants up her calves. Glittery sneakers covered her feet, and she wore a Reynolds Restoration hat on her head backward, her hair falling down her back. I thought she looked cute. Maxx would find her outfit over the top and sexy and demand she change it. She'd ignore him as usual, and he would glower at her all day. They'd make up later—if they lasted that long. Their foreplay amused everyone around them.

I arched my eyebrow at her. "You can't give Maxx a break today?"

She grinned. "He needs a distraction."

I chuckled. "Well, you're giving him one, I'm sure. The vehicles are due to start arriving shortly."

She smiled. "This is such a boon for the garage. For the

town. Maxx can employ more people. All that expansion we've done will be a great investment."

I patted her shoulder. "I know."

She poured coffee into Maxx's cup. "I'm going to go and see the big guy. Remind him how great we are. Today is gonna be easy peasy for us."

I watched her go with a grin. She was the perfect complement to Maxx's intensity. She always saw the bright side, took on any chore with ease, and knew how to bolster him. He would be worried about the garage, the finances, and the investment. She would assure him that everything was going to work out fine and distract him with her silly outfit, pretending she had no idea. She knew exactly what she was doing.

I got busy with some outstanding invoices, surprised when Dom appeared in my door.

"You better come out here, Chase."

I stood. "What's wrong?"

"Jim Albright is here. And he's not alone."

Frowning, I followed Dom through the garage. All the bays were full, and the waiting room had some people in it, the TV on and distracting them. Outside, I blinked at what I saw. Maxx, Stefano, and Charly were gathered with Jim Albright, who looked upset. The kicker was the man standing just outside the loose circle, smirking.

Dan Meyers.

"What the hell is he doing here?" I muttered.

"Causing shit," Dom replied.

I headed their way, Dan seeing me, his smirk getting wider.

I stopped a couple of feet away. "Problem, folks?"

Everyone turned in my direction. Jim's eyes narrowed when he saw me. He looked familiar somehow, but I couldn't place him.

"The thief shows his face," he sneered.

I was taken aback. "Excuse me?"

"You and your brother broke in to my tire store and stole from me years ago. Damaged the place while you were at it. Cost me thousands. Took me ages to rebuild and recover."

I searched my memory, shaking my head. "My brother may have done so, sir, but I wasn't with him."

"There were two of you. I chased you, but you got away."

Again, I shook my head. "I did a lot of things, but stealing wasn't one of them, and I never broke in to a tire shop. My brother had many other accomplices." I glanced Dan's way. "No doubt, Officer Meyers told you about me. But he doesn't have all the facts straight," I huffed. "Or he is twisting them to suit his own agenda."

"You're Chase Donner?"

298

"Yes, sir."

"You've been in jail?"

"Yes, sir."

"You're a convict. You expect me to believe you?"

"I'm not that person anymore. I was a mixed-up kid. I've grown up."

He snorted. "Leopards don't change their spots. Once a thief, always a thief."

"Chase is a trusted member of my staff," Maxx stated, crossing his arms. With his gravelly voice and intense stare, he looked like a giant next to Jim Albright.

"And a member of our family," Charly said with a frown. "I trust him implicitly."

Jim shook his head. "I don't. And it's my fleet." He turned to Maxx. "I've given you my ultimatum. Your choice."

"It's not much of a choice. It's grossly unfair," Charly said, sounding angry.

"What choice is that?" I asked, somehow already knowing.

Jim didn't flinch as I met his eyes, his dislike evident. "Maxx wants my business, you're out. I don't trust you."

"I don't work on your vehicles," I pointed out. "I'm the office manager, and I work on custom interiors," I said calmly, my mind racing. I had to fix this.

"I don't want you around anything to do with me or my business. You'll probably pad the account and steal from us both."

"I am not a thief," I pushed out through gritted teeth.

Charly grasped my arm. "Chase wouldn't do that."

Dan was almost dancing as he watched the spectacle unfolding in front of him. He had me exactly where he wanted me. How he'd done this, I had no idea. The why was plain. And someone was going to lose in this situation—big-time.

"Did Dan here tell you why he has a vendetta against me?" I asked. I kept talking before Jim could respond. "He's obsessed with my girlfriend, and he's been harassing me because of it. He doesn't care about your business—he cares about hurting me."

"You're talking about a police officer."

I shook my head. "Because he's a cop, his word is better than mine? Did he tell you he pulled his gun on me for speeding? That he threatened to throw me in jail for a DUI when I wasn't even driving? How about the fact that he vandalized my truck? Or that he bothers my girl every chance he gets, even when she says no?" I glared at Dan, who was leaning on his car, insolent and smirking. "I saw the bruise you left on her yesterday, you asshole. You need to be held accountable for that."

He shrugged. "I apologized. I didn't see her."

"Bullshit," I muttered, struggling to hold in my temper. "You did that deliberately."

Dom laid his hand on my shoulder. "Chase," he warned quietly.

I ignored him. I was fed up. My anger, which had been simmering for days, had reached its boiling point. Dan thought he would hurt me by hurting the people I loved? The people who were my family? I wasn't going to allow that to happen. I knew what Maxx stood to lose if Jim took away his business. I wasn't allowing Dan to have that power.

I faced Jim. "I made mistakes. I did my time. I'm sorry for what Wes did, but I wasn't part of it, no matter what lies Dan has fed you. I would never steal from Maxx or you. I am not the person I was when I went to jail. I changed, and I paid for my past. I lost everything because of it. I *never* recovered." I had to swallow around the lump in my throat, knowing I was about to lose everything again. "You don't want me around your vehicles? You don't trust me, and you're willing to let Maxx suffer because of it? He has bent over backward to accommodate you. Do you know that he has ordered special equipment, hired staff to make sure you are looked after—"

"Enough, Chase," Maxx interrupted.

"No. It's not enough. I am not sitting by watching your business pay the price because of me." I pulled my keys off my belt, pressing them into Maxx's large hand. "Thank you for everything you have done for me, Maxx. I'll never forget it. I quit."

"No," Charly gasped.

I turned and hugged her. "I have to," I whispered. "I have to do this for you and Maxx. Don't try to stop me. I love you."

I turned and walked away, leaving everyone stunned. I planned to keep going, not to stop, not to give Dan a chance of getting in the last word, but he refused to let that happen.

"Coward," he muttered. "Loser."

I stopped, pivoting. I headed in his direction, ignoring the warnings behind me. He watched me approach, his expression one of smug satisfaction.

"Coward?" I snarled. "*Loser?* I'm walking away so the people I love aren't hurt. I'm putting them above me. That's what a man does, Danny boy. He doesn't pry into people's pasts and make them pay again for something they regret. He doesn't harass women who don't want him and have clearly stated so. And he doesn't show up to gloat when he drives the final nail into someone's coffin." I glared at him, my hands clenched into fists. "But you didn't win, Dan. I have lost my job but not my family. I still have them. And I still have Hannah. Those are the important things. So you lose, asshole. Now go find someone else to harass. I'm done with you."

"Fucker," he muttered. "You think you're so much better

than me. You're nothing but a convict and a failure. Hannah will see that, and I'll be around to pick up the pieces when she does."

I snapped. My arm flew before I could stop it, catching him on the jaw and sending him sprawling. The crack of my fist meeting bone was loud, and I was sure I had just broken my hand, but I didn't care. "That's for the pain you've caused Hannah."

He staggered to his feet, and Dom was behind me, holding me back. "Steady, Chase."

"You attacked an officer of the law," Dan slurred, holding his face, blood seeping from his split lip.

I laughed. "You're in civilian clothes, asshole." I shook Dom off. "I'm not going to do anything else. He hurt Hannah, and that is unacceptable." I swallowed. "What he took from me today can't be soothed with some punching." I looked at Dan with loathing. "You wanna arrest me? You know where I live."

And I turned and walked away before I broke down.

I had the blinds pulled down, the living room dim in the afternoon light. I had turned off my cell phone, ignoring the constant calls and texts. The doors were locked, and since I had walked away from Maxx's, there was no car in the driveway to indicate I was home. I had hitched a ride into town and walked here. I drank some whiskey straight from the bottle, then wrapped my aching hand in ice and sat on the sofa, unsure what to do. My mind raced, going over the events of the morning. The dislike and derision in Jim Albright's gaze. His scathing remarks and threats to take his business away from Maxx. I knew if he did that, he would also talk about why he had done so, and Maxx's business would continue to suffer because of me. I refused to let that happen. The truth was, I didn't have to work, but the garage had been more than a job. It had been my fresh start. My second home. A place I was accepted. I only hoped I still had a place in their family. The thought of losing Charly and Maxx, Stefano and Gabby, the kids—it broke my heart more than losing my job ever would.

And Hannah—she was going to be so upset. I needed to straighten myself out before she got home later and I told her what occurred.

Unless, of course, OD decided to press charges. I guessed I would see her at the station then—from behind bars.

I flexed my fingers, wincing. I should take some painkillers, but I wondered if that was a good idea, given the whiskey I'd swallowed.

A thought occurred to me. What if Hannah was angry at me? What if I lost her because of this?

I shook my head. She loved me. She wouldn't do that to me.

I picked up the whiskey, peering at the bottle. Maybe another mouthful would take the edge off the pain. I unwrapped the ice, grimacing at my hand. It was a mass of bruises and the knuckles swollen and painful. I realized that although I was trying to flex my fingers, they weren't really moving. I probably needed to go to urgent care. Except I was sorta drunk and I had no car.

I leaned my head back. I would sleep off the alcohol, go to urgent care, and be home when Hannah arrived. I would be calm and tell her what had occurred, and she would help me figure out the next step.

That was a good plan.

If only I had the strength to execute it.

I woke up to the sound of hushed voices. Movement. I frowned, not opening my eyes. I was a little fuzzy about what was happening until my mind cleared and I remembered what had occurred that morning. How my world had blown apart.

My eyes flew open, and I sat up, the pain in my hand blasting out the last of the haziness. The living room was full. Dom, Hannah, Maxx, Charly, and Stefano were there, all looking at me.

"What are you doing here?" I asked, confused. "Why aren't you at the garage?" I swung my gaze to Hannah. "Or at work?"

"Because Charly called me and told me what happened."

I shook my head, ignoring the pain at the back of it. "You shouldn't have done that, Charly."

She sniffed. "And you shouldn't have quit."

"I had no choice. I won't let you and Maxx suffer because of me."

She glared at me. "Like losing you wouldn't make us suffer? We're a family, Chase Donner. We stick together."

"And I'm looking after my family."

"By walking away?"

"By walking away," I agreed. "You keep Jim's business. You keep the garage running. That is the most important thing. I'll find another job somewhere."

Charly crossed her arms. "I don't think so."

Maxx held up his hand. "Enough. Both of you. While I appreciate your sacrifice and decision, Chase, it is unnecessary."

"What?"

Maxx sighed, sitting back. "You know the day was planned. Work, home, family. No fights, no cops, no standoffs."

"Sorry," I muttered. I looked at Hannah, who was watching me with tears in her eyes. "Sorry, Cinnamon. I lost my temper."

She sat beside me, cupping my cheek. "I hate that this happened. That you're hurt. Those are the only things I'm upset about."

"Are you here to bring me into the station? Is Dan pressing charges?"

There were a couple of guffaws. Dom shook his head. "I doubt Dan is up to much today except licking his wounds."

"What?" I shifted and groaned. Hannah checked out my hand, gasping.

"Chase, we need to go to the hospital. I think it's broken."

Charly peeked at it, nodding in agreement. "I think so."

"I want to know what happened."

Charly frowned. "Did you really think you could just quit and walk away? That we wouldn't stop all this madness? I told Jim Albright if he was the kind of person who was so unforgiving and jumped to conclusions without all the facts, he wasn't the sort of person we wanted to do business with. As far as I was concerned, he could go away. Dan started up again, running you down, and I told him to shut up and get off my property." Charly's color was high, and she was talking fast. "I might have gotten in his face a little. He was stupid enough to mouth off, and when I challenged him, he raised his hand to me."

"Oh boy," I muttered.

She nodded in satisfaction. "Maxx took him down in a second. Dropped him like a sack of potatoes with one punch. Broke his nose."

I breathed out. "Wow."

Maxx looked livid. "You don't raise your hand to any woman. Especially my wife. I wasn't giving him a chance to touch her."

Charly tossed her hair. "I could have taken him, but whatever."

Maxx snorted, and Charly hid her smile. She loved it when he got protective.

Dom continued with the story. "Jim Albright looked shocked. And suddenly, he was questioning Dan's story. It turns out Jim's daughter was in an abusive relationship. Only things he hates more than thieves are liars and men who hit women. Dan had totally snowed him, but Jim was looking at him with different eyes, seeing how he reacted to Charly. What you said about him pushing Hannah and harassing her."

"How had he even made that connection between Albright, me, and the garage?"

"A couple of the guys were at the bar and talking about

their new job a couple of nights ago. We think Dan must have recalled seeing Albright's name in an old case file, put it together, and went to Jim with his whole concocted story. He took information from the files on you and Wes and conveniently tied them together, knowing what Jim's reaction would be, given the history."

"Where is Dan now?"

"At the station with the chief. Maxx called the cops," Hannah said. "And Charly called me. I took personal time and came home."

She leaned over. "The chief wants to talk to you. Today. But first, we're going to the hospital."

"Where does the contract stand with Jim?"

Maxx shrugged. "In limbo. He apologized. Explained his side and realized how he overreacted. He's called twice since he left. His wife called him an idiot when he told her about it, apparently. He wants to apologize to you as well. He regrets his actions. He was younger when the robbery happened. It hit him hard, and he took a huge loss because he didn't have much insurance. He was angry and bitter, and Dan knew exactly how to rile him up. Jim wants to talk to you. I told him the contract would depend on the outcome of that conversation."

"Maxx—"

He held up his hand. "Charly is right. We'll hurt a bit, but we'll recover. You are more important than the money,

Chase. Why don't you know that by now?" he demanded gruffly.

I blinked. "I just got it."

"Well, don't forget it." He stood. "We're taking you to the hospital. Then to the station. Stefano and Dom will head to the garage and make sure everything is good there. Tomorrow, you are back, broken hand or not. You can work with one." He met my gaze. "Your resignation is not accepted. You understand?"

I nodded. "Yes, sir."

"Okay. Let's go."

I had two broken knuckles. The doctor decided surgery wasn't needed but put me in splint and gave me painkillers. I was instructed to keep my arm immobile and above my heart as much as possible for the next forty-eight hours. Charly informed me I was off the rest of the week, refusing my objections. I was pissed. I couldn't work, I wouldn't be able to help with the deck, and I was feeling slightly ill from the whiskey I had gulped down earlier. The effects from the liquor were gone, leaving only the lingering aftermath.

Hannah stood beside me, stroking my head, her touch light and gentle. I leaned into her caresses. "What a shit day," I muttered.

"I know."

"Fucking OD."

"I know."

"Wish I'd kicked his ass a little more."

"It wasn't his ass you punched, Chase. Might have been softer."

I laughed, opening my eyes and meeting her amused gaze. "I'm sorry, Hannah."

She cupped my face. "You were defending me. Protecting your family. You have nothing to be sorry for."

"I still have to talk to your boss."

"And Mr. Albright."

I sighed. "Yeah. Him."

"Will you accept his apology?"

I shrugged. "He was out of line, but I get it. Wes did a lot of damage to people. The fact that Dan decided to add me into the scenario is on him. Not Jim. It brought up a lot of bad memories for him, and he reacted. I don't want Maxx to lose his business. I'll talk to him."

There was a knock on the door, and I looked up, seeing Chief Harper standing in the doorway. He looked serious, and I felt my nerves kick in. "Come in," I said. "Are you here to arrest me?"

He shook his head. "No charges will be laid on you or Mr. Reynolds. I came to assure you Officer Meyers will no longer bother you. He will be transferring out of the station, effective immediately."

"So he can become someone else's problem?"

The chief shook his head. "I don't work that way. I get enough misfits sent here that I would never pass along someone who is a problem. I had a long, frank discussion with Dan. I will tell you this in confidence. He will be getting some therapy. He is taking some personal time to reflect on a new choice of career. We agreed that policing is not what is best for him."

"That's good," Hannah murmured.

"Let's hope it helps. Not sure he knows how to reflect," I muttered, still upset but relieved he wouldn't be around to bother us anymore.

"Chase," Hannah admonished.

"He would like to make restitution for your truck."

"He admitted to it?" I asked, surprised.

The chief was silent. I waved him off. "No. I will pay to fix it. I don't want his fucking blood money. I just want him to stay away from us."

"Noted. He will not bother you again. I would like to talk to you, Chase. One-on-one, but perhaps on a day you are feeling a little less angry."

I barked a laugh. "Probably a good idea."

He stepped forward. "You got a second chance, son. You ran with it, and you have a good life now. I am trying to do the same for Mr. Meyers." He met my eyes. "We all have demons."

I nodded, his words somehow deflating my anger. He was right. "Tell Dan I don't need the money. I hope he finds what he needs."

He nodded. "I can do that." He glanced at Hannah. "Martha has tendered her notice. Effective the end of the month. Think it over." Then he left, passing Maxx and Charly coming in.

"You almost ready to go?" Maxx asked.

I nodded. "Just waiting for the prescription."

"Okay. We'll take you home then head to the garage."

"I could—"

Maxx cut me off with a glare. "No."

"Fine. I'll be in tomorrow."

"Next week," Charly huffed. "Don't make me mad again."

I rolled my eyes. "Whatever."

They left, and the doctor walked in. I blew out a breath. "Holy shit, it never stops."

He laughed, handing me the prescription. "Remember, up in the air over your heart as much as possible for the next forty-eight hours. It will reduce swelling. Keep it in the splint as long as you can."

"Can I take it off for a shower?"

"After forty-eight hours. Don't try to use it. Here's a follow-up appointment at the fracture clinic."

I nodded, and Hannah took the papers from me, putting them in her bag. She was still in uniform, and I grinned at her. "Escorting me home now, Officer Cinnamon?"

She laughed. "Yes. Behave. I can't even cuff you."

I chuckled, and we headed down the hall, rounding the corner. I stopped dead in my tracks, and Hannah ran into my back. "Chase! What the—"

She stopped speaking. In front of us was Dan, looking as shocked as we were. His nose was definitely broken, his jaw black and blue. His one eye was swollen, and he looked as bad as I felt. Part of me took great satisfaction in his injuries. He deserved those punches. The part of me that recalled the chief's words, "We all have demons," felt bad.

At least a little bit.

He held up his hand before I could speak. "I'm not following you. The chief made me come get checked out. I was just leaving."

"Us too."

He nodded, glancing between us. "I won't see you again. I'm sorry, Hannah." He drew in a deep breath. "You too, Chase. I was a jerk. I'm sorry." Then he turned and hurried away, disappearing around the corner.

I stared after him. "Unexpected," I grunted. "I had no idea hell was freezing over today."

Hannah tugged on my good hand. "Be nice. He's gone."

"Thank God for that."

She didn't disagree.

CHAPTER TWENTY-FOUR

Hannah

C hase proved to be a terrible patient. Despite what the doctor told him, he was restless and wanting to do things all the time. By noon the next day, I was at my wit's end. I had to go to work, and I was worried about what he would do while I was gone. I had already caught him trying to teach himself to use a drill with his left hand, testing out to see how a saw felt with his left arm, and attempting to measure something with his bad hand lifted into the air. The cursing I heard let me know none of those things was going well.

I walked into the kitchen, trying not to laugh at the mess of him making scrambled eggs. Shells and eggs were everywhere. Including the floor.

"What are you doing?"

"Making you something to eat before you leave for work. I

thought egg sandwiches would be easy. Cracking the damn things is awkward, though."

I shook my head. "You were supposed to stay sitting while I had my shower."

"I got bored."

"In fifteen minutes?"

He shrugged.

In desperation, I called Charly, and she told me to bring him to the garage on my way to work. Not long after I began my shift, she sent a picture. Chase was at his desk, his bad hand strung up on some sort of pulley system they'd added to a piece of garage equipment so it was over his heart. He was using his left hand to type, his face a mask of concentration. Charly's message informed me she'd given him the inventory sheets to work on. "It will keep him busy for hours with his hunt-and-peck routine," she assured me.

I had to laugh. That was better than leaving him on his own at the house. God only knew what he would get up to.

The hours crept by, with very little happening. I drove my routes, stopping once to help a woman who had fallen on the sidewalk carrying her groceries. I made sure she was all right and took her home. I had a call about a suspected intruder, but it turned out to be a neighbor's dog nosing around the back porch after he got off his lead. I found myself thinking more about Martha's job. I had read the posting and kept weighing the pros and cons in my head. I was certainly more productive in the office, organizing, filing, scheduling, tracking. When I was in Toronto, we were constantly busy as police officers—here, not so much. A small part of me wondered if I would like to return to the big city, but the more logical part knew I was better off here. Still, the thought cropped up on occasion.

Clouds began to gather as early evening fell. I was glad I only had another four hours in my shift. It was going to rain overnight, and it was miserable being on patrol in the rain. My radio crackled, and I responded, listening to the call for a possible domestic disturbance. A woman called in, she'd heard a scream and shouting plus a loud commotion coming from the unit beside hers where a new couple had moved in. I made a wide turn with the car and headed toward the address, my nerves already kicking in when I thought of the last domestic disturbance call I'd taken. Dispatch let me know backup was coming and to hold on as I arrived, then a moment later said they were delayed with a problem but would be there soon.

I sat in the car, staring at the complex. My heart raced, and I felt the sweat gather on my neck. If someone was in danger inside, the longer I waited for backup, the greater the potential for their life being at risk. It was my job—my duty—to help them. The reason I was a cop. I ran my hand down my chest, feeling the protective vest under my shirt. My hand shook as I radioed dispatch to say I was going to check it out. I placed my hat on my head and got out of the car, unclipping my gun as I approached the door. It began to rain, the drops hitting the ground hard, bouncing back up as they met the resistance of the cement. My thick shoes made a dull thump as I walked up the steps, my stomach in knots and my breathing coming faster. I felt the shudders that raced down my spine one after another. I could hear my heartbeat in my head, faster and faster. I listened, not hearing anything but the rain. No screams or shouting.

But I hadn't heard anything last time either. Everything had seemed normal until the door opened. I shook my head to clear it. That was last time. This was not the same situation, I reminded myself, trying to stop the waves of panic that kept hitting me.

The sound of metal hitting metal caught my attention, and I knew I had to proceed. My hand shook as I rapped on the door, announcing myself. My heart was racing, and I had to swallow the thick feeling in my throat. Flashes of memory kept taunting me, and I braced as I heard footsteps and the door swung open, revealing a man about my age. He was tall and lean, wearing a hoodie and sweats.

"Officer," he greeted me, looking confused. "Is there a problem?"

I was surprised how even my voice sounded. "We received a call about a disturbance in the home."

To my shock, a wide grin split his face. "You could say that." He turned. "Helen!" he called. "Come see what you've done now!"

Lights behind me indicated my backup had arrived, and to my utter surprise, he began to laugh. "Oh, she's really caused trouble."

A woman waddled down the hall. Waddled was the only word to describe it. She was hugely pregnant. She was tall and pretty, although she was covered in some sort of dust. She looked abashed. "Oh boy." She looked at the man holding the door. "Did you invite her in?"

"I was waiting for her partner, but yes, please come in," he said dryly. "I am sure you want to check and make sure everything is all right." He smiled again. "I'll let my wife tell you the story."

My backup was an officer I knew, and we walked in, our hands on our holsters. The woman was quick to speak. "You won't need those. There is a simple explanation. I assume Ruby next door called you. Warren was about to go over and tell her what happened so she didn't worry. I guess she heard."

"Heard what, exactly?" I asked.

"Come into the kitchen."

I followed her and her husband, and my eyes widened at the mess I saw. "What happened?"

Helen smiled, looking embarrassed. "I had a craving. I was making a snack, and Warren was teasing me. I got distracted, and the grease caught fire on the stove. He yelled at me to turn off the burner, and he ran for the fire blanket.

But I dumped salt on the flames. Then the smoke detector started. It startled me and I jumped. The baby kicked and I yelled. Warren was trying to get the smoke detector to shut off, and I waved a tea towel to help." She began to giggle. "Except it caught on the pot rack, and I tugged too hard. It was loose, and I pulled it out of the ceiling, and all the pots and utensils crashed down. I screamed. Warren yelled." She shrugged. "Ruby called you."

Jesse—Officer Owens—began to chuckle. I looked at the mess. Pots, pans, and utensils everywhere. The pot rack hung, lopsided and swinging from the ceiling, one hook keeping it in place. The ruined snack was still puffing a little smoke on the stove. I could see now that Helen was covered in flour, no doubt from when the pots fell into the bowl of whatever her planned snack was. Warren stood next to his wife, slipping an arm around her. "Oh, Helen," he murmured. "You troublemaker."

She laughed again, then her eyes went wide. "Oh God!"

We all heard it, and we all looked down. "My water just broke!" Then she grabbed his arm. "And here comes a contraction."

"Of course it did," Warren murmured. He looked at us. "Are we good here? I need to get her bag and get her to the hospital."

"I'll drive you," I offered.

Helen looked behind her. "The mess," she gasped.

Her husband kissed her. "I'll clean it later. We have to meet our girl now."

She smiled at him, her love brimming in her eyes. "Our girl. Yes."

He guided her to the table. "You sit, and I'll be right back."

She smiled at me. "I'm so sorry to cause you all this trouble."

"No. It's fine. I'm glad it was all a mistake."

She nodded. "Warren would never hurt me or even get mad at me. He's incredible. He was trying to get me to stop cleaning, and he was going to take me for fritters at Zeke's."

"Oh, those are good."

"Better than what I was attempting to make." Her eyes went wide. "Oh, another contraction."

"Those are fast," Warren said, coming into the kitchen. "I called the doctor. He'll meet us there. I got you a clean shirt to wear."

Jesse returned. He'd called in the report and talked to the neighbor. He spoke to me quietly. "You take them to the hospital. I'm going to stay here and see if I can rehang that pot rack. The neighbor is going to come over and help clean up."

"Great idea."

He grinned. "I know what life with a newborn is like. They

don't need that added stress. It's quiet out tonight aside from this unexpected call."

"Yeah. I'll do a couple drives in your area."

"Thanks." He paused. "You okay, Hannah? You look really pale."

"Just tired."

"Okay. Be safe out there."

I nodded. "You know it."

I got Warren and Helen to the hospital, listening to him coaching her to breathe and relax.

"I can't relax," she informed him. "Your daughter is determined to come now!"

I radioed ahead, and they were waiting for us. I watched them go, smiling at his fussing and her quarreling with him. I returned to my car and pulled into an empty spot in the parking lot. The rain beat down on the hood, its steady rhythm peaceful. I drew in a long breath, letting it out slowly. My hands still trembled, and I was tense. I told myself I was fine. Everything was fine. The call was a false alarm. An amusing story to tell one day.

But today wasn't it. I kept seeing another door. Another couple. A different scenario.

I shut my eyes and did all the tricks my therapist had taught me. I counted. Concentrated on my breathing. Tried to think of good things. Spoke out loud, reminding myself everything was fine. Today was a different day. I did that until I felt calmer. Then I radioed in and pulled out of the parking lot, praying I would remain calm until my shift ended.

By the time I got home, I was shaking again. Tamping down the panicked feeling in order to get my key into the lock and get inside. I shut the door behind myself, pressing my back against it. I was home. I was safe. Chase was here.

I let my coat fall to the floor. I had changed at the station, locking my gun in my locker. I rarely brought it home. I kicked off my shoes, taking a deep breath in. Chase came from the kitchen, stopping in confusion when he saw me.

"Hannah." He rushed toward me. "Baby, what's wrong? What is it?"

With a sob, I launched myself at him. He wrapped his good arm around me, holding me close. "Hannah, are you hurt?" he asked, panicked. "Can you tell me?"

I shook my head, unable to stop crying. He led us to the sofa, sitting down and cradling me on his lap. He held me tight, running his hand over my head repeatedly. "It's okay, it's okay," he murmured. "I'm here. You're safe. I have you."

Relief swelled, making me cry harder for a moment. He let me sob, making hushing noises and whispering that everything was okay until I began to calm down. He pressed some tissues into my hand, and I wiped at my face. "I'm sorry," I whispered. "I-I didn't mean to do that."

"Don't be sorry. I'm here, Hannah. Tell me what happened," he urged.

I told him everything. The call. The sudden fear. How it lingered. "I thought I was over it," I admitted. "But I'm not."

"I'm not sure you can ever 'get over' something as traumatic as that," he murmured, cupping my face.

I looked at him, seeing only understanding and caring on his face. "If it had been a real domestic violence call, my fears could have kept me from acting in time," I whispered. "I was so scared, Chase."

"You need to talk to someone," he said. "I think you left therapy too quickly."

"I felt so ashamed after. As if I was a coward."

"No." He cupped my face. "You are anything but. A very wise and beautiful woman once told me that it takes a great deal of strength to admit your fear. You're admitting them. You're feeling them." His grip tightened. "Maybe your fears are trying to tell you something, baby."

I knew what he was saying. I shut my eyes as another set of tears ran down my cheeks. "I can't be a good, effective police officer anymore. I need to do something else."

"Are you sure about this, Hannah? It's a big decision."

I opened my eyes and met his gaze. It was warm, hopeful, and filled with love.

"I'll support you no matter what you want to do," he assured me.

"I'm going to accept that job. I can still be an effectual part of the station."

"Yes, you can," he agreed. "Are you certain about this?" he repeated.

"Yes. I keep thinking about it. Thinking of the things I could do to help. Some community initiatives I could suggest. Ways to improve the reporting access."

"You'll be amazing."

I sighed, feeling exhausted. "I'll talk to the chief tomorrow. I'll ask about the job and more therapy."

He gathered me back in his arms. "Good."

"Be honest," I whispered. "Are you glad?"

"Glad about something that causes you pain? No. Selfishly, I am relieved. I know it's a small town, but bad things happen here too. I'm grateful, knowing you'll be a little safer every day at work."

I rested my head on his shoulder. I was pleased he was honest with his feelings. And I didn't mind him being selfish about me. I felt the same about him.

He held me for a while. "You want a bath or to go to bed?"

"Bed." I sat up, wiping my face. "How is your hand?"

"Good."

"Did you behave for Charly?"

He snorted. "Like I had any choice. They trussed me up so I couldn't put my arm down, and Charly was a taskmaster all afternoon." He grinned. "Then she fed me fried chicken and pie. So I forgave her."

I smiled at him. "You love it."

"I do. I love you too."

"I love you, Chase Donner."

A slight grimace passed over his face. "What?" I asked.

He shook his head. "I'm starting to hate my last name more all the time."

"Why?"

"People around this town hear the name Donner and immediately associate it with my brother and my dad. The bad seed and the man who let us go wild. Sometimes I think I should change my name. Become Chase Smith. Just be me."

"Did something happen today?"

"Someone asked me on the phone if I was related to Wes. I lied and said no. But it's the first thing that happens. Dan did it. Albright did it. Others do. I constantly have to prove I am not him. It gets tiring at times."

I kissed him. "Okay, Chase Smith. Not as catchy, but I still love you."

He stood, holding out his hand. "Let's go to bed. I need to hold you."

I followed him without an argument.

I needed that as well.

CHAPTER TWENTY-FIVE

Chase

D om stood back with a grin. "Done."

I looked at the deck, smiling in approval. "It looks great."

The day had gone by fast. Maxx and Stefano showed up, along with Manny and Bruce. I was even able to help, using my good hand to carry the cut pieces of lumber to them to fit onto the deck. With the composite decking, there was nothing left to do, no staining or sanding. It was ready to go. Hannah was in the kitchen baking with Cherry. Her mom had been overjoyed when Hannah shared the news of her new job. Cherry became emotional, and I left them to talk.

I had been horrified when Hannah came home so distraught. She'd been so pale that her freckles stood out on her face like wet sand. Her eyes were wide and panicked, and I was desperate to calm whatever storm was brewing around her. It hit me hard, listening to her talk of the terror she felt earlier. I hated that the anxiety still lingered in her voice and made her tremble in my arms even hours after the call. When she told me she decided to take the office job, it was all I could do not to shout in jubilation. Instead, I offered her my support, internally thrilled. She'd be safer. Happier too, I thought, in the long run. I knew Cherry would feel much the same way.

We cleaned up and sat around sipping a cold beverage and eating some of the cookies Hannah and her mom had been baking. Manny and Bruce left, their saddlebags filled with cookies plus leftovers from the lunch the girls had made. Maxx and Stefano left shortly after, leaving the four of us sitting on the new deck, enjoying the late-afternoon breeze. I carefully undid the splint, pulling it off and slowly bending my fingers. It still hurt like a bitch, but the fact that I could move them a little was an improvement. I let it rest on my leg as I relaxed. Hannah looked at me then at the hand, but she didn't say anything. I was pretty sure she'd given up.

"There's another band at Zeke's tonight," Dom said. "You up for some music?"

"Oh, I'd love that," Cherry replied.

I glanced at Hannah. She'd been quiet the past couple of days. In her head a lot. I knew I had to give her breathing room and let her work things through herself, even if it killed me to do so. She met my eyes with a slight shake of her head.

"We'll sit tonight out. I'm pretty tired, and my hand aches."

"Okay," Dom hummed. "I'll have Cherry back at a decent time." He paused. "Tomorrow."

I tried not to laugh at her outraged expression. The two of them were constantly at odds, yet their attraction was evident. Dom took it all in stride, grinning and teasing her about the stubbornness of the Gallagher women.

I stood. "I'm going to go take a shower." I held out my good hand and awkwardly shook Dom's. "Thanks for today. For everything."

He grinned. "Anytime, kid."

I stood under the hot water, the heat easing my muscles. I was surprised when Hannah slipped in behind me a few moments later, wrapping her arms around me.

"They left?" I asked.

"Dom said he wanted a shower and to change. Mom said she'd go with him to save him a trip back. They were going to eat dinner before the band started again." She grinned up at me, amusement filling her eyes. "I think she planned on doing exactly what I'm doing right now."

I bent and kissed her, our lips moving together. I slid my tongue into her mouth, deepening the kiss. I wrapped my good arm around her, pulling her closer, and I groaned when she dropped her hand, wrapping her fist around me. I loved it when she touched me. She stroked me, her fingers teasing and light.

"Jesus, Hannah, that feels good," I breathed into her ear.

"I need you," she replied. "I've missed you. Missed us."

We'd been affectionate and close since the Dan incident and the trauma Hannah had experienced, but we hadn't made love. I was waiting for my cues from her that she was ready.

It appeared I just got a big one.

"Take me to bed, Chase. I need this. I need you."

I turned off the water and backed her out of the shower, our lips once again locked together. We fell onto the bed, our wet bodies molded to each other. I rolled so she was on top of me. My left hand proved useful for once as I stroked and teased her until she was panting and pleading with me for release.

"Ride me, Hannah. Take everything you need."

She was beautiful as she sank down on me. She tossed her hair, placing a hand on my chest as she began to move. She rolled her hips, taking me deeper, making me arch my back. Her hand felt good before. Inside her was perfection.

I slid my hand along her thigh, anchoring her to me. The fingers on my right hand flexed and bent of their own volition, and I ignored the pain. It was worth it.

Her head fell back, and I felt her tightening around me. She was so stunning when she let go. Her cries were music to my ears. The way her muscles fluttered and her heat held me tight set off my own orgasm, and I thrust upward, shouting her name, gasping as I came hard. We moved and loved until we were exhausted. Sated.

Then she fell forward into my chest, and I held her close. I kissed her head, dove my hand into her thick hair, and lifted her face to mine, pressing kisses to her cheeks, forehead, nose, and lips. "I love you, Cinnamon. So fucking much."

She laughed softly, leaning into my lips pressed to hers. She loved affection. Being held. Kissed. Stroked and caressed. "I love you too. Equally as much."

"Good."

Hannah slipped into her role at the station easily. OD was gone, so that stress disappeared. I met with Jim Albright, and after a long, deep conversation, we agreed to leave the past behind us. He apologized to me for his actions, and I accepted his handshake. He also spoke with Charly and Maxx, and his business stayed with the garage. I had coffee with the chief, and he had some interesting stories to tell me. Some were about my dad and brother, some were his observations about the town in general, and a few included me—things I had no recollection of but were amusing when I heard them. He could recall a younger, not so troubled version of Chase. It was nice to know someone did. I had a good relationship with him and Jim now, and it helped heal me a little.

My hand began to get better, and life became somewhat normal for us. I loved coming home to Hannah. Filling our evenings with puttering around the house and the yard, spending time with friends and her mom on the weekends. The days seemed to pass quickly, and before I knew it, August had come.

We lay in bed on Sunday morning, the rain once again beating on the roof. I was glad I had replaced it when I did. Hannah's head rested on my chest, and we were quiet.

"Anything special you want to do next weekend?" I asked. "For your birthday? Go into Toronto for dinner or go to a show?"

She was silent for a minute. "No. Not really. My mom always made me a cake, but birthdays weren't really big. We couldn't afford much. Maybe a barbecue? Mom has to work on Saturday, so it would have to be Sunday."

"Okay. We can use the new deck—we haven't had a crowd over yet. Have everyone here and celebrate. Maybe we can do something on Saturday. I have the day off. There's a big yard sale—more like a town sale—over in Hedgewood. I know Charly loves going to it. She says she gets some great things."

"That would be fun. We still need a couple of things for the house."

I ran my fingers through her hair. "Sure. We could have lunch out and explore. Corn is in season. We'll get some to cook on Sunday."

"Sounds like fun," she said. "A nice, quiet day." She paused. "I would like a cake, though."

I bit back my grin. "I can do that." I already had plans, and there was nothing quiet or nice about them. I wanted to celebrate Hannah big-time, and she had said something a few weeks back that gave me an idea. I hoped she liked it as much as I did. And there would be cake. Lots of it. Lots of all her favorites.

Including me.

Hannah kicked off her sandals with a groan. "My feet are killing me."

I chuckled and patted her leg. "Great day, though, right?"

"Yes. We got so many awesome things!"

I glanced at the rearview mirror. The back of the truck was piled high with her "awesome things." There was a set of side tables and a coffee table she planned to restore. Baskets, pieces of crystal, plant pots, material, all sorts of crafty things. Pictures, frames, knickknacks. Homemade jams and jellies. A crock for pickles. Items I had no idea we needed or that even existed. But it kept her busy and happy. I loved to see her smile.

She scrolled through her phone. "My mom didn't call."

"You said she was working today. She'll call tonight."

"I guess." She scrolled a little more. "A couple of texts, but that's it."

"I got you flowers. And some bath stuff."

"I know and I loved them. I just thought Annette might call or, you know, Charly."

"They know we're having a barbecue tomorrow," I soothed.

She nodded. "You're right."

She glanced out the window, and I bit back my grin. Everything was going according to plan. She was quiet for a while, and when I looked again, she was asleep. I tugged her over, and her head fell to my shoulder. She didn't even stir. "Sleep, Cinnamon," I murmured. "You're gonna need it."

She woke up as I parked the truck in the parking lot behind Zeke's. She sat up, blinking. "What are we doing?"

"I'm craving some nachos. I thought we'd grab a bite and head home."

"Oh. Will our stuff be okay?"

"It'll be fine."

I got out and went to her door. I held out my hand, and she

slid from the truck. We headed toward the front, almost bumping into a girl coming around the corner. She shook her head at us. "Bar is closed," she said. "Some private party."

Hannah stopped. "Oh. Well, I can make us nachos at home."

I tugged her hand. "Zeke will give us an order to go."

She followed me reluctantly. At the door, she pulled on my hand. "Chase, it says closed." She read the sign. "Private function."

"It's fine."

I towed her behind me. "I don't think—" she started, then gasped as everyone yelled, "Surprise!"

I grinned at her. "The party is for you, Cinnamon." I bent and kissed her. "Happy birthday, baby."

HANNAH

I looked around in shock and astonishment. All of our friends were there. People from work. My mom. The local band, the Frozen Tundra, we had been to see and enjoyed so much was onstage, currently playing "Happy Birthday." The place was decorated, the air smelled incredible, and the bar was open. A table had presents piled on it. Balloons were attached to chairs and flowers everywhere. It was incredible. I was hugged and kissed, going from person to person. When I got to my mom, she hugged me fiercely.

"He did it all," she whispered. "Organized everything. That boy is crazy about you."

I looked over at Chase, who was watching me, his eyes soft, his smile wide. The love I felt for him filled me up totally. He was it for me. He winked, and I blew him a kiss, which made his smile even wider. I finally made my way back to him, and he pulled me close. "Hey, birthday girl."

"You did all this?"

"I had help."

"You are amazing. I love you."

He grinned. "I love you. Now let's get a drink and enjoy your day."

Chase made sure my favorite items from the menu were on the large buffet Zeke set out. The drinks were plentiful and cold. The music rocked. I ate and danced. Laughed and talked. Drank some of the delicious concoctions Charly had Zeke make up, but I didn't go overboard. I wanted to remember every minute of tonight. I'd never had a party before. No one had ever given me one either. But Chase had. Quietly. Without a fuss and without spilling the secret. I never had a clue.

I laid my head on his shoulder as we swayed to a quiet song. I loved being held by him. He pressed a kiss to my head. "Having a good time?"

I tilted my head up. "The best." I leaned up on my toes and kissed him. "Thank you, Chase. For all of this. It's been the best birthday ever."

He smiled. "The night isn't over."

"What?"

He chuckled. "There's cake."

He turned me, and I gaped at the large cake being carried from the kitchen. Sparklers and candles glittered. Pink and purple flowers adorned the layers. Everyone started to sing, and Chase wrapped his arms around me, holding me tight to his chest. He sang in my ear, his voice low and slightly off-key but still perfect. It took three tries to blow out the candles, and then the kitchen cut slices for everyone. They all wanted me to open the gifts, and I enjoyed the whole thing. I received some wonderful, thoughtful gifts. Some fun ones. Useful items. I loved them all.

Then I heard a voice clearing in the microphone, and I turned to see Chase onstage. He waved me closer so I was in front of him. He smiled down at me.

"Today, we celebrate Hannah's birthday. Some of you have known her a long time, some are fairly new, and of course, her mom has that special connection. We all know a different Hannah, and she means something unique to each of us. The one thing we all have in common is that *we* love *her*. The difference there, though—" he stopped and swallowed, meeting my eyes "—is that I love her more."

There was a chorus of oohs, and I had to wipe my eyes as tears slid down my cheeks.

"So tonight, I want to wish the love of my life a happy birthday. Thank you, Hannah, for loving me. For giving me a home. Because where you are is home." He paused. "I love you."

"I love you," I replied.

He stepped off the stage and stood in front of me. He cupped my cheeks and kissed me, then stood back. He smiled at me. "I have a gift for you too, Hannah."

I shook my head. "You gave me this party."

He winked. "That was for our friends, so they could celebrate with you. This gift is only for you."

My heart began to beat harder. My breathing picked up. He looked intense. Serious.

"It sort of comes with a request. I want to give you my heart, Hannah. Forever. I want to share my life with you." He dropped to his knee and opened his hand, a small box resting on his palm. "If you accept that, I would also like to give you this."

I heard some gasps around me. My mom said my name, her voice filled with wonder.

I met Chase's eyes.

"My request is that you marry me, Hannah Gallagher. Give me that gift. Your love forever."

He looked at me with so much love. Tenderness. I saw our life together reflected in his eyes. There was only one response I could give.

"Yes."

He opened the box, and I stared at the pretty ring inside. It glittered under the lights, the center diamond flanked by smaller ones on each side. He slid it on my finger, his hand shaking as he did so. "Perfect fit," he whispered, a tear sliding down his cheek. He lifted my hand to his mouth. "Mine. Forever."

"It's beautiful."

He stood, touching my face. "So are you."

Then his mouth was on mine, and everyone was clapping.

It was the best birthday ever.

And one, thanks to Chase, I would never forget.

CHAPTER TWENTY-SIX

Chase

After rounds of hugs, backslaps, and congratulations, I danced with my fiancée. She was lit up with happiness, only one arm around my neck, the other on my chest so she could see her ring.

"I love it," she whispered.

"I've had it a while," I admitted.

"You have?"

"Yeah. I bought it after the first night I held you. I knew you were it for me."

"Chase…" she breathed out.

"I asked your mom for permission a couple of weeks ago. That day I told you I went to Toronto for parts, I actually went to see your mom. I took her to lunch and asked her blessing and told her I was having this party for you."

"She never let on."

"I know. We work well together."

The door to the bar opening and a voice calling out startled us, and I turned, meeting the amused gaze of Brett. He was grinning widely. "Someone told me there was a party going on!" he yelled. "Celebrations were happening!"

A moment later, I was engulfed in a bear hug, and Hannah was lifted off her feet and twirled. Kelly watched, amused, giving me a far less hard hug. "Congratulations, Chase."

"What are you doing here?" I asked. "You're not due back for a couple of weeks."

"And miss my boy getting engaged? When you called and told me you were asking Hannah tonight, I knew I had to come."

I clapped his shoulder. "Thanks, Brett."

He chuckled. "I was there when you fell in love with Occifer Cinnamon, remember? Your dream girl?" He pointed to the back. "Right out there. Inebriated or not, you were smitten."

I glanced at Hannah and winked. "Still am."

Hannah slipped her arm around me. "Inebriated or smitten?"

I kissed the end of her nose. "Drunk on love. Your love."

She beamed. "Good answer."

I woke up, the stillness of the morning surrounding me. Hannah was beside me, but she wasn't asleep. Her head was on my chest, but her arm was raised and she was moving her hand in that way women did to catch the light on their rings. Hers caught it easily and sparkled brightly, casting a shower of light on the opposite wall. She giggled softly, enjoying herself. I tightened my arm, and she glanced up at me. "Hi," she whispered.

"Having fun?"

"It's so pretty, Chase. I love it. I can't believe you bought it weeks ago."

"I saw it in the jeweler's window. You and your mom had been looking in a magazine, talking about some ring styles of celebrities. You mentioned this sort of ring. I went in and bought it."

"It's perfect."

I trailed a finger down her cheek. "When do you want to get married, Hannah?"

"The sooner, the better."

I bent and kissed her. "I like the sound of that. Where and when?"

"I love the little church in Littleburn. There's a hall attached. We could rent it and get married there and have a party. I mean, we're not religious, but I'd like that. And the stained glass is so pretty for pictures. I was hoping Kelly could take them."

"I'm sure she would if we asked. I like that idea. We'll go talk to them." I paused. "I have another question to ask you, Hannah."

She sat up and faced me. "This sounds serious. I'll sign a prenup if you want—you don't have to ask."

I sat up as well and shook my head. "No prenup. I don't care about that. This is far more personal and important."

She shifted closer, taking my hand. "Okay."

"I want to take your last name instead of you taking mine."

She blinked. "Really?"

"I hate the constant explaining associated with Donner. It upsets me when the first impression someone has meeting me is that I'm from bad stock. I don't want to deal with it anymore, and I certainly don't want you to either. Or our kids. I looked into it, and I can change my last name as easily as you can change yours." I swallowed. "I asked your mom last night. She was okay with it. In fact, she got a little

345

emotional thinking we would carry on the Gallagher name with our kids. She said your dad would have approved."

"Chase Gallagher," she said softly. "I like it."

"Me too."

"I would love for you to take my name, Chase. And you keep saying kids. How many are you wanting?"

I grinned. "As many as you'll give me, Cinnamon. A bunch of freckle-faced little rug rats running around would be awesome." I looked around. "We'll need a bigger house, though."

She laughed. "How about we start with one?"

I pulled her onto my lap. "How about we start practicing?"

She wrapped her arms around my neck. "Yes."

Later that afternoon, we sat on the deck, surrounded by friends. Burgers were grilling on the barbecue, corn was roasting. The little ones were kicking a ball around, Theo, as usual, sticking close to where Vivvy was. Protecting her. Thomas was far more interested in getting the ball past Mack. Kelly was taking photos.

"So, Chase Gallagher," Charly mused. "I like it." She'd been a little emotional today, generous with her hugs, effusive in her happiness. Every time she looked at Hannah and me, her eyes became bright. She stayed close to Maxx, her hands wrapped around his. He knew she was feeling all of this deeply, and he pressed kisses to her head and teased her gently about her "boy" growing up. I was lucky to have them in my life. To have their support and love.

"Me too."

"You know you're not like Wes," she pointed out. "You've left that far behind you."

"But others haven't. I like the idea of starting off my married life with a new name. I won't have to deal with it, nor will Hannah. Or our kids."

"Something you want to tell us?" Brett said with a smirk.

I laughed and winked at him. "I'm working on it."

"You've been busy," Stefano remarked. "Buying rings, planning a party, deciding on a name change. All on your own, all under the radar." He clapped my shoulder. "Our boy has grown up."

Brett leaned his head back with a pretend sob. "He doesn't need us anymore."

Everyone laughed, even Charly, and I met Hannah's eyes. I linked our fingers together and kissed her hand. "I'll always need you guys. But now I have someone who needs *me*. I like that."

Hannah leaned forward and kissed me.

"We need each other."

Brett lifted his glass. "To Hannah and Chase. A new name, a new life."

I lifted my glass, smiling widely.

I liked the sound of that.

Very much.

EPILOGUE

Chase

The sun streamed through the stained-glass windows of the church, the colors bright and shimmering on the pews filling with people. Outside, the November wind blew cold, but inside, it was warm and filled with light.

Our friends, colleagues, and family were all there to celebrate Hannah and me getting married. We had done nothing traditional. A church wedding with no pastor. Instead, Brett took the course to become ordained.

The groom taking the bride's name was another anomaly. Our friends had been surprised when I'd explained I was taking Hannah's name but, as usual, supportive. They understood the stigma attached to the name in this town, even though I was doing my best to erase it. I only hoped by the time my kids were around, the name would be just a memory and they would be judged on their own merits. I hoped to be one day as well. It felt right taking Hannah's name.

The bride's mother was her maid of honor. My best man—a woman. We didn't want a huge wedding, and when Hannah said she really only wanted her mom with her, I knew who my choice to stand beside me had to be. The person who had shown me more love, forgiveness, and support than I ever expected to receive. My sister, mother, and friend all rolled into one. Beside me, Charly sparkled as bright as the sun, excited and happy. She wore a rich green dress that suited her coloring. She looked beautiful. Cherry wore a deep blue gown, and I had a feeling Dom wouldn't be able to take his eyes off her. His hands either, once he got close enough to her.

Charly met my eyes. "Nervous?" she whispered.

"Not anymore," I answered honestly. "Now I know Hannah's here, I'm good. I'm ready to marry her."

Charly laughed. "As if she'd change her mind."

I had to laugh with her. "You ready to do this?" I asked.

"I am. I hope I don't trip."

I squeezed her hand. "You'll be fine."

Even our service was different. I wasn't going to be waiting for Hannah at the front. We would meet at the back, Cherry and Charly walking ahead of us. We would walk down the aisle together. The same way we would face the world from now on.

"Thanks for doing this, Charly."

"Of course."

"And thank you for everything. Your forgiveness. Your trust. For always being there." I smiled as her eyes got bright. "For loving me."

"Holy moly. I need to look good in the pictures. Stop with the sweet stuff." She swatted my arm then leaned up and kissed my cheek. "I love you, Chase Donner—Gallagher—whatever name you want to go by," she whispered. "You were meant to be part of us. I'm as lucky to have you as you are to have us. We're family. I am honored to stand beside you today."

The room suddenly got a little misty.

The door opened, and Brett walked in, looking anxious. "We're ready to start." He glanced at Charly. "You have the rings?"

"Of course I do," she scoffed. "Right here." She patted her side. "Pockets. I love pockets."

"You okay, Brett?" I asked. "You look a little nervous. I'm the one getting married."

He wiped at his forehead. "I don't want to mess this up. You should have gotten Stefano to be your officiant. He's used to crowds with his family."

I chuckled. "You're my guy."

He squared his shoulders. "And I'm proud to do it. I won't let you down."

I shook his hand. "I know."

He grinned and reached over to hug me. "Be happy, Chase. You deserve it."

I returned his grin. "I know."

It was the first time I really believed that.

The music began, and Charly opened the door, standing in front of me. On the opposite side of the small church, framed by the door, was Cherry. Her hair was piled on her head, and she looked happy and every inch the proud mother. She smiled and nodded, and she and Charly began to walk, meeting in the middle and turning to slowly begin to head to the front of the church. I stopped in the door, getting my first glimpse of my bride. The sunlight behind Hannah highlighted the red in her hair as she waited for her turn to begin. The pretty ivory-colored dress clung to her torso and exploded in a froth of lace that hit the floor. Her hair was up, and I saw glints of pearls and sparkles woven into the red-gold of her tresses. A few tendrils hung around her face. She was spectacularly beautiful. And soon, she would be my wife.

She carried a bouquet of lilies, matching the one pinned to my lapel. Tears stung my eyes as we walked toward each other, stopping as we met at the aisle we would walk down together.

"You look so handsome," she whispered.

I tugged on my white cuffs, straightening my shoulders. I had never worn a tux before, but I was glad she liked it.

"You take my breath away."

She smiled, the color highlighting her cheeks at my words. The light caught the diamonds in her ears I had sent her.

"You got my gift."

"I love them." She paused. "I love you."

I bent my arm, offering it to her. "Then, shall we get married?"

She slid her hand into the crook of my elbow. "Yes."

I swayed with Hannah in my arms, breathing her in.

My wife.

Mine now. Always.

The ceremony had been brief but heartfelt. We both got emotional during our vows. Charly wept openly, making Maxx stand to hand her a handkerchief. Once he did, Vivvy decided she needed to join her mother. Theo came to get her, and they ended up sitting together behind Charly since that was as far as Theo could convince Vivvy to go. The way they sat and held hands in the front pew made everyone smile, and we carried on with the ceremony.

Kelly made the pictures fun. I found it easy to smile every second. I was surrounded by people who loved me. Something I never thought I would experience. I had a family I had been given instead of born into. It made them all that much more precious to me. I now had a beautiful wife whom I adored beyond measure to share my life with.

Hannah sighed, and I pressed a kiss to her head. "Okay, Mrs. Gallagher?" I teased. "Are you tired? You want to escape?"

She laughed, tilting her head up. "No, I'm having fun. But I am tired."

"You've been tired all week. Too many wedding plans."

She pursed her lips. "That too."

"What else? The other night?" I teased. "I tried to keep my hands to myself. It's not my fault you look sexy trying on bathing suits for our honeymoon."

Hannah shook her head, laughing. "You know, I kinda have a gift for you too. It's not diamonds, but I think you'll like it."

I pressed my lips to her ear. "Did you order that little number I saw you looking at? The mechanic one?"

When I saw it the other night, I suddenly understood Maxx and his obsession with Charly's outfits. The frilly, barely there mechanic's uniform was what wet dreams were made of.

At least mine.

"Well, I may have ordered it."

"Can we leave now then, please?"

"Chase," she admonished, frowning at me. "Get your mind off sex."

I kissed her head. "Sorry, Cinnamon. The thought of making love to *my wife* is rampant in my head." I pulled her closer. "Both of them."

Her breath caught. "Oh yes. I mean, wait. I want to give you my present."

"Okay."

"We need a little privacy."

I looked around. The dance floor was busy, people laughing, talking, drinking. Kelly had finally stopped taking pictures, and for the most part, everyone was ignoring us for a moment while we danced. I shuffled us into a darker corner, my back to the dance floor. "Okay?"

"Yes."

She took my hand and slid it between us. "The baby is making me tired."

I was confused. "What baby?"

She lifted her eyebrows, and I froze, her hand holding mine to her stomach. "Baby?" I repeated.

"Yes. *Our* baby."

It took me a moment. Then it hit me. I gave her diamonds. She was giving me a child.

I pressed my forehead to hers, my voice thick with emotion. "*Hannah*. Oh my God, Hannah."

"You're going to be a daddy."

I didn't care where we were. Who was watching. All I cared about was the words she shared and what they meant. I picked her up, holding her tightly, and kissed her. I kissed her until she was breathless and people were clapping. No one knew why, thinking we were simply acting like newlyweds, and I was happy to keep it that way for now.

I buried my face into her neck. "Say it again."

"We're going to be parents, Chase. You, me, and Baby G."

I began to laugh. "*Baby G*. Perfect. You're okay? How far? Do you know what it is?"

She cupped my face. "I'm fine. About six weeks, and no, I don't know yet. We'll find out together."

I nodded. "Together." Then I grinned. "This sort of makes Charly a nan. When can we tell her?"

She smiled. "Soon. Until then, just us. I haven't even told my mom." She looked at me. "Can you keep Baby G a secret?"

"I can try. It might be a good thing we're going on our honeymoon tomorrow. I can last two weeks." I smiled. "Or at least try to."

I slipped my hand between us again, resting it on her still-flat stomach. "He or she is right here. Baby G is in da house."

"That name is going to stick, isn't it?"

I kissed her. "Just like me. Forever."

She kissed me back. "I like forever."

"Me too."

We began to move again. My heart was full. I was married to Hannah. We had a baby on the way. Another twist to our unconventional relationship. An amazing one.

I pressed my lips to her ear.

"Just so you know? Best gift ever, Cinnamon."

She bit her lip, her eyes swimming with tears. Mine were watery too.

I tucked her close.

My baby. Our baby.

The start of our family.

Hannah, me, and Baby G.

Perfect.

Thank you so much for reading UNDER THE RADAR. If you are so inclined, reviews are always welcome by me at your retailer.

This was a fun story to write with these secretly crushing roommates. Chase worked so hard to overcome his past, and Hannah's openness made her the perfect match for him.

If you haven't guessed, Dom and Cherry are the next couple in Full Throttle of Reynolds Restoration world. You can add to your TBR on Goodreads.

If romantic comedy is your favorite trope, Liam and Shelby, from my novel Changing Roles, would be a recommended standalone to read next. It is a story of friends to lovers set in the bright lights of Hollywood.

Enjoy meeting other readers? Lots of fun, with upcoming book talk and giveaways! Check out Melanie Moreland's Minions on Facebook.

Join my newsletter for up-to-date news, sales, book announcements and excerpts (no spam). Click here to sign up Melanie Moreland's newsletter
or visit https://bit.ly/MMorelandNewsletter

Visit my website www.melaniemoreland.com

Enjoy reading! Melanie

ACKNOWLEDGMENTS

It takes a village… we have all hear that expression, and the same applies to writing a book.

To Beth, Deb, Trina, and Melissa—thank you.

Lisa, as usual, thank you for all your patience and humor.

Atlee and our girl George— thank you for making Karen's life easier

and making me smile with your support.

Karen—there are never enough words to encompass all you do for me.

Thanks and love are all I have—and they are in abundance.

To my Minions, my Literary Mob—

Thank you for all your efforts and support. I appreciate and love you all.

All the bloggers and book lovers—thank you for sharing your passion.

And Matthew—my rock, my shoulder, and my love.

It is you who inspires.

Always.

ALSO AVAILABLE FROM MORELAND BOOKS

Titles published under M. Moreland

Insta-Spark Collection

It Started with a Kiss

Christmas Sugar

An Instant Connection

An Unexpected Gift

Harvest of Love

An Unexpected Chance

Following Maggie

Titles published under Melanie Moreland

The Contract Series

The Contract (Contract #1)

The Baby Clause (Contract #2)

The Amendment (Contract #3)

The Addendum (Contract #4)

Vested Interest Series

BAM - The Beginning (Prequel)

Bentley (Vested Interest #1)

Aiden (Vested Interest #2)

Maddox (Vested Interest #3)

Reid (Vested Interest #4)

Van (Vested Interest #5)

Halton (Vested Interest #6)

Sandy (Vested Interest #7)

Vested Interest/ABC Crossover

A Merry Vested Wedding

ABC Corp Series

My Saving Grace (Vested Interest: ABC Corp #1)

Finding Ronan's Heart (Vested Interest: ABC Corp #2)

Loved By Liam (Vested Interest: ABC Corp #3)

Age of Ava (Vested Interest: ABC Corp #4)

Sunshine & Sammy (Vested Interest: ABC Corp #5)

Unscripted With Mila (Vested Interest: ABC Corp #6)

Men of Hidden Justice

The Boss

Second-In-Command

The Commander

The Watcher

The Specialist

Reynolds Restorations

Revved to the Maxx

ABOUT THE AUTHOR

NYT/WSJ/USAT international bestselling author Melanie Moreland, lives a happy and content life in a quiet area of Ontario with her beloved husband of thirty-plus years and their rescue cat, Amber. Nothing means more to her than her friends and family, and she cherishes every moment spent with them.

While seriously addicted to coffee, and highly challenged with all things computer-related and technical, she relishes baking, cooking, and trying new recipes for people to sample. She loves to throw dinner parties, and enjoys traveling, here and abroad, but finds coming home is always the best part of any trip.

Melanie loves stories, especially paired with a good wine, and enjoys skydiving (free falling over a fleck of dust) extreme snowboarding (falling down stairs) and piloting her own helicopter (tripping over her own feet.) She's learned happily ever afters, even bumpy ones, are all in how you tell the story.

Melanie is represented by Flavia Viotti at Bookcase Literary Agency. For any questions regarding subsidiary or translation rights please contact her at flavia@bookcaseagency.com

facebook.com/authormoreland

twitter.com/morelandmelanie

instagram.com/morelandmelanie

bookbub.com/authors//melanie-moreland

Printed in the USA
CPSIA information can be obtained
at www.ICGtesting.com
LVHW010348150624
783213LV00014B/625